D1133487

THOUGH DARKNESS DESCEND

JANET JOANOU WEINER

All rights reserved.

United States of America

Copyright © 2022 Janet Joanou Weiner

All Rights Reserved.

This book has been published with all reasonable efforts taken to make the material error-free after the consent of the author. No part of this book shall be used, reproduced in any manner whatsoever without written permission from the author, except in the case of brief quotations embodied in critical articles and reviews.

THE HOLY BIBLE, NEW INTERNATIONAL VERSION®, NIV® Copyright © 1973, 1978, 1984, 2011 by Biblica, Inc.® Used by permission. All rights reserved worldwide.

Dedication

To Dudley, whose listening ear made all the difference.

Praise for *Though Darkness Descend*

"Bravo! A truly great story, full of light in a very dark time in history! Beautifully written! Powerfully told! A must read! Five stars!"

-Bodie Thoene, *Best-selling author of more than 75 novels*

"With its lush historic detail and passionate story of strength in the face of oppression, *Though Darkness Descend* captivated me from the first page. These memorable characters 'struggles became my own and my heart is stronger for having delved into this beautiful tale."

-Tara Johnson, author of *Engraved on the Heart, Where Dandelions Bloom* and *All Through the Night*

A Note from the Author

The context of this novel is the conflict between the Catholic King Louis XIV and the Huguenot Protestants in 17th century France. It was a different era, one full of much fear and misunderstanding, as well as actual differences in faith practices. At that time, each side thought the other to be heretical.

The author wishes to make it very clear that she does not hold this opinion.

PREFACE

On October 31, 1517, Martin Luther nailed 95 theses to the church door in Wittenberg, Germany. His only intention: to bring correction to an increasingly corrupt Catholic church. Instead, the Protestant Reformation was born.

In his theses, Luther denounced, among other things, the practice of "indulgences," the widespread practice of parishioners paying the church for the pardoning of sins. Instead, he held to the biblical truth that man is saved by God's grace through faith in Jesus alone.

As the Reformation spread throughout Western Europe, millions chose to follow God in a new way. The Protestants, or the "Reformed," believed they had a personal connection with their Savior. They were free to read the Bible and pray to God directly themselves, without the intermediary of a priest. This belief shaped their value of individual responsibility, which affected all areas of their lives. Protestants valued literacy, education, and hard work.

By 1562, there were an estimated two million Protestants in France, concentrated mainly in the western and southern regions. Catholic hostility grew as they gained influence and prosperity, causing the "Wars of Religion," first fought intermittently from 1562-1598. The Edict of Nantes ended the conflict and granted the Huguenots, as they came to be known, the legal right to meet and to follow the Protestant faith. The Edict was also significant for paving the way for the separation of church and state, as the King and the majority of France remained Catholic.

Protestants flourished until the mid- seventeenth century when Louis XIV rose to power. Under his rule, the Huguenots experienced increasing persecution in the form of legal restrictions. Edicts were issued forbidding them from holding public offices, such as the vital role of town *notaire* (lawyer/notary.) Further decrees placed strict monitoring systems for court lawyers, doctors, and midwives, severely limiting the scope of their practices. They were also required to report all activity to Catholic officials or priests.

By the 1680s, the King also restricted the Protestants' right to meet for worship or to build new *temples* (churches.) Despite this, the Huguenots of St. Hippolyte de la Planquette, in the Languedoc region of southern France, continued to come together every Sunday. As a result, in 1681, the order came to tear down their temple with their own hands. The stones were used a few years later to construct the Catholic church. Four thousand strong, the Huguenots of St. Hippolyte met instead on the rubble of their *temple* until forbidden to do so.

Forced to attend services in nearby villages, they overflowed the existing buildings. When the King banned them from enlarging those structures, the stubbornly faithful St. Hippolyte Huguenots refused to give up. They held open-air services in a vast field on the edge of town. Neighboring villages were convicted by the courage of the St. Hippolyte Huguenots and resumed their services despite pressure from the King.

Further royal edicts soon forbade meeting—contrary to the Edict of Nantes guarantee of this freedom. Also, the Huguenots of St. Hippolyte could no longer have a pastor.

In 1683, King Louis XIV sent his special forces, the dragoons, to suppress the Protestants in the south of France. Starting in the Dauphiné region, Huguenots were tortured, hung, and burned alive for their faith. Then, in early October 1683, the King turned his focus to the largest population of Huguenots: those in the 'Cévennes region, and in particular, St. Hippolyte de la Planquette.

TABLE OF CONTENTS

CHAPTER 1
TODAY IS THE DAY

Day One
Wednesday, 6 October 1683
Château de Planque
Tessier family home
St. Hippolyte de la Planquette

Branches whip and scrape like claws across her face. Her feet pound the forest floor, going in which direction she does not know. They're coming. They're coming after her. She must stay ahead, elude detection. Exposure would cost her everything. Trees thin out; divergent paths appear. Heart beating wild, pulsing fear into frozen limbs, she veers right. Deeper in, surrounded by chestnut and pine, a black-dark hole emerges from the ground like a waking animal: a cave. Hide and wait? Run like the wind?

Whirling sharp, a crashing volley of musket fire, then shrieks of terror surround her and fill the smoky air. She ducks into damp darkness and regrets it instantly. Trapped, no way out. Horror wells and bursts. Suppressed screams rise through her chest and spill forth. Garbled, strangled sounds alone emerge and mount into a whine unequal to her panic.

Blanket clutched against her pounding heart, Jeanne sat bolt upright. Dread encased her even as the dream dissipated. She forced herself to focus on the room: the tiny shafts of early morning light seeping through high shuttered windows, the scent of beeswax on the ancient oak armoire, the even breathing of her sleeping sisters. What this day would hold, she did not know. No one did. Only one thing was crystal clear— massive change was in the wind.

1

The news came yesterday. Twelve hundred dragoons, King Louis XIV's fiercest soldiers, were on their way to suppress the Huguenots of St. Hippolyte de la Planquette. Jeanne drew a deep breath. How had their tiny town of four thousand drawn the attention of the King? Yes, the entire population, save a handful of Catholics, were Huguenot Protestants. But all of them remained fully loyal to their Catholic King. Brow furrowed, she shook her head, still unable to comprehend. Why did he deem it necessary to send an *army* against them? They only desired to maintain their legal rights to worship and to live in line with their beliefs.

With one swift motion, Jeanne threw off the covers and jumped to her feet, the wooden bed frame creaking as she rose. No more time for sitting and thinking. There was much to do. Judging by the slant of gentle autumn sun trickling into the room, their departure was drawing near. In one brief hour, they would leave their home, the Château de Planque. She'd been born under its enormous roof and lived inside its thick limestone walls her entire eighteen years. She inhaled deeply and exhaled with force, as if the swirling questions would wash away with her breath. Papa and the elders' plan would work. It had to. They'd all return to their homes soon. Why then did her chest squeeze tight?

Jeanne pulled her forest-green woolen traveling skirt up over her shift, then added a plain cotton blouse; lace was not appropriate for what lay ahead. She tugged on her warmest stockings, then drew on her linen waistcoat, fumbling with the buttons, nerves making her clumsy. Time was ticking away.

Action suited her. During the night, when sleep eluded her, she'd packed for herself and her siblings. The eldest of four, the family depended on her. Glancing across the wide, high-ceilinged room where the younger Tessiers slept, Jeanne blinked back the sting of tears.

With a practiced hand, she wound her dark brown hair up and splashed a bit of brisk water from the basin on her face. She added her linen bonnet, letting the wide white ties hang loose. A quick check in the mirror reflected hazel-green eyes ridged with tension. She brushed the back of her hand across her forehead as if to smooth away the anxiety.

Unbidden, Etienne's face came to mind and a faint blush warmed her cheeks. What would it take for him to notice her, to see her as more than his sister's closest friend? She frowned and banished the thought.

2

There were far more important things at stake today. But was the life she dreamed of sharing with him over before it even began?

She didn't know what to think of his audacity yesterday. A messenger had brought her father the news that the dragoons were up the road in Anduze, stopping there before descending on St. Hippolyte. Word spread like wildfire from one neighbor to another. The entire community dropped what they were doing and hurried to the vast fields on the southeast edge of town. Ever since the King had forced them to tear down their *temple*, the Bedos brothers had welcomed them to gather on the uncultivated portion of their land for worship. With the river on one side and the flat-topped Pie de Mars mountain a bit farther away on the other, it was their spiritual home, where they instinctively pulled together to figure out what to do.

The elders had called everyone to order. Standing in the late afternoon sunshine, on the wooden podium used for their services, they presented a plan prepared in advance for just such an eventuality. A tiny spark of hope had trickled up through Jeanne's numb interior, and she sensed it ripple through the community, despite their panic and cold terror. Maybe it would work, and they would get through this ordeal and return to their everyday lives.

Then, as quickly as it rose, her optimism crashed. Led by Etienne, several of the younger men insisted they *fight* the dragoons, arguing with force against the elders' plan of passive resistance, despite the fact that the elders included his father. No one had ever before publicly disagreed with them. It simply wasn't done. Obedience to pastors and elders was second only to God. Jeanne bit her lip. It was still hard to believe Etienne had disputed them so boldly.

Today, the Huguenots would move to Le Cengle mountain, on the other side of town, for strategic advantage and the safety of being together. Jeanne figured once they all settled onto the mountain, the young men's dissent would fully die down, and they would stop their campaign to fight the dragoons.

Yet, the thought of passively waiting didn't settle well with her either. It felt like being stuck with no way out. The possibility of action, of fighting for their rights, caused her breath to catch. Something awakened in her soul: a flash of longing for…for something *more*. Usually, she went along with her father and the elders, not wanting to create problems, not wanting to risk rejection. Anyway, it didn't matter. She couldn't imagine

Etienne and his friends actually carrying through with any of it. What did they know about fighting trained soldiers?

The hint of a smile tugged at the corners of her mouth. Once they were on the mountain, she'd tell Etienne she sympathized with his point of view, even if it seemed impossible to carry out. It would be a good starting point for conversation, and hopefully, a new connection between them.

Jeanne took one last look around her bedroom, taking in every line, curve, and detail: the terracotta tile floors, the high ceilings, and especially the tall windows with a view across the vineyards onto the river Vidourle, which flowed gently or wildly, depending on the season, past the front of the château. Today, due to recent rains, the river roared and splashed, rushing down from the mountains and on through the town, reflecting the tension-filled air. She crossed the room to the windows and flung open the wooden *volets*, not minding the crashing sound they made as they banged against the rocky limestone walls. Brisk air poured in, causing her younger sisters to stir in their beds.

"*Arrête!*...stop! Jeanne, that's enough!" Of the four Tessier children, Catherine needed her sleep, even more so at age fifteen. Three years younger than Jeanne, they were worlds apart in just about every way. And Catherine certainly didn't appreciate being touched or talked to first thing in the morning.

"It's time, Catherine. We must be on our way soon," Jeanne stated. She braced herself for an onslaught of bad attitude and no action. But Catherine merely grumbled, got up, and started getting ready.

Their little sister, Anne, rose without a word and began to put on her clothes. Tears streamed down her face. Wise beyond her eleven years, she held a special place in Jeanne's heart. She reached for her little sister and pulled her close, kissing the top of her head. A small leather-bound book of Psalms lay next to her pillow. Anne loved the hand-illustrated family heirloom and kept it close since Maman taught her to read. Last night, she'd even slept with it. Jeanne's throat tightened, but she forced her face to stay neutral. It was her job to be strong.

Paul, the youngest Tessier, jumped out of bed. He grabbed the chamber pot kept under his bed and stepped behind the screen in the corner to use it. Within minutes, he threw on his clothes and headed out the bedroom door. To Jeanne, he was still the baby of the family, a role he protested vigorously, especially since his tenth birthday. Always

4

dreaming of adventures, today was full of promise as far as Paul was concerned. It was no surprise he rose quickly and was ready to throw himself into the battles of the day.

"Time for breakfast! *À table!*" Maman's voice, high-pitched and tight, called down the hall from the *grand salon* where they dined and spent most of their time. Jeanne helped the younger girls with the ties to their skirts and coaxed them along as they scrambled into woolen stockings and slid on leather walking shoes. The girls grabbed their linen bonnets and pulled them on as they hurried down the corridor.

They burst through the family entrance into the spacious room where Paul was already seated at the impressive oak table near one of the two fireplaces attempting to warm the space. Busy jousting an invisible dragoon with the bread knife, he didn't notice his sisters' arrival.

A few seconds later, on the opposite side of the room, Papa arrived through the formal entrance, firmly shutting the tall double doors of carved chestnut behind him.

"Isaac! There you are!" Maman motioned for him to take a seat at the table in one of the high back chairs. "We need to eat now if we're to be on time to meet the others."

Jeanne wished they would skip breakfast and go. Even the warm fragrance of the freshly baked wheat loaf did nothing to awaken her hunger. Marion, the housekeeper, had also filled the table with a crock of recently churned butter and a bowl of jam made from the end-of-summer berries they collected together along the river. Plus there were bowls of warm milk to wash it all down. Jeanne usually had a healthy appetite, but today she wasn't the least bit hungry and doubted if anyone, except maybe her little brother, would eat a bite. It seemed silly to her and a waste of time, but Maman had insisted, thinking it might be their last proper meal, seated together like this in their home.

"*Désolé*, Suzanne," Papa said, kissing his wife's cheek. "Sorry I'm late. I've been with the Lacombes. André, Pierre, and I needed to figure out how to keep the animals and the vineyards cared for while we're away."

Maman's eyes darkened. "But it should only take the soldiers a half-day to march from Anduze to St. Hippolyte. They could be here as early as noon today."

"But we don't know how long they'll stay in Anduze. It's best to bring enough supplies for more than one day on Le Cengle."

Papa and Maman held each other's gaze. Maman spoke in a low voice. "None of that may even matter if the dragoons choose to wipe us out as they did to our kind in the north."

"Those Huguenots attacked the King's men. As I've said, if we do not move aggressively against the soldiers, we'll avoid disaster."

"But you heard Etienne and his friends yesterday, advocating we do just that. I think they still intend to initiate a battle with the dragoons."

"Young Gamond and the others will most certainly *not* fight the soldiers. We'll keep them occupied on the mountain and under our watch. We cannot have them inciting the dragoons, giving them an excuse to...." Papa's voice trailed off as all four of his children were listening. He pulled out his chair and took his place at the table. "Above all, we trust in God's strong protection. Let's eat. We leave soon."

Heads bowed, hands folded, Papa gave thanks for the food set before them. Usually, breakfast was full of chatter and at least one bowl of spilt milk. Not today. In silence, the Tessiers ate quickly; only Paul seemed oblivious to the gravity of the situation and helped himself to a second serving.

Jeanne chewed on the corner of her bread. Her parents took Etienne's desire to fight seriously, and her father planned to stop him. Of course, she'd heard of the dragoon's atrocities in the Dauphiné. The Huguenots had held the soldiers off for longer than expected, but eventually, the soldiers trapped them in a barn. The dragoons then set fire to the wooden structure. At least fifty of the Huguenots died, courageously singing psalms until the end. Jeanne shuddered. She'd tried to avoid thinking about it too much—until now.

A fragment of her dream flashed before her, like the thunder that so often struck their land. This tempest was human: mounted, armed, and charged with suppressing them. Her hand still holding a morsel of bread dropped to the table. Would the soldiers sweep through the Huguenots of St. Hippolyte with the same violence as in the north? Would fighting provoke them or prove their point? What if Etienne was right and Papa's plan for passive resistance didn't work?

Jeanne glanced around the *grand salon*, stopping at the wood-frame upholstered armchairs in front of the marble fireplace where Maman and Papa sat nightly, discussing their day. There was so much to be lost.

It was one thing to take a stand for their way of life, but she was certainly not ready to die for God. Why should she? Sure God existed,

6

but that was about it. Certainly, he was not involved in or cared about their lives in any significant way.

He hadn't protected the Huguenots to the north and they suffered violent deaths. Closer to home, despite all their efforts, all their fervent prayers, God hadn't saved her baby sister two years ago. By the time Papa returned with the doctor, little Marie had died in her arms. And God hadn't helped Maman, who had never been quite the same.

She'd successfully hidden her lack of any faith or trust in God from her family and the Huguenot community. There was no other option in her world. One was Protestant, believing in a personal relationship with the Almighty, or one was Catholic and depended upon the priests to connect with God. There was no middle ground, no room for doubts to be voiced. And certainly no possibility to be an unbeliever.

Papa stood from the table and picked up the large family Bible from the shelf above the mantelpiece. It was their practice to read the scriptures together after dinner; never had Papa done so after the morning meal. Now, he voiced the familiar words as a prayer:

"Whoever dwells in the shelter of the Most High
will rest in the shadow of the Almighty.
I will say of the Lord,

'He is my refuge and my fortress, my God, in whom I trust.'"

Jeanne listened, eyes shut, head bowed, enclosed in herself. Papa trusted in God's protection above all. More than any plan, he trusted the Almighty to rescue them out of this danger. Her eyes flew open. That didn't work for her. God deeply disappointed her in the past. She would *not* let that happen again.

As Papa finished reading, Jeanne made her decision. Her respect and love for Papa remained, but she couldn't passively go into this day, trusting in God's deliverance. The stakes were too high. Either way she might die, but at least she'd go out fighting. What that would look like, she didn't know.

Despite her churning stomach, something deep inside woke up. For her, there was no other choice. Never in her life had she outwardly gone against her father's wishes or beliefs. Today that changed. She'd tell Etienne she was on his side. Then she'd encourage and support active resistance in any way possible.

---

[1] Psalm 91:1-2 (NIV)

7

CHAPTER 2
DRAGOONS IN ANDUZE

Day One
Wednesday, 6 October 1683
Anduze

Colonel Raymond Arnault stood alone, motionless, staring at the water. Far from the multitude of dragoons camped along the broad banks of the Gardon d'Anduze, he strained to see the current of the river meandering through the hilly Cévenol town. The absence of odor and the occasional tiny ripple proved the water was not stagnant, despite its appearance of stillness. He scooped up a handful of smooth river rocks and hurled them one at a time into the water. Each landed with a gratifying splash that seemed to provoke the water into a forward jolt of movement. If only he could achieve a similar result with General De Tessé.

Arnault walked farther down the riverbank, his steps pounding out his frustration. Newly promoted to the rank of colonel after his success over the Huguenots in the Dauphiné region, he now led a regiment of five hundred mounted dragoons. The increased responsibility did not concern him. He wore authority as well as he did his magnificent emerald blazer with its yellow velvet cuffs and golden embroidery. The problem was his superior.

General De Tessé commanded fear and respect over the entire detachment of twelve hundred men, including seven hundred foot-soldiers. Yesterday, they'd easily secured compliance among the Huguenots of Anduze. This Protestant village was not the problem. With a growl, Arnault yanked a wayward lock of dark hair back into place. By now, they should be on their way to their primary target: St. Hippolyte de la Planquette.

Arnault glanced upriver where his men milled about. Another layer of tension lined his face. Yes, they'd effectively crushed the Huguenots to the north. So why couldn't he celebrate the victory? Was it the humiliation of the Huguenots holding them off for hours despite being outnumbered and untrained? Or was it that certain members of the King's court were calling their recent campaigns "ignoble butcheries"?

They were Louis XIV's soldiers and did what needed to be done. It was proper and correct to honor their King, God's representative on earth. Integrity and loyalty ran deep in his blood, which were the very characteristics leading to his promotion. Why then did his soul freeze with every remembered image of that particular battle? Arnault stopped and threw more stones into the placid river.

And that sound! Haunted by the echo of other worldly Huguenot voices singing hymns as they burned alive, Arnault longed to erase the event from history. Especially his part in it. He'd only been following General De Tessé's orders. What else could he do but set the barn on fire when the command came?

Nor could he wipe away the memory of the fearless proclamations of faith of De Tessé's remaining prisoners as they faced slow, vicious deaths, broken into pieces on the rack-like Wheel. Why hadn't they given in, converted to the religion of the King, and lived?

Arnault swiveled abruptly and began pacing along the riverbank as the most troubling picture of all rose in his mind. Etched on his brain was the image of a Huguenot woman rising from the forest floor while her rapist, his soldier Rossel, sniggered nearby. It wasn't the disheveled hair, the torn clothing, nor the gash across her face that tormented him. It was her eyes, the haunting gaze that penetrated and unsettled his soul. Despite her anguish, something radiated from her that he still couldn't define. *Defiance?* Arnault shook his head. That wasn't it. It was something more like strength but laced through with—and this shocked him—*courage.* How could that be, and why couldn't he forget it?

Attempting to dispel the disturbing images, he started back towards the dragoon camp, refocusing on the task at hand. Their new orders were to sweep even farther south, to the rocky, wooded Cévennes, the most significant stronghold of Huguenots. There was no good reason they couldn't be on their way by now to St. Hippolyte, the most critical stop.

They would be there by mid-afternoon and commence reigning in the most stubborn Protestants of all. Arnault reached down and lifted a large rock from the path and hurled it into the river, his whole body involved in the effort. The stone created a satisfying thump and he watched the ripples spread and fade away. He couldn't wait to bring the Cévenol Huguenots into submission to the King. Maybe then his soul would be at peace.

Waiting did not suit him, nor his men. The longer they tarried, the greater the opportunity for his soldiers to engage in further debaucheries. It didn't help that the reason for the delay resided in a slightly faded manor home at the edge of town. General De Tesse's favorite paramour in all of France, a renowned auburn beauty, lived in Anduze.

"Sir! Colonel Arnault!" An approaching messenger jolted him from his thoughts. Arnault nodded his permission to approach.

"Sir, I carry a word from the Duke de Noailles, Governor of the Languedoc region."

Arnault received the sealed document, quickly scanning its contents. Once finished, he gazed into the distance for a moment, then read it again. Finally, he rolled it up slowly, then slapped it against his open palm. His piercing stare bore down on the messenger. "Do you know anything about this? Is the report true?"

The younger man hesitated. Arnault barked, "I'm aware this was a sealed missive. Speak now! That's an order!"

"Sir, it's rumored the Huguenots move today to a mountain which overlooks the Route de Lasalle, the road your men will use to access the town."

"Anything else?"

"They..." The messenger paused, then drew himself up. "They're calling themselves the 'Lord's Army.'"

The colonel's nostrils flared. "Just as they did in the north, in the Dauphiné?"

"Yes, sir."

"Unbelievable," spat Arnault. "One would think they'd learn from the mistakes of their neighbors."

"It seems they're asking for a fight, which is incredible given how easily your squadron suppressed their fellows."

Arnault's jaw clenched. He scrutinized the young man.

"Excuse me, sir, if I spoke out of turn."

10

The colonel studied him in silence. Somehow in the chaos of the battle in the Dauphiné, it had never become common knowledge the Huguenots had held his men off for *hours*. It was not a secret there had been fierce resistance, resulting in dragoon casualties. But in the end, as the Huguenots went up in flames, the campaign was deemed a success. And to ensure there was even less opposition as they swept south into the bastion of Protestantism, the King had sent four times the soldiers. Twelve hundred dragoons would quickly bring the Huguenots of St. Hippolyte in line.

But that was the problem. What would it entail? How far would they have to go against their countrymen, even if they were heretics? Unbidden, the Huguenot woman's eyes, as she rose from the forest floor, appeared in Arnault's mind.

His scowl deepened and he began pacing while the messenger waited, casting a glance over to the dwindling number of his men still in camp. Suddenly, he stopped and stepped towards the young man.

"Go, now, to General De Tessé, by my orders. Deliver this news to him. Do not leave until he receives it."

"Sir, excuse me, but, uh, he gave explicit orders not to be disturbed."

"This information *must* be given to him. Tell him I sent you."

The fire in Arnault's eyes brooked no argument. The messenger gulped and managed a "yes, sir."

"I'll send my man Lieutenant Lefèvre with you. He's utterly fearless," added Arnault.

The colonel turned and strode towards the rows of white triangular tents making up their camp. Following the scent of food cooking and the pillar of smoke from an open-air fire, he searched for his right-hand man.

Lieutenant Lefèvre jumped to his feet at the approach of his colonel. "We're moving out?" Relief lit his craggy face under the standard issue green stocking caps.

"Not yet. But I've received new information that will possibly speed us along. Lieutenant Lefèvre, accompany this man and his message to General De Tessé. Add the following from me: 'It's Colonel Arnault's opinion that if we depart for St. Hippolyte today, we'll have the advantage of disrupting the Huguenots before they organize themselves on the mountain.'"

11

Lefèvre saluted his colonel, turned on his heel, and walked at a brisk pace towards the home of De Tessé's mistress, the messenger struggling to keep up.

Arnault glared after them. With any luck, this new information would rouse the general from his distraction, and they would soon be on their way. There was still time today to make the journey. A slow smile crossed the colonel's face as he gazed at the river, which suddenly seemed to pick up speed.

CHAPTER 3
CHEZ LACOMBE

Day One
Wednesday, 6 October 1683
La Planque quartier
Lacombe family home
St. Hippolyte de la Planquette

Pierre Lacombe stomped the mud off his boots, then stooped through the low doorway into the warmth of the family kitchen. All his senses were on high alert. The door crashed against the limestone wall, every gesture containing more energy than usual. His mother stopped stirring the milk warming in the iron pot hanging over the fire, eyebrows raised at her adult son. Pierre shot her an apologetic look. Normally, his brother Gabriel was the boisterous one but today was not anywhere near normal.

His father followed him through the door. The pair appeared more like brothers than father and son, enhanced by the fact that Pierre stood a head taller than his papa.

André bent to kiss his wife on the cheek. "*Desolé*, Isabeau! Sorry, we're late. The château's fields and animals have never been left entirely alone, so Isaac accompanied us as we worked out how to best leave everything here."

Isabeau nodded at her husband, then turned her gaze to Pierre. All three understood the gravity of the situation and the potential consequences to all they managed for the Tessier family and the Château de Planque estate. Their own home was on château land, just across the Route de Lasalle from the Tessiers. The vineyards stretching through the terrain just outside their front door and down to the river belonged to the château and were worked by fifty men, all overseen by Pierre. Every aspect of their lives was under threat.

Pierre joined his younger siblings at the kitchen table while his mother slid the long-handled wooden plank into the brick oven, and pulled out a steaming loaf of wheat and rye bread. The yeasty aroma filled the room, but he barely noticed. His body was present *à table,* his mind elsewhere. Staring intensely into the distance, he pictured the various possibilities of the day ahead as if they were sketched in the air.

For most of the night he'd examined every aspect of the coming hours: what could happen when the dragoons arrived and how best to deal with it, plus the logistics of settling thousands of Huguenots onto the narrow rocky ledges of Le Cengle mountain. They all needed food, cooking supplies, and bedding. Pierre sighed. At the community gathering yesterday, some insisted they needed to bring their most precious goods, such as books and furniture. The elders had tried to dissuade people from packing more than the essentials, but no one knew how much damage the dragoons would inflict. Protecting their lives and faith were the main priorities, but they couldn't afford to lose their property. His father and Isaac depended on him to help manage it all.

What about his fermenting blends of grapes and the casks of experimental wines he was leaving behind? During this first month after the *vendanges,* they needed to be taste-tested twice weekly. He could then adjust the acidic balance by adding yeast if needed. What if the dragoons came into their homes while they were away? And what would happen if they found and disturbed—or even *drank*—the new wines? He batted the thoughts away like pesky flies. Although dreaming up and caring for his creations was his passion, he needed to concentrate on what was happening today.

Pierre observed his young sisters, sitting in silence, waiting for their *petit-déjeuner.* Usually, their chatter dominated the breakfast table. Their parents had tried to protect them from the full impact of the impending arrival of the dragoons, but danger was in the air, and they could sense it. They sat on their wooden bench like statues, frozen with fear.

At the opposite end of the table, seventeen-year-old Gabriel was ready to spring into action. Even more tightly wound than usual, he was a blur of motion even while seated. Warm milk sloshed into his bowl; the jug slammed back onto the table. He grabbed the wooden plank holding the hot loaf too quickly, sending the bread knife flying across

14

the room. The energy coursing through his veins threatened an imminent explosion. Pierre reached across the table and placed a calming hand on his brother's arm. A forceful brush-off was his reward.

Although Gabriel resembled their mother with his wiry sand-colored hair and green-blue eyes, his temperament was his own. Pierre recognized the determination on his face. Gabriel was born for a day like this, a warrior longing for battle. One was finally coming his way, and he was ready to jump in with full force. With his flair for the dramatic, it was not hard to imagine he pictured himself in some heroic role. Worried his brother's need to prove himself would result in foolish action, Pierre determined to keep an eye on him.

As if he could read his older brother's mind, Gabriel glared at him, pushed back from the table, and sprang to his feet.

"I'm not hungry! Let me go and join the others now," he pleaded. "I can be of help!"

Isabeau met André's eyes and continued coaxing her daughters to eat something. They had no illusions about their younger son's intentions. Gabriel planned to join the other young men preparing to fight the soldiers, even though this conflicted with all André and Isabeau believed. As a midwife, Isabeau focused on bringing life into this world, not taking it out.

"Son, we've discussed this already," said André. "We are taking the family gun, but for self-defense if absolutely necessary. Only Pierre or I will carry it. *Not* you."

"But I'm a better shot than you both! You know that!" replied Gabriel, banging the bread knife back onto the table, causing his sisters to jump. "Why are we even calling ourselves the Lord's Army if we don't plan to fight?"

"It's no use arguing, Gabriel. *Only* your brother and I will be responsible for the gun, which we will use *only* in self-defense. That's final."

Pierre observed the exchange in silence. Yesterday, judging from the community's reactions, he wasn't the only one stunned by visiting Pastor Boyer's encouragement to take up arms and fight. He'd proclaimed, "We can now attack the King, who has forced us to act in line with our consciences." This radical idea had robbed Pierre of sleep. He'd examined it like a foreign object throughout the night, observing it from every possible angle.

15

They *had* remained loyal to the King, despite recent years of one royal edict after another restricting their fundamental rights. All they wanted was the freedom to live according to what they believed; most importantly, to read the Bible for themselves and pray directly to God without the intermediary of a priest. Pierre had tossed and turned at the injustice of the King sending his soldiers, to force them to convert. But to take up arms, to fight the royal army? Could that possibly be God's will for them?

Yet, Pierre chafed at the passivity of the elders' plan. Would moving to the mountain to wait and watch for the dragoons work? Once the soldiers arrived, the elders planned to assure them of their loyalty to the crown and explain they only wanted to maintain their legal rights.

During the depths of the night, neither fighting nor passive resistance seemed like a good option. In the end, he couldn't shake the sense that they'd invite disaster if they took aggressive action like the northern Huguenots. Most were killed, either in battle or afterward, like Pierre's cousin, in horrific displays of public torture.

Such thoughts circled, swirled, and swooped back around again in endless loops like evening swallows searching for a place to land. By morning, Pierre settled on going along with the elders' plan.

André cleared his throat and opened the family Bible.

"You will not fear the terror of night, nor the arrow that flies by day." [2]

Pierre raised his head; his soul leaned in.

"Nor the pestilence that stalks in the darkness, nor the plague that destroys at midday.

A thousand may fall at your side, ten thousand at your right hand, but it will not come near you." [3]

There was another element in this battle, unseen but powerful and real. He inhaled deeply. Faith became tangible and coursed through his veins, refreshing and restoring his strength.

Today was the day, and it was in the Father's hands.

---

[2] Psalm 91:5 (NIV)

[3] Psalm 91:6-7 (NIV)

CHAPTER 4
CHEZ GAMOND

Day One
Wednesday, 6 October 1683
Centre Ville
Chez GAMOND
St. Hippolyte de la Planquette

Louise Gamond let her gaze linger on each member of her family sitting around the polished oak dining table. Would this be the last time they all sat there together? Grief engulfed her, and she was unable to keep hot tears from spilling over.

For all her sixteen years, the stately family villa in the center of St. Hippolyte de la Planquette with its expansive gardens leading to the foot of the mountains, had been her home. Her great-grandfather built this house and knowing it had housed generations of her family was a source of security for Louise. Today, she imagined her Huguenot ancestors sitting around the table with them, shoulder to shoulder, connected across the generations as they prepared to face the ordeal ahead.

The dragoons were coming, and all the awful possibilities passed through Louise's mind like terrible portents. Her sky-blue eyes threatened to fill again but she blinked back the tears, not wanting to upset her younger siblings. With her mother swept away by fever two years earlier, Louise carried a substantial load of maternal responsibilities. Observing her frightened little brothers and sister half-heartedly eating their bread, listening to Papa read scripture, she could scarcely breathe. She'd face whatever lay ahead of them, but no harm must come to the children.

"You will only observe with your eyes and see the punishment of the wicked. If you say, 'The Lord is my refuge,' and you make the Most High your dwelling, no harm will overtake you, no disaster will come near your tent.'"[4]

Louise blinked. It was as if God was speaking directly to her. Right to her fears. Papa's voice spoke just what she needed to hear from her heavenly Father. She absorbed the words and let them settle her soul. How could she help take care of the others if she wasn't in a stable place herself?

Louise straightened up and nodded encouragement at each member of the family, finishing with her older brother Etienne. Her face fell despite her deep affection for him. Ignoring his breakfast, oblivious to everything going on around him, Etienne stared off into the distance, his body tightly wound. Typically, Etienne fully engaged in the daily Bible readings, often debating a theological point with their papa. Louise admired his thirst to understand and his razor-sharp mind that raised questions she'd never considered. But today he wasn't even listening.

Guillaume Gamond, the town's lawyer and one of the church elders, cleared his throat in the direction of his son. No response. Louise noted, not for the first time, the resemblance between the two went beyond their rich brown hair and intense green eyes. Both were extremely stubborn and strong-willed. Normally they sparred like the bulls in their neighbor's field; she could never quite tell if they locked horns in play or battle. If she had to guess, they enjoyed refining their arguments, debating finer points on many topics, each challenging the other to defend their position thoroughly. Although Papa had practiced law for over twenty years, Etienne could hold his own, not backing down, and deftly proving his point. Louise knew this was a source of pride for their father.

But for many months, layers of unresolved tension had mounted between Papa and Etienne. They'd argued loud and long on his choice of profession. Papa desired his son to follow his footsteps into the law, but Etienne was determined to be a pastor. Royal edicts now limited the ability of Huguenots to enter into either one, adding even more obstacles to Etienne's dream. Being blocked by anyone, king or father, was not acceptable to Etienne.

---

[4] Psalm 91:8-9 (NIV)

Fresh in Louise's mind was their dispute yesterday in the Bedos' family field. As usual, Papa and Etienne held opposing views, but never before had they argued in public. Never had a son of an elder openly disagreed with a decision. It had sent shock waves through the community, and she wasn't the only one who had felt extremely uncomfortable. Then, adding more fuel to the fire, Pastor Boyer proclaimed it was their right and their duty to fight the King's dragoons. Etienne and his friends had cheered him loud and long.

Now, the only sound in the room was the soft swishing of the children's feet swinging under the table as Guillaume finished the reading and prayed for their safety. Despite the reassuring words of faith, mounting tension filled the air like an atmospheric shift before a storm. No one seemed capable of rising from the table knowing that once they did, they would be stepping into the unknown.

"Etienne, it's time to go." Guillaume's voice deepened into the one he used in the courtroom. "Son, to be clear, there will be no question of you or any of your friends fighting the dragoons. We intend to keep you out of trouble—for your own sakes, as well as for the safety of the community. Don't even *think* of going against us!"

Etienne locked eyes with his father. The pair stared at each other for what seemed like an eternity.

Guillaume broke the silence. "If you involve yourself with the minority who still plan to fight the dragoons, understand this: if you live through such folly, there will be serious consequences."

Louise gulped back a gasp. It was no small matter Etienne openly defied their father. But what did her papa have in mind?

Etienne pushed back his chair with such force it clattered to the ground, splintering one of the legs. Guillaume rose to face his son.

Silently placing a hand on her brother's arm, Louise stood between the two men. Not for the first time, her quiet strength calmed Etienne. Understanding passed between them and he finally gave his father a curt nod.

Louise sent the children to grab their bundles and go down to the wagon, then saw to it the servants finished the final preparations for their departure. She paused and observed Etienne going through the motions of preparing to leave. His tense shoulders and the too-loud clunking and clattering of the trunks he stacked were all the confirmation she needed that his opinion had not changed.

19

There was no time to find out what he was planning to do. Perhaps on the mountain, she would be able to talk with him, to help him be reasonable. She would do her best to convince him not to do anything rash that would put himself, and others, in harm's way.

With a deep breath, she squared her shoulders, took one last glance at her beloved home, and walked out the door.

CHAPTER 5
PREPARATIONS

Day One
Wednesday, 6 October 1683
Château de Planque
St. Hippolyte de la Planquette

Tension crackled through the atmosphere inside the Château de Planque as everyone bustled about, bumping into one another, finishing preparations to leave. Housekeeper Marion stood in the middle of the *grand salon* on the second floor, capable hands placed on broad hips. She relished barking out orders to the other servants: sending one to finish clearing the breakfast table, another down to the kitchen to gather the bundles of food supplies, and yet another to bring the needed blankets into the dining room. And to get it done in a hurry.

Jeanne stared blankly at the growing piles of supplies. Maman wanted help deciding which items were essential. But who knew what would be useful on the mountain or how long they'd be there. She glanced out the side window to the narrow terraces of Le Cengle mountain. Was there even enough space for them all?

Decisions needed to be made and swiftly. Time was running out. She counted the bedding, making sure there were at least two woolen blankets for each family member. At least there would be something between them and the cold hard ground.

"Maman! Why can't I take the book of Psalms?" Anne clutched the small volume to her chest. Clearly, she couldn't imagine leaving behind their most prized possession besides the family Bible. It was a privilege to own both.

Glancing at Maman's weary face, Jeanne replied in her place. "We can only take what's essential for survival. I mean for our *stay* on the mountain. Only so much will fit in the wagon and on the terraces." She fought to smooth the tremor from her voice.

Anne slowly put the book back on the shelf by the fireplace. Jeanne understood that for her little sister, it was an item of vital importance.

"On second thought," Maman said, "We should take some of our most valuable items as well. But hurry!"

Jeanne met Maman's eyes across the room, reading there what they were unwilling to say out loud. Would it even matter once the dragoons arrived? Whether they were on the mountain or in their homes, the soldiers would most likely sweep through, pillage, and destroy everything in their way.

Anne carefully wrapped the book in a clean linen cloth and placed it on the table next to the family Bible, in one of the "Maman approved" piles.

"Jeanne, please let Papa know we're almost ready. See if he has finished his preparations," said Maman.

Jeanne leaned out the *salon* window, glorious fall color filling her vision: amber, crimson, ochre-gold. Her favorite season in full array. How could the world go on as usual? Every stable thing she'd ever known was being uprooted like the recently fallen tree below, its deep roots exposed.

Inside the wrought-iron fence enclosing the front courtyard, the Tessier's silver-gray gelding stamped and snorted, impatient to go as aged stable-master Martin hitched him to the wagon. Despite his constantly aching and somewhat fragile back, he insisted on helping.

To the right, the Lacombe family assembled in the Route de Lasalle. All except Pierre. He was most likely out in the vineyards, for one last check. Belongings piled high onto their horse-drawn cart; the Lacombes were ready to help. Papa often said he didn't know what he would do without André, who managed the Château de Planque and served with him as an elder. Papa also greatly appreciated their friendship.

She could just make out what the two men were discussing. "We've got hoes and a few trowels to fortify the rocky terraces lining the mountain." André gazed across the vineyards to Le Cengle rising majestically on the other side of the river at the far end of their land. "Those ledges were built to last, but it's been a while since anyone used

22

them for cultivation. I expect they'll need some reinforcement. Do we need any other tools, anything else?"

"It's hard to say what exactly we'll need," Papa replied as he handled the pitchfork he had also stowed in the wagon.

For the first time, the thought came to Jeanne that they might use the tools beyond their designated function. Would they become weapons as events unfolded?

Slowly Papa uncovered one of the baskets sitting in the wagon, revealing the family gun and ammunition. Jeanne drew back, inhaling sharply. The elders had stood firm yesterday against the young mens' arguments. But there was Papa's musket, packed and ready to go with them to the mountain, despite their proclamations that passive resistance would convince the dragoons of their loyalty. Why then had they packed the gun?

She'd decided to support Etienne in actively resisting. So why did the sight of an actual weapon make her feel she couldn't breathe?

Gripping the inside of the window frame, Jeanne leaned out a bit farther. She didn't want to miss a word.

Papa placed a small lambskin on top of his gun and closed the lid on the basket.

"This is only for self-defense, of course. I'm leaving my grandfather's musket here." He said something else to André, which Jeanne didn't catch.

The vertical line between Papa's eyes deepened as he tugged on his short gray beard. "It's still so hard to believe the King and his court, in their new Versailles palace, would even be concerned about us down here."

André shrugged his shoulders slightly.

"You heard what Pastor Boyer said yesterday, but I still don't think God would have us attack the soldiers. Scripture is full of the deliverance of his people from the hands of fierce and numerous enemies without them having to fight at all."

"True. Yet I also think of times God led them to fight and to *kill* their enemies." André sighed. "But, then again, Jesus taught us to turn the other cheek."

"There are many who disagree with our plan. One of my servants brought word that several hundred men will stay in town with Josué Noguier, preparing to fight the soldiers. They're calling him *Capitaine*."

23

André's frown deepened. Josué Noguier's grandfather had served the Duke de Rohan in battles for Protestant rights earlier in the century. St Hippolyte was full of young and not-so-young men whose great-grandfathers had also fought in Rohan's army. They carried their forebears' arms and their bitterness at being on the losing side in that round of the religious wars. Jeanne suspected André was also thinking of his own son. Gabriel had been almost as vocal as Etienne yesterday regarding fighting the dragoons.

"Their choice," said Papa, his jaw set. "We need to concentrate on the majority who are with us and how to best protect them while standing firm on the question of our legal rights."

Servants appeared laden with baskets and bundles of food, clothes, and bedding to add to the Tessier wagon. Papa caught sight of Jeanne in the window.

"Tell Maman it's time to go."

Jeanne exhaled the breath she hadn't known she'd been holding and shut the window tight. She couldn't help the ripple of anticipation rising within her. There were others besides Etienne and Gabriel who planned to fight! She could bring this news to Etienne and maybe even help him get away to join Noguier's men.

Her excitement dissipated as the reality of flagrantly disregarding the elders started to sink in. Ever since a royal edict banned the stubbornly faithful Huguenots of St. Hippolyte from having their own pastor, the elders' authority had increased. Individual pastors visited and preached from time to time, but overall it was Papa, André, Guillaume Gamond, and Louis Bedos, who led the Huguenot community. Never had they been so overtly challenged. For a second, Jeanne shut her eyes, trying to process the implications, then remembered Papa's message.

"Maman! Papa says it's time to go. Catherine that means you too," Jeanne called down the hall to their bedroom where her sister had gone to avoid working. "Papa's waiting."

Catherine emerged with a huff and stomped down the hall to join Jeanne in the *grand salon*. The sisters adjusted their white linen bonnets, threw neck scarves over their shoulders, grabbed their cloaks, then hurried down the majestic central stairway to the ground floor. They passed through the chilly foyer, then emerged out through the massive double entry doors to the front of the château, blinking at the bright sunlight. Maman and the younger Tessier children appeared next, with Marion and the housemaids close behind with the final baskets of food.

André and Pierre stepped forward to relieve the servants of their burden and, with stable-master Martin's help, hoisted it up onto the wagon. Hinges creaked with the weight at precisely the same time Martin groaned with a spasm of pain from his aged back.

Jeanne gazed up at the château, trying to impress the image of the three-story structure with its wine-colored *volets* into her memory. Would they ever return? And, if so, what would have changed by then? Longing for what already seemed lost wrung through her, squeezing her heart tight. It was not just the estate and possessions she would miss, but their whole pattern of living, their family life.

Love strengthened into resolve. She would fight for her life, for their rights, even if she didn't hold the same beliefs. No matter the cost. No matter if women weren't usually involved in such things. Today, she would let nothing stop her from telling Etienne the news of Noguier's fighting men and then concoct a plan for them both to join the *Capitaine's* army.

CHAPTER 6

PIERRE

Day One
Wednesday, 6 October 1683
Château de Planque
St. Hippolyte de la Planquette

The silver-gray gelding hitched to the Tessier wagon stomped and snorted. In response, the Lacombe mare tossed her head and took a step or two. Pierre jumped forward and caught a small barrel of wine jostled loose from their wagon. He stroked the horse's neck, speaking soothing words over her. The animals weren't the only ones who were on edge, ready to go. The dragoons should arrive within hours, and they absolutely needed to be settled on the mountain before that happened.

Pierre surveyed the vineyards spreading out wide across the front of his home and the château. Thankfully, the men who worked under his supervision had already finished the *vendanges*. This years' grapes were gathered, pressed, and casked. Still, he regretted leaving it all behind. Blending the new Morvèdre grape with the traditional Carignan was starting to yield exciting results. Pierre inhaled deeply and blew it out as he turned away from the fields. What they were facing today was far more critical than his passion for bringing the flavors of the *terroir*, their land, with its hints of wild thyme, sage, and even lavender, into each vintage.

Finally, the Tessiers all assembled outside the château. Isaac helped his wife up onto the wagon seat. Settling onto the wood plank, Suzanne swiveled abruptly, searching the length of the road.

"Where's Paul? I haven't seen him all morning."

"I thought he was with you," said Isaac. Their eyes locked, adding a layer of tension onto Suzanne's pale face.

"And I thought he was out here helping you."

Both parents stared at each other blankly.

"And where did Gabriel get off to?" asked André.

Pierre's face hardened. Had he already failed at keeping track of Gabriel? It had been at least a quarter of an hour, probably more, since he'd last seen his hot-head brother.

All forward motion came to a standstill. Pierre rubbed the back of his neck and peered down the road leading from the château into the Planque *quartier.*

"I bet I know where Gabriel went." Pierre glanced at the Tessiers, then continued, "Paul might be with him. I'll go and get them."

Isaac reached for Suzanne's hand and he nodded at Pierre. "Go then. But quickly. We should be well on our way to the mountain by now."

"I'll go too," volunteered Jeanne, her voice determined.

Hoping no one noticed his suddenly flushed face, Pierre took off down the road in the direction of the *moulin à huile,* where olives from the groves on the terraces behind the château were pressed into the oil used daily in their cuisine.

"Hey, wait! Slow down a bit!" Jeanne called, out of breath, struggling to keep up with him. "Your legs are *a lot* longer than mine!"

Pierre slowed down, trying to keep his face neutral despite the stir she created in him.

They passed by the *moulin* used to grind their wheat into flour, the closer of the two water-powered mills belonging to the Château de Planque.

"We're going to the olive mill, right? You think they've gone to see Emmanuel Marolle about fighting?" said Jeanne.

Without changing his pace, Pierre glanced at her, eyebrows raised. He nodded. She never ceased to surprise him.

"I thought so. Paul talked about battling dragoons all last evening. Gabriel too?"

"That's all he can think of," replied Pierre, turning his focus back towards the destination.

He'd always known Jeanne and been part of the Tessier family—both as an employee of her father and through the close-knit Huguenot community. Their paths often crossed as he helped his father and Isaac

27

manage various aspects of the château estate, in addition to overseeing the vineyards. Although he was four years older, they'd always had an easy rapport.

"Pierre? What do you think of all that happened yesterday at the gathering? The disagreements, the decisions made? I know we've always followed the elders. But then Etien..."

Pierre winced as she gulped back the name, reluctant to say it out loud. She met his eyes, then drew a deep breath, letting her words rush out like river water through the mill wheel. "But, well, I think the younger men are right. We should make the first move and attack the soldiers. Like Pastor Boyer says, it's our *right* because the King has taken away so many of ours." Her brow furrowed. "I'd rather fight to defend ourselves than sit around on the mountain waiting passively. What do you think?"

Pierre studied her and marveled, not for the first time, at how quickly her brain worked, formulating and articulating thoughts in rapid succession. Was she even breathing? Her hazel eyes fixed on him; he was obliged to answer.

"Despite our loyalty to the King, it's most likely we'll be attacked when they arrive."

"So, you think we should attack them first?"

Before Pierre could respond, they arrived at their destination. Emmanuel Marolle's wife stood outside their home next door to the *moulin à huile* he managed for the Château de Planque estate. Françoise held their youngest child on her hip, another one evident in her swollen belly. The two young Marolle girls ran to greet Jeanne with *bisous,* three kisses as was tradition.

"*Bonjour* Françoise! Have you seen my brother Paul?" Jeanne called. "And Gabriel Lacombe?"

Not waiting to hear the answer, Pierre strode into the stone mill house.

Sure enough, Gabriel stood talking with Emmanuel, and young Paul listened nearby. Pierre grabbed each brother by the arm and silently led them out of the building. Taken off guard, the boys did not resist.

Once outside, Pierre demanded, "What do you two think you're doing?"

He turned to Jeanne. "I found them in the middle of a gun demonstration from Emmanuel." Jeanne glared at her little brother, who wisely avoided making eye contact.

28

Pierre continued. "Gabriel, you know what Papa told you about guns. Only to defend ourselves, and *only* he or I will do so."

Gabriel exploded. "That's ridiculous! We can take them! God is on our side. What did Papa read this morning from Psalm 91? We have nothing to fear! The enemy can approach, and they'll fall before us!"

"I understand that scripture to mean we stand firm, trusting in God. He will take care of the enemy. I do not see a mandate for an attack in those words."

Pierre looked straight at Jeanne. Here was the answer to her question.

Gabriel continued. "We call ourselves the Lord's Army, meaning we *fight!* The dragoons will surely attack us. So, we must prepare; be on the offensive."

"And how did that work out for the Huguenots in the Dauphiné? They attacked the dragoons, and they all died—horribly."

Gabriel sputtered, "You can't understand; you're an old man at twenty-two. Always the cautious one. So boring."

Pierre's lips compressed, his eyes shot daggers at his brother. He did not appreciate the fact that Jeanne was overhearing this interaction. Blood rose to his face, and his grip tightened on Gabriel's arm.

Jeanne spoke up. "Our families are waiting for us in front of the château. We need to get going. The dragoons should arrive soon." She took Paul firmly by the hand. He jerked it away and stomped past her in the direction of their home. The Lacombe brothers scowled at each other, then followed close behind.

Pierre had nothing more to say to Gabriel for the time being. They moved along swiftly, in silence, as Jeanne attempted to talk sense into Paul.

"And *you,* young man! What do you think you were doing back there? Discussing gun battles? You're only ten years old!"

Paul glanced back at Gabriel, hoping for encouragement, but received none. He drew himself up. "I *am* old enough to fight!" Pierre restrained himself from knocking both younger brothers' heads together.

"We'll see what Papa says about that," said Jeanne.

As they approached the château Suzanne let out a small cry of relief at the sight of her son. Anger quickly replaced her anxiety. "What on earth were you doing, going off on your own? Today of all days?"

29

Paul's bravado of a minute earlier evaporated. "I, uh, I just wanted to see," he stammered, stopping short. Finally, he pointed at Gabriel. "I followed him!"

André stepped forward. "Where were you, son?"

Gabriel threw him a hard look and refused to answer.

"We should go," said Pierre.

His father stared at him for a second and started to press the matter, then stopped. André turned back to Gabriel, his eyes boring into his younger son. "Pierre's right. We must leave now. But don't think we won't be discussing this later."

Suzanne ordered Paul up onto their wagon next to her. He climbed up and plopped down on the bench seat with such force the horses startled and reared. Isaac calmed them, then gave Martin the signal to go.

Jeanne took hold of Anne's hand and gave it a little squeeze as they set out on foot. She nodded encouragement to Catherine to keep up with them. Isaac walked alongside his family, moving up to the wagon and glancing back to his daughters, keeping watch over them all. Pierre and the rest of the Lacombes brought up the rear.

Within a minute the two families arrived at the *Pont de Planque*, allowing them passage across the Vidourle river. Together they crossed the bridge that gave the château and the town its name.

Immediately on the other side, they passed under the arch marking the town side of the bridge and then turned right onto the narrow road towards the village of Cros, merging with hundreds of Huguenot families streaming out of town. Little more than a five-minute walk to go before they would start the trail up the mountain.

Practically stepping on the heels of his brother, Pierre determined again not to let him slip away. How exactly he would manage to do this was unclear, especially in the chaos of settling thousands of Huguenots on the mountain. One glance at Gabriel's stony face confirmed Pierre's belief his brother was more resolved than ever.

If he was judging correctly, so was Jeanne. She'd kept her distance from him as they approached the mountain, her shoulders set, her eyes straight ahead. Was she avoiding him? Her desire to support the fighters didn't entirely surprise him. But had she thought it through? The dragoons did horrible things to the Huguenots in the north. Was she facing the reality of the violence involved? And, what made her so intent on taking action, even against her father's leadership?

The mountain loomed near. Pierre kept his eyes on Jeanne as she darted through the crowd, corralling siblings, acting the *maman poule* like always. Only one motivation seemed possible for her to break with her family. Sighing deeply, he made his decision. He would have to keep track of her as well.

CHAPTER 7

THE MOUNTAIN

Day One
Wednesday, 6 October 1683
Le Cengle mountain

One family after another converged at the diagonal path leading up onto the mountain. The chirping of birds filled the air, indifferent to the precarious steps of the people below.

On their left, the cliffs of Le Cengle mountain soared into the sky, the rocky granite and limestone *façade* a reassuring presence. A lone eagle floated on the fresh currents high above, reminding more than one Huguenot to see things from a heavenly perspective.

Inspired by the birds' melodies, several of the beleaguered community began to sing Psalms, as was their tradition. The music washed over them like a wave of peace and gave them courage as they climbed up the mountain.

"I lift up my eyes to the mountains—where does my help come from?
My help comes from the Lord, the Maker of heaven and earth."[5]

The Huguenots spread out onto the first big terrace at the end of the path, sheltering horses and wagons in a copse of green oak trees at the far end. Each able member of the community piled as many necessities as possible into their arms and onto their backs, then continued up the steep trail. Slowly, they moved toward the higher and narrower ledges carved into the side of the mountain and held in place with short rock walls. Such terraces were familiar to them as they covered mountains and hills all over the Cévennes region and were used to reclaim the land for

---

[5] Psalm 121:1-2 (NIV)

agricultural production. Le Cengle mountain's terraces had not been used for such purposes in years, which suited the Huguenots' present needs well. It was definitely something new and different to install people on the narrow, flat surfaces.

Jeanne strained to see through the crowds. Usually, she didn't mind being petite, but it certainly made it difficult today to locate anyone among the throngs of Huguenots. She doubled her concentration as Pierre passed by, choosing to ignore him for reasons she didn't fully understand. She needed to find Etienne as soon as possible and tell him about Josué Noguier's fighting men in town. From there, they could make plans.

Jeanne moved through the community, greeting friends and neighbors as she went. She might as well keep up the illusion of compliance with the elders' leadership as long as possible. Craning her neck to see through the masses, she passed right by Louise, who was sitting on her family's wagon.

"Hey you," Louise called, then jumped down next to Jeanne. "Are you trying to ignore me?"

"Oh! No! I was just looking...I mean thinking..."

Louise put her hand on her friend's arm. "Jeanne, he's up ahead with Gabriel Lacombe and the others."

"He? He is?" Jeanne stopped and stared at Louise. "Wait...you *know*?"

Louise tilted her head a bit. "Of course!"

One of the many things Jeanne loved about Louise was her ability to see and understand.

"Does *he* know?" Jeanne asked, clamping her mouth shut when her voice rose a pitch higher than usual.

"Are you kidding? My brother's focus is most often on his goals, his plans for the future."

The two friends walked on, arms linked. "But do you mind?"

Louise paused. "Well, to be honest, I did at first."

Jeanne's throat constricted. She hadn't realized how much her friend's opinion mattered.

Louise continued, staring at the ground. "Part of it was envy, I suppose. Not wanting to share either of you. I'm not proud of it." She lifted her chin and looked Jeanne in the eye. "I wonder if you know how challenging he can be? Once he makes up his mind about something, he's not easily swayed."

Jeanne liked Etienne's firm opinions and strong will. She hoped that once they were in a relationship, his confidence and faith would conceal her lack.

Louise continued. "But, I love you both, and if it goes in the direction I think you want it to, well then we'd be sisters in every way." She reached her arm around Jeanne's shoulders in a warm hug.

Elation flashed through Jeanne, thinking of a future where her last name was Gamond, followed by the settled feeling of calm after a storm, an effect Louise often produced in those around her.

"So, what did you think of Etienne speaking out against the elders yesterday? It seemed like the world stopped and froze in place. No one knew what to do or say," said Jeanne.

Louise rubbed her chest with the palm of her hand. "It was so awkward! It's nothing new for him to disagree with Papa, but he's never done so in public! I wanted so badly to disappear, to blot out what was happening." She gulped air and let it out in a slow sigh. "Everything is already so complicated right now. I wish they'd agree for once."

"You know we've always followed the elders, who just happen to also be our fathers," Jeanne said, meeting her friend's eyes, her head tilted slightly. "But this situation is completely different: an army of soldiers sent to do what? Repress us further? Force us to convert? To kill us if we resist? I think…" she paused, pulling herself tall. "I think the young men are right about fighting." Jeanne's heart rattled like a trapped animal against her ribcage.

Louise's eyes grew wide. "You agree with them? I thought you were shocked they argued with the elders."

"I was, and I still am, but the more I think about it, I find myself agreeing with their ideas."

Well, Etienne thinks it's the right thing to do, of course. Pastor Boyer's statements only strengthen his position. He'll not be easily swayed. In his mind, God will provide a miracle, or we'll die for our beliefs."

"I know!" Jeanne exclaimed with force, surprising them both. "I'd really like to talk to him about all this."

"So, you truly plan to support him?"

Jeanne held Louise's gaze until understanding passed between the two.

"But what if fighting the dragoons provokes them to do more...to murder us like in the Dauphiné?" Louise asked.

"I think there's an excellent chance we'll die either way. And I, for one, cannot sit by passively, without at least *trying* to fight for our lives." She could hardly believe she was saying such things out loud. Jeanne hoped the turmoil in her soul couldn't be heard in her voice. Deep down, she still wished this would all go away.

Louise stood silent, then looked her friend in the eye. "Well, then, you should go and find him now. Take advantage of all this chaos."

Jeanne drew her friend into a warm embrace and held on a bit longer than usual. "Let's find each other once our families are settled. I want to know where your camp is."

"I bet you do," Louise replied, nudging Jeanne in the ribs before taking off up the mountain.

Jeanne wove her way through the multitude of Huguenots, dodging those who couldn't see past the piled possessions in their arms. Etienne was nowhere to be found on the first terrace. She started up the steep incline to the next levels, stopping to survey the crowd below one more time. Disappointed, she continued the ascent, with families all around her staking their claim to a bit of land, trying to settle in for the duration. How were they all going to fit? Would anyone roll off the steep ledges during the night if they were still here? Jeanne trudged up the rocky path, feeling the weight of what they were doing increase with each step.

"Jeanne! Over here!" Her mother's voice pierced through her swirling thoughts and tangled emotions. "Where have you been?" Maman barely looked up as Jeanne approached, then handed her some bedding without waiting for an answer.

From a stone outcropping farther up the mountain, Papa called out in a loud voice, "Settle the women, children, and the elderly on the uppermost levels." He repeated the instructions, directing his voice to his right and left and up and down the steep slopes. "Men, station yourselves on the lower terraces; keep watch for any signs of danger."

"I'd prefer we all stay together," Maman said to no one in particular.

Jeanne shrugged. Papa and the elders made the decisions.

"Maman, look here!" she said, attempting to divert her mother's attention. Her arms still filled with blankets, Jeanne pointed with her elbow at an unoccupied rock-lined nook. "This is perfect for the family."

Maman nodded, her eyes blank, her face like marble.

Jeanne led Maman and her sibling towards it and helped them unpack. The sooner they were settled in, the sooner she could get away to talk with Etienne.

A quick quarter-hour later, Jeanne stood, arms crossed, and surveyed their work. The blanket beds were all spread out and ready to go. Marion squawked and fussed and finally directed Anne and Paul to collect wood for the fire needed for warmth and to prepare simple meals. Catherine was nowhere in sight. Why did her sister always disappear when there was work to be done? Jeanne sighed. She glanced at Maman, sitting like a statue on a large boulder. Anxiety rippled across her face, alternating with blank fear. Jeanne couldn't think of anything to make her feel better.

Papa joined them, looked over their little camp, then met Jeanne's eyes. He rested his hand on her shoulder, gave her a slight nod. She smiled in return while her stomach churned. Once he knew her plans, that approval might disappear forever.

Papa continued across their terrace until he joined André. Together they moved down a level to where the Gamonds were settling. Jeanne trailed behind to watch and see what she could learn. Louis Bedos soon joined the other men.

As the elders started in on their discussion, Louise waved up at her. Her lifted eyebrows and slight shake of her head answered Jeanne's silent question. No, she'd not seen Etienne.

Jeanne checked on her family one more time. Everyone was still bustling about with tasks or were lost in their thoughts. With Papa occupied, here was her chance. She found a small passage in the rock wall to the terrace above. Where could Etienne be? He was not with his family, so he must be with his friends somewhere. Perfect!

She wove her way through clusters of Huguenots, now filling the narrow ledges like herds of goats clinging to the mountainside. She pulled her linen bonnet forward and kept her head down. She really didn't want to be pulled into any conversations, or worse, be asked uncomfortable questions.

Finally, she found Etienne at the far end of the highest terrace, where the ridge narrowed and blended into the mountain's rock face. Jeanne scooted around the families camped there, focused straight ahead as if on an important errand.

With each step, the drumming of her heart increased like a call to battle. The men, lost in heated debate, didn't see her coming.

"We should go *now* to join Noguier's men in town," said Gabriel, with force. Jeanne stopped cold. They already knew! They were aware of Noguier's makeshift army! The hope of using this information to impress Etienne tumbled out of reach, like a spray of loosened rocks down the steep mountainside.

The men fell silent and stood watching her. Now, what could she say? Words had rolled away with her hope.

"Jeanne?" Etienne said.

Well, at least he knew her name and had said it out loud. That was something, wasn't it?

"Jeanne, what are you doing here?" he asked again, not unkindly.

She stared at him, then at the others: Gabriel Lacombe and Jean Bedos. They were all sons, or the brother, of the elders currently conferring on a lower terrace. Yet, here they were, in a parallel meeting, making their own plans. Since they were already aware of Noguier's men, she needed a new strategy.

"I've come," she swallowed hard, marshaling her thoughts. "I've come because I know you want to fight. I do too."

The men gaped. Finally, Etienne spoke. "Jeanne—you agree with fighting the dragoons? You know it's against the elders' direction."

Jeanne lifted her chin. "I was at the same gathering as you yesterday."

Gabriel jumped in. "You want to fight? What use would you be? You're a girl!"

Fists clenched, Jeanne took a step towards him, eyes ablaze. His words were like tossing dry kindling on a growing fire and provided a convenient target. She couldn't care less what Pierre's annoying brother thought of her.

"I may be small, but I am mighty," she said, then instantly regretting the words—her father's favorite description of her—as they left her lips. It had spilled out without thought, and to her horror, Gabriel suppressed laughter and Jean Bedos appeared confused.

She focused on Etienne, silently begging him to refrain from mocking her. He studied her intently. What was he thinking?

After what seemed like an eternity, he took a step towards her. "Jeanne, I appreciate that you support fighting the dragoons."

A glimmer of hope rose in her heart.

"But, it's a dangerous business, with an uncertain outcome," he continued.

"Of course, it is! Just as it is for all of us here on this crazy steep mountain." She gestured wildly, arms flying as she spoke, teetering on the edge of the rock wall as if to prove her point. "There is no 'certain outcome' following the elders' plan either." Her words fired off like bullets. Etienne tilted his head slightly, reminding Jeanne of the same gesture in Louise, bolstering her courage. "Either way we might die. I, for one, would rather fight and die than sit around and do nothing but wait." She drew a deep breath, a little taken aback at the passion, the clarity she had once she said it aloud.

Etienne raked his fingers through his hair and turned towards his friends. Their silence and indifference conveyed disapproval. Clearly, they were anxious to get on with their business.

He turned his gaze back to her. "Jeanne, I agree with your thinking. But, I cannot allow you to fight alongside men. You wouldn't know the first thing to do!"

"Do *you*? Have you ever trained for battle?" Jeanne sensed the irritation of the men rising into anger and didn't care. It matched her own. "None of us has! But I'm willing to fight, and you don't have a whole lot of others on your side."

"Which is why we'll see if Pastor Boyer can convince the elders to change their minds. He's supposed to show up here today sometime. If that doesn't work, we'll join Noguier and his men," stated Etienne. Gabriel and Jean Bedos nodded.

"Then I'll also join Noguier," Jeanne said.

"No, you won't! It's not safe for you. Don't you know what dragoons do to women? Anyway, I couldn't present a woman to Noguier. He'd laugh in my face."

Jeanne glared at them, sorting through the possible answers in her mind.

"Hey!" hissed Gabriel. "Here come the elders."

"Let me take care of this," Etienne muttered under his breath.

"There you are," called Papa. Jeanne wasn't sure if he was addressing the men, her, or them all. What explanation could she give for her presence up here alone with Etienne, Gabriel, and Jean?

André walked the narrow ledge right behind him; his eyes fixed on Gabriel. Her stomach clenched at the rage in Guillaume's face as he approached Etienne. Only Louis Bedos appeared calm, but then he was always the stoic one.

"*Bonjour!* Hello, Monsieur Tessier!" Etienne said, avoiding his father. "What brings you to the upper terrace?" Jeanne had to admire his attempt to deflect attention.

"We could ask the same of you, young man," replied Papa, his burning stare bearing down on Etienne, then the others. "But, it doesn't take much imagination to discern what you're doing here."

Etienne said nothing, wisely.

Papa continued. "Listen, we've no time to lose. The dragoons could arrive any minute, and we must be ready. We're posting guards on each terrace to protect people and to sound the warning when the soldiers arrive."

"So you'd like us to do the job?" asked Etienne.

"No, son," replied his father, stepping forward. "We want trustworthy men who follow our leadership." Jeanne shrank back at the fierceness of Guillaume's demeanor.

"Go to the second terrace. Your task is to strengthen the rock walls where they've crumbled," said André, addressing Gabriel first, then the others. "Report to Pierre *now*. He's waiting for you three."

Gabriel started to speak, then stopped. He turned on his heel and headed toward the lower terrace, Jean Bedos following close behind.

"What are you waiting for, son? Go!" said Guillaume.

Etienne's nostrils flared, his stance widened; then, with a glance at Jeanne, relaxed slightly. Surprised, she studied his face. Then, running his hand through his hair, Etienne let out a noisy sigh and followed his friends down the hill.

"Jeanne?" Papa's attention turned to her. "I don't know where to begin. What on earth are you doing here?"

"Papa! There's no need to worry! I was just exploring the mountain. I wanted to see the view from as high as possible. The men were already here talking." A weight, heavy as one of the surrounding stones, descended on her chest.. Lying did not come naturally to her, and here she was doing it easily, right to her father's face.

Before he could comment, she rushed on. "And, I was thinking, why don't we gather everyone for worship and prayer. It would do us all good."

Papa studied her, unanswered questions written across his face. Jeanne waited until he appeared to set them aside, at least for now.

"Yes. We were about to send a message to meet for those very reasons, on the lower terrace. You can help spread the word," Papa said, his eyes intense.

Jeanne ducked her head, then turned and followed the length of the terrace, finally remembering to breathe. She relaxed slightly. This was good! She'd find Etienne at the service and make plans.

But his comments on women fighting! Her brow creased, her jaw clenched a bit. None of them had ever fought, so what difference did it make that she was a woman? Even if she didn't directly enter the battle, surely there were many ways she could help. With each footstep, she became more determined. She'd just have to change his mind.

CHAPTER 8
SERMON ON THE MOUNT

Day One
Wednesday, 6 October 1683
Le Cengle mountain

Word passed through the Lord's Army that it was time to gather for a worship service. The Huguenots of St. Hippolyte streamed eagerly to the meeting place on the largest terrace, glad to come together to find comfort in God and one another.

Back at the Tessier camp, Jeanne grabbed Paul by the hand, determined not to let him wander off. He tugged and twisted, struggling to free himself. She threw him her sternest look and he gave up the fight. Jeanne led the way down to the meeting place on the lowest and widest terrace. Catherine, Anne and Maman followed. Papa and the other elders were already at the far end, waiting for everyone to arrive. The Tessiers made their way through the crowd to join him.

Butterflies flitted through Jeanne's stomach as the Gamond family arrived, Etienne included. Louise winked almost imperceptibly as they joined the Tessiers. Jeanne squeezed her friend's hand and avoided eye contact. Now was not the time to blush or worse, giggle.

André and Isabeau appeared with their sons, who came straight from fortifying the lower terraces, Gabriel glowering as usual. Jeanne leaned forward to observe Etienne on the other side of Louise. His stony face and the set of his jaw conveyed his discontent. She sat back but sensed someone watching her. Pierre! Jeanne looked him in the eye and he turned swiftly away, an emotion on his face she couldn't quite identify. She blinked hard. So much was happening, there was no time to process anything. For now, she pushed away the confusing thoughts and feelings.

Pastor Privat, whom they called La Roquette, moved to the front to preach. From the neighboring village of Monoblet, he had been covertly acting as their primary pastor since the King forbade the Huguenots of St. Hippolyte from having one of their own. Jeanne liked La Roquette and the way he taught. Even though she didn't trust God, she found comfort when they gathered to sing, to listen, and be together. Among the many other pastors in the region who traveled to preach for them from time to time, like the fiery Pastor Boyer, she most appreciated La Roquette's steady presence.

A hush rippled over the crowd, and the Huguenots of St. Hippolyte collectively leaned forward to hear what La Roquette had to say. He spoke on Psalm 33.

"We wait in hope, and we trust in God's presence with us. *He* changes everything. Our heavenly Father is always good and always trustworthy, even when our circumstances are uncertain and appear utterly bleak. Our hope is unwavering because of *who* He is and because He loves us."

The Huguenots glanced at one another, nodding in agreement. They drew these words into their hearts and souls, strengthened by this reminder of the truths they believed.

Jeanne peeked at Etienne and found him watching her, with what? Surprise? She decided it was a good thing.

Suddenly, a collective gasp rifled through the crowd like wind rushing through wheat. Pastor Boyer strode to the front and vaulted onto the large boulder serving as a podium. La Roquette backed away as Boyer waved overhead the long iron bar he'd been carrying since they had gathered yesterday. Boyer peered across the assembly, his eyes wild.

"We must protect our rights!" he cried. The Huguenots jumped to their feet and stood in utter silence. Boyer continued, ramping up his orations when no one responded. In a frenzy, he again brandished the iron bar overhead like a demented warrior, promising to defeat "all the swords" of the King's army with this very weapon!

"God is on *our* side, and we will not be vanquished!" he roared across the crowd.

His actions did nothing to promote his cause. Jeanne and Louise grabbed each others hands and stumbled back as he leapt from the boulders and began striding through the crowd. Still swinging the iron rod, his rant grew simultaneously louder and less coherent. Finally,

42

sensing he was alone, he repeatedly exclaimed God would give them victory with this one weapon.

Agitation sparked and spread like wildfire through the assembled Huguenots. Fathers moved to protect their families, and with every wave of Boyer's rod, screams and shouts erupted, hysteria rose. Snatches of conversations drifted past Jeanne: Boyer had gone too far, had moved beyond reason. He had lost any hope of influence.

The elders acted swiftly to restore order. Guillaume and André corralled Boyer off to the side and attempted to calm him down. Louis Bedos walked through the crowd uttering words of reassurance while Papa motioned for Pastor La Roquette to address the people and pull their focus back to God and the plan.

Waves of anger radiated from Etienne. One glance at his blazing face and clenched fists told Jeanne all she needed to know. Boyer was his hero. Etienne had counted on him to sway the Huguenots, including his father, to fight. There was no hope of that now. Jeanne waited a moment, then stepped around Louise, and rested her hand on Etienne's arm. For a long moment, he stared into the distance, then at her, but without seeing. Finally, he turned abruptly and disappeared through the crowd.

Jeanne stood cold in his wake. Now what?

A small hand rested on her arm. "My brother's hero has fallen," Louise said. "I don't know what he'll do now. I'm sure everyone is firmly on the elders' side after that display."

"I think I know what he'll do," said Jeanne, gazing in the direction Etienne had disappeared.

Louise waited, brows raised.

"He'll go join Josué Noguier in town. The *Capitaine*, as they're calling him, is training men to fight the dragoons from there."

"How do you know all this?"

"It doesn't matter, but I'm sure that's his idea—especially now."

"But, if our father has his way, Etienne will never be out of his sight unless he's working under Pierre's supervision. Even though it breaks his heart to consider it, Papa's threatening serious consequences if Etienne continues in this direction. I'm not sure what Papa meant exactly, but he made it sound like something life-altering."

"I don't think Etienne cares about any of that right now," Jeanne said, hands falling to her sides.

"Then go after him, Jeanne! Now, while everyone's still distracted here."

Jeanne stared at the ground. Louise gave her a gentle push. "Go!"

A glance at her preoccupied family and the busy elders confirmed it was now or never. Jeanne squeezed her friend's arm, then melted into the crowd as La Roquette's reassuring baritone flowed from the rock pulpit. "The elders have stationed watchmen on every terrace to survey the route from Lasalle where the dragoons will arrive. Once they're visible, Isaac Tessier and Guillaume Gamond will go down to greet them and assure them of our loyalty to the crown. We'll convince them we are acting in peace, *with no intention to fight.*"

Murmurs of approval rippling through the crowd affirmed her thoughts. The entire Huguenot community firmly embraced the elders' plan after Boyer's debacle. Now fully united, they held to passive resistance and hoped to negotiate a truce. It had worked in the past, most significantly last summer. The King had issued yet another proclamation, this time forbidding them to meet for worship at all. But, they had never missed a Sunday service despite the increasing restrictions. They assembled, as always, in the Bedos' field. La Roquette had preached on loyalty to crown and God, using Jesus' teaching on giving back to Caesar what is Caesar's and to God what is God's. Even the Catholic priest and local governor had approved.

But this time, the part Jeanne couldn't count on was God helping them, delivering them from the inevitable onslaught of the dragoons. For the rest of the Huguenots, faith and trust in God's good and trustworthy involvement were the critical components. If only she trusted God like everyone else. She wished to believe he'd come through for them and there'd be no bloodshed. Life could then carry on with their freedoms reinstated. But, she knew God couldn't be depended upon.

Anyway, she'd already staked her position, forcefully, in front of Etienne and his friends. There was no backing away, even now, without any hope of Boyer influencing the elders to change their course of action. *Something* was going to happen when the soldiers arrived, most likely violent and terrible. Jeanne sighed. It all seemed to be a lost cause, but at least she'd go out fighting. Taking action suited her, and fighting with Etienne was a bonus. But first, she must find him before he left to join Noguier without her. Too bad if he didn't think the *Captaine* would accept her. She wouldn't give either man a choice.

CHAPTER 9
WAITING AND WATCHING

Day Two
Thursday, 7 October 1683
Le Cengle mountain

Early morning sunshine reflected off the eastern-facing cliff hovering protectively over the sleeping Huguenots. Men, women, and children stirred as the coral-hued light attempted to warm the frosty air. More than one woke with a jolt, forgetting where they were. Consciousness seeped into foggy brains as it dawned on them. They were on the terraces of Le Cengle and had made it through the first night on the mountain.

Jeanne lay still under her blanket, reflecting on the many events of the previous day. Pastor Boyer's outburst, Etienne's angry departure, and how her father had thwarted her search for him. Somehow Papa had seen—or sensed—what she was up to and cut her off, directing her back to their family's corner. They had eaten a quick cold supper of chewy chestnut bread and sausage, then gone to bed with the sun.

Jeanne rolled on her side toward hushed voices murmuring nearby. Marion bustled around the fire, warming the last of the milk they had brought along and kept cool wedged in rocks overnight. Her siblings slept on, but Papa and Maman were up. They huddled together, sitting on the fallen pine log they had dragged close to the fire.

"I don't know why the dragoons have yet to arrive or when they will," Papa said. "So early this morning, we sent Marc Massador and Jacques Rafinesque to Monoblet to spy on the route from Anduze."

Maman's eyebrows raised. Papa reached his arm around her, then continued, their heads together. "First, they'll go to Pastor La Roquette;

he returned home last night to tend to his parishioners and family. With his advice, they'll find a suitable place for a lookout and install themselves. Once they sight the soldiers marching on the road from Anduze, they'll return swiftly on horseback with the news, taking the back roads, of course. This way, we'll have advance warning of the dragoons arrival."

"That sounds dangerous," said Maman softly, her face now permanently pale. "Our Massador? The sheepherder? Is he up to the task?"

"Ah, yes, I do believe he is. There's a quietness about him essential for the job. What's more, he has a way with horses I've seldom seen."

Maman pondered this. "Well, it's a good thing Rafinesque is with him. He knows the land like the back of his hand. His people have always lived here."

Papa tugged on his beard. "It's true Massador is untried. Of course, he might be tempted to do something impulsive, but we all know the Rafinesques don't get carried away," Papa added, a small smile tugging at the corners of his mouth but not reaching his weary eyes. "We believe together they'll carry out the mission well. Massador, especially, felt the honor of being chosen. He won't let us down."

Jeanne rolled this new information around in her mind, biting the inside of her lip. Could this be helpful information for the fighters' cause? But how was she going to get away from her family? It seemed like Papa kept a sharp eye on her as if he intuitively understood she was up to something. Her empty stomach twisted into knots. She still wasn't ready to declare her intentions to his face. Also, what if Etienne had already left and joined Noguier and his men?

As if reading her mind, Papa continued. "We've sent Etienne, Gabriel, and Jean Bedos down to the river to fetch water for our families, under Pierre's tight supervision. We've got to keep those three, plus any others with the same foolish ideas, out of harm's way." Feigning sleep, Jeanne sensed his glance linger, his concern weighing on her like a too-heavy blanket. "All will be well," he stated. To Jeanne that sounded like forced hope, probably meant to reassure them all.

Taking her time, Jeanne sat up to meet the day, racking her brain for a new plan. She stood and greeted her parents with the customary three *bisous,* then rolled up her blanket bed. To appease Marion's grousing about the lack of decent food, she pulled a clump of wild thyme from the rocky ground and presented the bouquet to the housekeeper. Earthy and fragrant, it would add a nice touch to their midday meal of boiled chestnuts. After that, there would only be dried sausages and there were not too many of those left. Butchering the autumn pig was meant to happen later in the month; their current stock was close to depletion.

The Tessiers gathered around their simple morning meal of day old bread and warm milk. Only twenty-four hours had passed since they'd last eaten breakfast within the security of the château's limestone walls, but that seemed a lifetime away. Now they sat on chilly boulders, waiting. There was nothing else to do.

Like exuberant angels, the bright blonde heads of Emmanuel Marolle's children bounced into the Tessiers' corner. Bursting with energy, they'd come for Anne and Paul to play away the boredom.

"Maman, where's Paul?" asked Anne, as she looked around the nearby terraces.

Everyone stopped what they were doing. He had been there during breakfast but now was nowhere in sight.

"I thought he'd just gone to relieve himself," Maman said. "But now that I think about it, that was a while ago." Her habitual anxiety etched deeper across her face.

"Not again!" Jeanne cried, rubbing her forehead. "Why won't he stay put? Enough's going on around here without him sneaking off every two seconds."

Shoulders tight, Maman walked to the edge of the terrace, leaning and craning as she searched the levels above and below them. Papa and Jeanne moved into action, each going in the opposite direction, asking families along the way if they'd seen Paul. But, no one had, and it occurred to Jeanne that Paul was becoming an expert at slipping away unnoticed.

Finally, she returned, shaking her head.

Anne piped up. "When I got up this morning, he was already awake. He seemed to be listening to you and Papa talking."

"Then he knows we sent spies to Monoblet and some of the young men to fetch water at the river with Pierre," said Papa.

A slight strangled sound escaped Maman as she folded in on herself. Afraid she'd crumple completely, Jeanne put an arm around her shoulders. "Papa, I don't think he'd attempt to go all the way to

Monoblet by himself, but it's possible he followed Pierre and the others to the river."

Papa stared down the mountain, then at Jeanne.

"Papa, you're needed here." She tilted her head towards Maman. "As the lead elder, everyone depends on you. Let me go down to the river and fetch him." Maman mutely shook her head. The line between Papa's eyes deepened.

Before he could object, she continued. "I know the way, and I'm small and can easily hide should the dragoons arrive. I'll be quick." Jeanne rushed through the words, hoping to quell her parents' fears.

Papa cast one last glance around the terraces as if willing Paul to appear, then agreed. "Go, Jeanne, be swift and be safe. God will be your fortress to protect you and your brother." His voice grew stronger as he spoke out his faith.

Jeanne held his gaze, hoping he only read confidence in her eyes. A quick *bisous* for Maman, and she hurried away before he could change his mind.

With perfect timing, Françoise Marolle appeared to check on her children, along with Isabeau Lacombe carrying her ever-present midwife supply basket. At the end of the terrace, Jeanne glanced back and a faint smile tugged at the corners of her mouth. Isabeau was already applying her expert hands to Françoise's eight-month pregnant belly. The rest of the morning's visit would revolve around the coming baby and all three women's previous birth stories.

Descending the narrow, steep trail down one side of the terraces, Jeanne had time to think. What if Paul wasn't actually at the river? Where else could he be? And, what could she say to persuade Etienne? Should she suggest they leave straight away for Noguier?

Then she remembered that Pierre was also at the river. How would he react? Also, she'd promised to get Paul safely back to camp. Irritation mingled with the stress of it all and squeezed around her head like a too-tight bonnet. She adjusted her head covering, then pulled it forward to shield her eyes from the mid-morning sun.

As she went, Jeanne surveyed each terrace, occasionally asking if anyone had seen Paul. There was still no sign of him.

Along the rocky limestone path, her feet crushed the wild mint and purple-blue thyme as she went, their fragrances filling the air. She stopped for a moment, savoring the pungent scents. Memories from childhood appeared in her mind, triggered by aromas anchoring her to the land. Nostalgia for simpler times surged through her in a wave of longing. Hot, stinging tears pricked behind her eyes. She blinked hard and continued on her way.

She focused on the scarlet, amber, and golden-green colors of autumn blazing their glory across the mountain and into the valley below. Breathing deeply, she drank in the beautiful sights and scents like an elixir of courage.

Her feet jostled and skidded on the rocky trail. She grabbed hold of a flaming red grapevine for support. Steadying herself, she searched the Route de Lasalle across the valley. No sign of dragoons, at least not yet.

The shadow of a golden eagle soaring high above crossed her path, drawing her gaze upwards. She followed its course as it honed in on the river. She, too, had a goal. How everything would work out, she still didn't know. There was only one way to find out, and with a last glance up the mountain, Jeanne let go of the vine and hurried on her way.

CHAPTER 10

THE RIVER

Day 2, Thursday
7 October 1683
Le Cengle mountain

Pierre stood tall, stretching his cramped back muscles. In other circumstances, this would be a perfect autumn day. Gentle sunshine shimmered across the river Vidourle, its waters flowing steadily on, replenished by recent rains. Gone was the parched summer river bed and the floods of winter were not yet upon them. Today, plenty of fresh water splashed over river rocks, gathering in deeper pools where a prism of colors sparkled to the surface.

Pierre rubbed the back of his neck. If only this were an ordinary day, a routine trip to fetch water. Glazed clay water jugs lined the riverbank and were all nearly full, the young men's task nearing completion. Pierre wiped his brow, then waded in deeper to fill the last of his containers, straining to stay close to his charges. It wasn't an easy assignment. Etienne and Gabriel continually repositioned themselves just out of earshot. Thankfully, Jean Bedos worked steadily on his own, sticking to the same spot. While the water was necessary for their families, it was even more essential that none of them ran off to fight.

Pierre pieced together snatches of overheard conversation. Etienne had counted on Boyer swaying the elders' position away from passive to active resistance. But, without the pastor's influence, there was no longer any hope of that happening. To Pierre's relief, Etienne appeared conflicted about losing his father's approval, possibly permanently, and the other two young men were reluctant to go on to Noguier without him.

Voices drifted across the current. "So, now, they've sent Massador and Rafinesque to Monoblet to watch for the arrival of the King's troops? Too bad they didn't trust us to go," muttered Etienne.

Gabriel's scowl deepened. "We'd be excellent spies!"

Pierre plowed through the water until he stood directly in front of the pair. "That's confidential information! You *must* keep it to yourselves."

Gabriel rolled his eyes. "Why are you always so serious, brother? What difference does it make if we talk about it?"

"There's wisdom in being discreet." Pierre waved his free arm wide. "If it becomes known that we've sent out spies, it could come to the attention of the King's officials in town. You must have noticed people coming and going from the mountain since we arrived." He paused for effect. "Whether they're merely curious or gathering information about our activities, it's hard to say."

"And what of it?" Etienne asked, leaning down to scoop water into his jar.

Pierre narrowed his eyes. "It's to our benefit that the King's men, and the handful of Catholics who live in St. Hippolyte, think we're merely camping out on the mountain to protect ourselves. If they discover the scouts, it could be perceived as an act of aggression." Pierre leaned forward. What did it take for them to understand what they were up against? "It would take very little to provoke the dragoons into a full-scale attack on us. Just like in the Dauphiné."

"Of course, they're planning to attack us! Exactly what I've been saying all along," said Etienne. "*Just like in the Dauphiné.*"

Pierre planted both feet firmly in the chilly river. "If we attack the dragoons, we can expect a massacre—as in the Dauphiné."

Silence filled the air, save the occasional burble of water against rock. Pierre drew a deep breath, then continued. "We're not soldiers, and they are the King's fiercest, most highly-trained forces. What chance would we ever stand against them?"

"I thought you trusted in God," replied Etienne, his head tilted up, his eyes locked with Pierre, who towered over him by several centimeters. "Can we not expect *him* to deliver us from our enemies?"

Pierre shifted his water jar to his hip. "I do believe God will deliver us from our enemies. But I do *not* think that justifies attacking the dragoons. Time and again in the Scriptures, we see the Almighty deliver his people by surprising methods."

When the inevitable retort didn't materialize, Pierre's eyebrows raised slightly. Maybe he was finally getting through. "Don't you remember the victory recorded in the Old Testament, where the Israelites, led by God's word, entered a battle with the worshippers in the front? And, don't you remember the outcome?"

Gabriel could not hold back the sarcasm. "Look who's a preacher!"

Unfazed, Pierre carried on, focusing on Etienne. "The people trusted in God and followed his directions, and their enemies turned on one another! Victory came to God's people that day, without them taking up arms or fighting."

Loud snapping sounds suddenly emerged from the brush lining the river, followed by a piercing yelp, overriding Etienne's response. All heads swiveled downstream as a small boy leapt from behind a sizable prickly bush.

"Oh! Oh! Oh! Ow! OUCH!" Hopping from one foot to the other, Paul Tessier beat at his pants legs, stomping, crashing about in a frenzied dance. He held a homemade spear in one hand, adding to the overall spectacle.

With most of the fiery ants brushed away, he slowly grew aware of his audience. Lifting his chin, he pretended to ignore their bemused expressions.

Pierre waded out of the river and poured a bit of cold water on the stings. Once assured the boy was all right, he lay into him. "What on earth are you doing down here? You should be up on the mountain with your family! They must be worried sick you've snuck off *again*."

Paul scoffed, "It doesn't matter. We need to prepare for battle!" Throwing out his chest, he spread his arms wide. "And, I'm here to help!" he added, thrusting his spear at the ground for emphasis.

Etienne and Gabriel suppressed smiles. Pierre threw them a dark look; the last thing he needed was the boy to be encouraged.

"Paul, we admire your determination and courage. It will serve you well in the future." Placing his hand on the boy's shoulder, he waited until Paul looked him in the eye. "But for now, *none* of us are initiating any fighting. If necessary, we'll defend ourselves *if* the dragoons turn their full force on us. But even then, you're not old enough to fight. You've not had anywhere near the necessary training, nor the equipment," he added, glancing at Paul's makeshift spear lying on the ground, "to take on the King's men."

The boy turned to Etienne and Gabriel, his face full of hope. Under Pierre's scrutiny, they shook their heads. Kicking the dirt, Paul grunted in exasperation.

With the sun indicating the approach of midday, Pierre's blood raced at the thought of the dragoons showing up with the extra responsibility of Paul on his hands. Also, if the soldiers arrived now, it was highly likely his brother and Etienne would do something rash.

"Come, let's waste no more time. Finish filling the jars so we can get them, and Paul, back up to the camp," gesturing to the mountain behind him. "We're vulnerable enough as it is down here on our own, and his family…"

A cascade of rocks suddenly rumbled down the hill behind him, cutting off his words. Pierre whirled around just as another red-faced Tessier slid in a final rush down the steep path. He sucked in his breath, and his face turned crimson. Jeanne!

CHAPTER 11
DISCORD

Jeanne regained her footing, then stopped for a moment to take in the scene. Her eyes narrowed at the sight of Paul, half-hidden behind Pierre.

"I'll deal with you later," she called to her little brother. "Don't even think about going anywhere."

Jeanne turned towards Etienne. She stood straight and walked up to him, ignoring her frantically beating heart.

She swallowed hard. "Can we talk in private?"

Etienne stared at her, then glanced at the other men, all watching, all eyebrows raised.

Pierre broke the silence. "I assume you've come to fetch your brother? We're almost done here and must return to camp quickly."

Jeanne tried to meet his gaze but couldn't. Her lips compressed.

"Pierre, give me a few minutes with Jeanne, then we'll go," said Etienne.

Pierre hesitated, then responded, his voice tight. "Make it quick."

Jeanne and Etienne moved farther downstream and stood on the rocky bank. Jeanne looked back to where the others filled jars, her brows knit tight together.

"Well, what is it?" asked Etienne.

"I came to tell you the elders have sent spies to Monoblet," she stated.

"I know."

Jeanne's heart sank. This wasn't going well. She hadn't been sure what Etienne was going to do with the information, but she'd wanted to be the one to tell him.

"What's this all about, Jeanne? What do you want?"

"I already told you! I want to join the fight against the dragoons. We cannot—at least I can not—sit by passively and do nothing."

Etienne's silence stretched out. Finally, she plunged ahead, "I know, well, I think, Pastor Boyer's fall from influence discouraged you." She looked him in the eye. "I don't want you to give up."

He shook his head. "You don't understand. My father is livid at the thought of me fighting. Which may be irrelevant if we don't live." He brushed back a wayward lock of hair. "Yes, I'd thought Boyer would sway the elders, and we'd all agree to fight. But that's not going to happen now. And despite our differences, I'm not ready to break so completely with my family." His last words squeezed out soft and low.

Jeanne stepped back, studying Etienne's face, processing what he'd just shared. She'd been counting on him to choose to break away, a choice she would support and encourage. Yes, she was determined to fight, but in her mind, it had been them doing it together.

But how could she not understand his predicament? Didn't she feel much the same way? And, there was simply nowhere else to go if one broke away from family or faith. They both truly loved and valued their families. "I know how close you and Louise are," she began. "She's important to me too. Maybe it will help you to know that we've discussed my opinion about fighting, and I have her support."

He raked his hand through his hair. "But the consequences are not the same for you as they are for me."

"Aren't they? My family will be shocked when they know my plans." She ignored her shaking insides at the thought of it.

"Your plans?"

"To go with you to Noguier and join the fight!"

Etienne gaped. "You cannot be serious! I already told you, women don't fight. It's all complicated enough without your interference."

"Our cause is just, and the soldiers greatly outnumber us. I should think you'd welcome help from any source."

The pair stared at each other, the impasse broken only by Pierre's call to leave. Finally, Etienne turned away, grabbed his water jars, and moved towards the mountain. Gabriel and Jean exchanged a look, then followed.

Jeanne stood, hands on hips, her jaw clenched. She'd not expected Etienne to be quite so difficult, despite Louise's warnings. Now what?

The sound of approaching footsteps on gravel broke through her thoughts. Pierre. Why wouldn't he just go on his way and let her figure this out?

"Let's go, Jeanne. Your parents need to know that you and Paul are safe." He gestured to the path. She stiffened then started back up the mountain. Pierre and Paul trailed behind.

They all climbed back up Le Cengle in silence. As the terraces of the Lord's Army came into view, Jeanne let out a noisy sigh. Tears rose and, despite her best effort to hold them back, spilled over.

Pierre moved to her side. "Do you want to talk about it?" he asked after a moment.

Startled, Jeanne looked at him blankly. She'd forgotten he was there.

"Jeanne, what's going on?"

She flicked her gaze away. "Wait. Where's Paul?" It'd been a while since she'd last seen her little brother next to Pierre.

Pierre stared at her as if she was an unknown species. Heaviness at disappointing him settled on her like an unwelcome load. She shook it off. They'd all have to get used to her not being the perfectly responsible big sister, always doing the right thing.

"I sent him on ahead to your family with Jean Bedos," Pierre said with care as if speaking to a cornered animal.

"Oh, all right. I did promise Papa…"

"I trust Jean to deliver him safely to your family."

"Thank you. I, uh, I was distracted."

Jeanne finally met his eyes. "I know you're wondering about what I had to say to Etienne. And I think you know I'm upset." It was a relief to speak a bit more honestly, a bit more like their usual rapport. The flecks of gold in his brown eyes glinted, and his silence encouraged her to go on.

"I wanted to…." she began. "I thought I had some information that would help Etienne."

Pierre stopped abruptly. "What information?"

The sudden sharpness in his voice scraped and startled her. She looked away. "I don't want to go into the details, but it doesn't matter. He already knew."

"Jeanne, what are you doing? The stakes couldn't be higher today; the dragoons should arrive anytime. Etienne and Gabriel continue spouting off about fighting. But what is your concern with all this?"

Would no one take her seriously, believe she had an opinion and could be of use in the coming battle—however it played out? Eyes ablaze, Jeanne glared up at him, "I know you don't think we should fight the dragoons except in self-defense. But that's not what I believe!" She bit her lip. How much was she willing to reveal?

The planes of Pierre's face smoothed calm. Jeanne tilted her head. Why wasn't he more alarmed? Also, why was she simultaneously drawn to and resisting what she saw in him? He seemed to respond to her small step towards honesty.

Banishing the distracting thoughts, she continued, forcing conviction into her voice. "Of course the soldiers are coming to attack us. We must be ready to fight!"

When he said nothing, she continued. "And God will win the battle for us!" Not that she trusted God to do any such a thing, but she knew this was what Pierre believed. In her mind, the outcome was entirely up to what they did for themselves.

Pierre studied her. She spun away, starting up the hill again. Why did it always feel like he saw more than she was sharing?

Pierre followed her silently for a while before speaking. "You know, that's exactly what Etienne says. When we last talked, I thought you were unsure of what was best."

"Is that a statement or a question?" asked Jeanne, jerking her bonnet farther up over her forehead. She couldn't even remember what she'd thought or said to him earlier. And she definitely didn't like him pointing out her use of Etienne's words. With each step up the rocky path, her real reasons and motivations seemed less clear.

The last minutes on the trail passed without further discussion. The wind rustled through autumn leaves over their heads, occasionally sprinkling them in crimson, amber, and gold. The twirling beauty went unnoticed, each of them lost in tangled reflections.

Jeanne and Pierre slowed as they approached the Lacombe camp, then turned to the other to speak, words crossing and tumbling unheard.

"Go ahead, you first," said Pierre.

"No, you go."

Pierre's words came out with intensity, laced with sincerity. "Jeanne, why did you *really* come to the river? And what do you plan to do now?"

She stared at an ancient green oak tree, clinging to the side of the mountain, struggling to stay attached.

"Now? I'm going to my family's camp to see if Paul is safely home," she replied. She then lifted her chin and walked away before he saw the tears spilling down her cheeks.

CHAPTER 12
GONE!

Day 2
Thursday, 7 October 1683
Le Cengle mountain

With each step towards her family, Jeanne struggled against the north wind cutting across the terraces of Le Cengle mountain. Nothing was going according to plan. How could Etienne be conflicted about joining Noguier after all his bold words about fighting? She hadn't expected Etienne's hesitation to be so strong when Boyer failed to sway the elders. Jeanne brushed away the tears. She had been counting on him to lead their defection to Noguier's camp. Maybe she should simply go on her own. But her idea had been for them to do it together, for so many reasons.

And Pierre. Why was being around him so…what was it exactly? She couldn't put her finger on it, on why his opinion left her feeling unsettled. Maybe it was best to give up on fighting and go along with the elders. Maybe whatever was going to happen was going to happen. She brushed the tear tracks from her cheeks and sighed heavily.

Papa's voice reached through her jumbled thoughts. "Jeanne! There you are!" He stood waiting for her at their camp, with Paul by his side.

Maman and the rest of the family sat by the fire while Marion finished preparing the midday meal. Boiled chestnuts and the last bits of bread were on the menu, with some sheep's milk cheese to finish. Jeanne's stomach growled, and normally at least one sibling would have commented and teased her, but no one said a thing. Was it fatigue or the overall shock of their situation? Either way, they were definitely hungry. The Tessiers were used to more substantial fare for the biggest meal of the day, including fresh vegetables from the *potager* behind the château: especially the sweet Cévennes onions. There simply had not been time to dig up the current harvest before departing to the mountain.

Once the meal was ready, Papa led them in blessing the food, thankful for his reunited family and the simple meal in front of them. Jeanne kept her eyes on the wooden bowl balanced on her knees, struggling to keep it stable as she dipped chunks of slightly stale bread into the tepid chestnut broth.

Golden-breasted blue tits chirped and chattered overhead in the green oaks, waiting to swoop in for any wayward crumb. With a sudden, collective swoosh, they fled as Pierre approached their camp, picking his way around the countless Huguenots lining the terraces.

"Ah, *bon appétit!*" Pierre said.

Jeanne's head shot up. What was he doing here? What would he tell her father?

"Merci, Pierre," the Tessiers replied more or less in unison.

"Sorry to interrupt your meal, but it's urgent. Isaac, may I please have a word with you?"

Papa rose, his left eyebrow raised high. He set his bowl on a boulder and motioned for Pierre to follow him to the far side of their campsite.

Jeanne tried to calm herself. Pierre didn't know her actual plans. Even if he suspected she'd leave, her father was going to find out eventually anyway. No longer able to sit, she jumped to her feet and began gathering the family's dishes. Marion protested, but Jeanne insisted the housekeeper take a break. She hoped no one noticed that the washing up bucket was in hearing range of Papa and Pierre.

Jeanne stacked the plates next to the water, then plunged the first one in, taking her time cleaning it. She kept her back to the men. Maybe they wouldn't realize she could overhear their conversation.

Pierre spoke up. "Somehow, Gabriel's gone missing. He was ahead of me on the path back from the river. But now he's not with our family, and we've searched everywhere and not been able to find him. He's just disappeared." Frustration filled his voice.

Pierre paused. Did he know she was listening? She didn't dare look. Thankfully, Papa faced away from her.

"And..." said Pierre.

"What is it?"

Jeanne pictured the line between Papa's eyes deepening.

61

"So has Etienne. He's vanished too."

A bowl slid through Jeanne's grasp, clattering to stony ground. Before she could stop herself, she glanced up at the men. Then, quickly ducking her head, she grabbed the dish off the ground and went back to washing up, hoping they would continue their conversation and not ask questions.

"You're sure of this?" Papa asked.

"I've checked with his family, and they've not seen him since he left this morning to fetch water. Like Gabriel, he was ahead of me on the path back up the mountain. I thought, that is, I assumed he'd gone back to his family's camp."

When Papa finally replied, disappointment laced through his voice, drawing it tight. "It was your job to ensure their safe return! What could have possibly distracted you?"

With each minute of silence that followed, Jeanne's heart sank further, leaving her hollow. Carefully, she spread the clean dishes across the boulders to dry under the weak autumn sun.

Finally, Pierre replied, "I'm very sorry, Isaac. I've let you down."

"Any idea where they could've gone?" asked Papa, his voice flat.

"I'm guessing they've gone to join Noguier and his men in town or possibly to join the spies in Monoblet. Earlier at the river, I heard them discussing their desire that you'd sent them instead."

Done with her dishes, Jeanne started gathering twigs for the fire. She caught a glimpse of Papa combing his fingers through his beard, head tilted, gazing skyward, as he listened for divine wisdom. She found Pierre watching her. Flicking her eyes away, she moved on to gathering larger branches.

Papa cleared his throat. "This is what we'll do. First, go to town and see if they've joined Noguier. If they're not with the *Capitaine*, then they might have gone to find Massador and Rafinesque in Monoblet. Take the back route behind the château, through the hills, and then the vineyards below. Once in Monoblet, find Pastor La Roquette. He'll be able to direct you to where the spies are hiding out. Find your brother and Etienne and bring them back before they get themselves, and all of us, in trouble."

"Thank you, Isaac. Thank you for trusting me. I won't let you down."

"I believe you, Pierre. You're a good man. But focus is more important now than ever. Let *nothing* deter you from bringing them back—all the way to me."

"I understand."

"I don't like sending you alone, but you should be able to move rapidly and with stealth. Should the dragoons arrive while you're out there, well, I don't need to tell you to lay low. Conceal yourself well and wait. Now, go with God, and be careful."

Jeanne bent and gathered another branch as Pierre brushed past, leaving a slight whoosh of cool air. He strode down the hill on his way to find Etienne. Drawing a deep breath, she made her decision.

Her heart hammered hard, but it was now or possibly never. While Papa went to update André and Guillaume on this new development, and with Maman exhausted and preoccupied with the younger children, now was her chance. She stole away and started her own path down the mountain.

CHAPTER 13
SPIES IN MONOBLET

Day 2
Thursday, 7 October 1683
Monoblet

Marc Massador reigned in his bay mare, leaning over to pat her dark mane for a job well done. The shepherd of Château de Planque loved all animals, but his connection with this one was special. Ma Belle was more than a horse to him. She served as his second set of legs and as a loyal friend. They functioned as one; the mare had an uncanny ability to read his intentions. Especially grateful for her companionship today, the young man stroked her velvety neck, murmuring his thanks.

The first golden rays of the sun peeked over the valley. Massador pushed his stick straight hair off his face and drew in a deep breath of the sweet morning air. It was good to be alive. He still couldn't quite believe the elders had chosen him to spy out the dragoons' arrival. Once again, a thrill flashed through him. He'd been waiting for just such an adventure all of his young life.

He reached around to the back of his waistband to check if the pistol was still where he'd put it earlier. Despite the elders' orders to simply wait for the dragoon's arrival on the road from Anduze and then return swiftly through the small back roads, Massador needed some action. Dragoons had killed two of his uncles in the Dauphiné, burning them alive in a barn. A wave of revulsion passed through him, and Ma Belle twitched and stamped the ground. He hoped taking out a soldier or two might bring some relief from the sting of their loss. How he'd carry this out wasn't clear, but he figured he'd know when the time came.

"We made good time," said Jacques Rafinesque, pulling his stocky dappled mount to a halt alongside Massador. "Monoblet is just ahead. We'll arrive at Pastor La Roquette's house in a quarter of an hour. To avoid drawing attention to ourselves, we must be inside before the villagers are up and about."

"Good. I'm famished!"

Ma Belle tossed her pretty head and whinnied in agreement.

The men smiled. They could all do with some breakfast.

Just as Rafinesque predicted, they arrived at the pastor's home at the edge of town within fifteen minutes and quickly led the horses around to the stables in the back.

The family dog did her job well, barking up a storm to announce their arrival. La Roquette's wife, Elisabeth, welcomed them into the warmth of her home, despite her surprise at their appearance. Massador removed his cap and shifted from foot to foot while she greeted her cousin Rafinesque with three *bisous*, for the Father, the Son, and the Holy Spirit.

The Rafinesque family had been in the southern Cévennes for centuries and were well-known, if not related, to almost everyone. Several of their men had served in royal armies. Others were pastors; all were fervently Protestant. Massador was relieved the elders had sent Rafinesque along, his knowledge of the people and the land would continue to serve them well as they moved surreptitiously across the back roads. Not to mention his wry sense of humor, which lightened the more tense moments.

Elisabeth sent the older boys to the barn to tend to the horses and announced they'd wait for La Roquette to return before discussing the reason for their visit. The men sat *à table* with the three young children who took it all in with wide eyes. She placed warm bowls of milk in front of each of them and passed around the rest of the fresh bread. Massador's belly responded loudly, causing a ripple of suppressed giggles from the children.

La Roquette joined them midway through the meal, straight from praying with a parishioner. Elisabeth shot them all a pointed look, her wooden serving spoon poised midair, making it clear nothing was to be discussed in front of the children.

Once the young ones finished their breakfast and ran off to play, Elisabeth joined the men at the table. Seated next to her husband, she leaned forward, fixing her vibrant gaze on the pair.

Massador made eye contact with Rafinesque and then tilted his head a bit in Elisabeth's direction. She was *his* cousin, after all. Rafinesque cleared his throat and started to explain why they were there and the mission they'd been given by the elders in his steady, methodical fashion.

La Roquette listened patiently, and Massador saw that Elisabeth also took the information in stride. A glimmer of concern crossed her otherwise peaceful demeanor as she glanced at the door as if she saw twelve hundred dragoons on the other side. But strength and resolve won the upper hand almost immediately. Like most of the Rafinesques, her faith was deep and rendered her unshakeable.

"Where do you plan to situate yourselves?" La Roquette asked. "You need to do so in haste. The dragoons could arrive at any time."

Rafinesque's lips pressed tight in his inscrutable face. He paused to consider, then spoke. "I know the area reasonably well from Sunday afternoon walks when I've visited. But I haven't landed on the best spot to establish our look-out."

Massador was surprised by all this. He'd assumed they'd find a big rock to hide behind and from there it would all work out somehow.

"I have an idea," Elisabeth said, glancing at her husband. "Just outside the town, as the road curves towards Anduze, there's a hill. It's sprinkled with huge boulders and rocky ledges and covered over by trees. I often walk there to think and pray."

The pastor steepled two fingers under his chin as he mulled over her suggestion. "I don't often walk as far as you, my dear, but I believe I know where you mean. I've seen it from the road below, right where it bends before heading off towards the fork between Lasalle and Anduze." He covered her hand with his own.

"Yes, that's the place," she said. Then, turning to Massador and Rafinesque, she continued, "I believe you could arrive at the location unseen. The forest is quite dense there. Then, when the time comes, you can depart the same way. Also, there's an abandoned stone shepherd's hut nearby where you can hide the horses."

"Sounds perfect," Rafinesque answered for them both.

66

"Excellent! Now I have a question for you." Elisabeth looked Massador in the eye. "Do you plan on using that gun only for self-defense or have you other ideas?"

Massador involuntarily touched the pistol shoved into the top of the back of his pants, covered over by his loose shirt. He thought he'd concealed it well. Apparently not. Clearly, it hadn't escaped Elisabeth's notice.

Rafinesque scowled at the young man, his bushy eyebrows raised high. "We were not to bring arms! There must not be the slightest hint of intent to attack dragoons!"

Massador hung his head.

"Can you explain yourself?" La Roquette asked.

Massador found it impossible to put his thought process into words. Grief and a vague desire for revenge, plus a dash of adventure, had clouded his judgment. "I'm sorry," he managed.

"Be assured *I* will take charge of the gun. We certainly do not intend to incite the soldiers to violence as in the Dauphiné," stated Rafinesque.

All sat silent for several moments. Not everyone agreed the Huguenots' aggressive action had provoked the dragoons' vicious attack in the north. But whatever one believed to be the truth of it, the soldiers had crushed Huguenots without mercy.

La Roquette studied Massador. "Would my trust be misplaced were we to allow you to keep your weapon? Do you promise not to engage the dragoons?"

Warmth spread through Massador's chest. He lifted his head. "Yes, Pastor, I give you my word."

"That's good enough for me," La Roquette said. He glanced at Rafinesque, who did not appear happy with this turn of events but gave a slight shrug. He would acquiesce to the pastor's decision.

La Roquette stood. "I'll take you to the area we mentioned. We should depart immediately and avoid the main road. May our God give you both wisdom," he said, throwing a concerned glance in Massador's direction. "And keep you hidden from the eyes of the enemy."

"Amen," the men replied in unison.

While Elisabeth gathered some food to add to their supplies, the three men walked to the barn to prepare their horses. The younger children had fallen in love with Ma Belle. And, as usual, the mare knew how to adapt to whoever was around her. Massador let them hug her neck one last time, and promised to bring her back to visit.

La Roquette's horse had pulled a tendon during yesterday's trip back from St. Hippolyte, so Massador suggested they ride together on Ma Belle. She wouldn't have a problem carrying the two of them for a short distance. The pastor could then walk home on foot, which meant he could hide more easily if the dragoons arrived.

"Will there be a problem if any of your parishioners see us?" asked Rafinesque, leading his horse out of the barn.

"The villagers *are* worried. I encountered several of them gathered at the central water fountain yesterday. They've heard rumors that the King's dragoons are on their way to St. Hippolyte and will most likely pass through Monoblet."

"Do you think any of them would inform the soldiers of our presence here?" asked Rafinesque.

"It's true there are those in opposition to my decision to preach and serve as a substitute pastor in St. Hippolyte these past few years. The general opinion is you're all foolishly stubborn in your refusal to stop meeting for worship service, and that I shouldn't put myself at risk by serving you. I have to say, though, some of them begrudgingly admire your courage and faithfulness, even if they prefer not to draw that kind of attention to themselves."

La Roquette settled onto Ma Belle behind Massador. "But, there's no way to be sure what people will do once the soldiers arrive and start applying pressure. I hope no one would betray you, but it's best we keep your presence here as much a secret as possible."

Elisabeth handed the scouts bundles of dried figs, raisins, and *saucisson*. Then, with words of thanks and a wave, the men departed, moving swiftly around outlying farms, entering the forest.

Men and horses climbed the gentle slope of the hill, silent save the crackling branches under their feet and an occasional bird call. As the woods grew denser, all three breathed a collective sigh of relief. Ma Belle nickered softly. Mixed in with the green oak and chestnut trees were evergreens, their resinous scent filling the air. At the crest, they dismounted and studied the area. Elisabeth's suggestion ideally suited their needs.

La Roquette pointed out the limestone shelter nestled back in the trees, just large enough to hide the horses. Massador and Rafinesque walked farther out towards the highest point. They tried out several large boulders, settling on a cluster with a good view of the road from Anduze. Surely they would go undetected here. And, when the time came, they would depart down the back of the hill and ride like the wind to alert the Lord's Army on Le Cengle mountain.

CHAPTER 14
ON HER WAY

Day 2, Thursday
7 October 1683
Between Le Cengle mountain and Monoblet

Jeanne crouched behind a scrabbly bush, her pounding heart reverberating in her ears. She darted from boulder to tree, avoiding the main path, then stopped and ducked back into the brush whenever someone passed nearby. The last thing she wanted was to be seen or to need to explain her reasons for going down the mountain. With so many Huguenots crowded onto the terraces, progress was slow.

Jeanne had lost sight of Pierre, but it didn't matter. He was on his way to the center of town, to Noguier's home on the rue Blanquerie, where he hoped to find and extract his brother and Etienne. She was headed to the same place, but with the opposite desired outcome. How either of them would achieve their goal, she wasn't sure. For now, her problem was remaining undiscovered by Pierre or anyone else. And if the dragoons arrived during her journey? Terror jagged through her, and her legs rippled like water. Jeanne knelt behind a boulder, placed both hands on the ground, and took several deep breaths. She must stay focused.

After a few moments, she continued on her way, reminding herself to take her time and be careful not to be seen. Moving at this pace did not come naturally to her; slow was not her usual speed. Everything in her wanted to move swiftly as possible, arrive at the destination, and accomplish what she set out to do.

Flushed and slightly relieved, Jeanne finally arrived on level ground, where the mountain ended and merged with the edge of town. She stepped into the granite *lavoir* hewn into the lowest portion of the hill and caught her breath in the damp, cool shade. She sat on the edge of the stone cistern, filled to the brim from recent rainfall. Jeanne dipped her hand in and scooped up several mouthfuls, then pressed chilly fingers gently against her eyelids and cheeks.

Revived, she crossed the road in front of the *lavoir* and disappeared into a tiny passage between the houses on the other side. She wound her way through familiar gardens and alleys, stopping and taking cover at every barking dog or any other suspicious sound. Although the streets were empty as almost the entire population was on the mountain, she took great care not to be seen. A handful of townspeople had stayed behind, some to prepare to fight alongside Noguier, some for unknown reasons. She'd overheard the elders talking about those who might even side with the dragoons and turn immediately from their Protestant faith to avoid repercussions.

Anticipation rose in Jeanne as she approached the town center. Thankfully, the normally bustling area was quiet. Still, it was impossible to know if anyone was watching her from the windows of the townhouses circling the main fountain.

She waited several minutes in the narrow passageway next to a stately home. Hoping the Catholic noble who lived there would not choose that moment to emerge, she ran across the town's principal street. A little bit farther to her right, and she arrived at the top of the rue Blanquerie. Finally!

Pressed flat in a recessed doorway, she carefully peered down the road to Noguier's house, the tallest on the street. Her breath caught and she pulled back. A familiar figure strode up the road towards her and *away* from the *Capitaine's* home. Pierre! Which could only mean Etienne and Gabriel were not with Noguier.

In a matter of seconds, Pierre would pass by her hiding place. Compressing herself farther into the rough-hewn limestones, Jeanne shut her eyes as if this would render her invisible. His steps drew near and then passed by. How he did not see her or hear the pounding drumbeat of her heart, she didn't know. As Pierre's steps receded, she counted to thirty before daring to move.

Jeanne slowly opened her eyes, then leaned out. She could see Pierre, striding quickly towards the other side of town. She practically leaped from one doorway to another and into narrow passageways, trying to keep up. Finally, he arrived at the Planque bridge. Across the river, the Château de Planque rose above the vineyards. Her home! Was it only yesterday morning they had departed, crossed this bridge, and moved to the mountain? It seemed like an eternity had passed since then.

Jeanne hid in a small alley between two homes, then peered out and around the corner. Pierre, bent low, moved swiftly across the bridge. Once he arrived on the far side of the river, he stopped and stood still next to her favorite tree, the grand ginkgo. Lifting his head slightly, he seemed to sense something in the air. Her stomach tightened. Did he know she was following him? She shrunk back into the passageway. Or was it possible he heard the distant sound of dragoons? Anytime now, they would come down the road where he stood, the Route de Lasalle, the narrow street separating her home and his.

Jeanne peeked out again in time to see Pierre cross the small area in front of the château and edge along the left side of her home. He arrived at the entrance to the grounds behind the château, pulled open the gate, and disappeared from her view.

She scurried swiftly across the bridge, scrunching down as small as possible. Following Pierre's footsteps, she stepped through the same garden gate and into the kitchen *potager* just in time to see him head up the terraced hill behind the château. She darted from tree to tree, determined not to be left behind.

A pain grew in her side. She pushed her hand hard against it, gulped air, and forced herself to keep up. Once they left the walled property behind the château onto the wild hills and *garrigue* scrublands, she wouldn't know the way. There had never been a need for her to take the back way to Monoblet. Today, of course, the main road was out of the question; over a thousand dragoons would soon march down that route.

Just past the *bergerie*, where Massador penned their sheep on the second terrace, she lost sight of Pierre as he disappeared into the thick forest of trees covering the hill. Not surprised that his long legs outstripped her, she sped along an existing trail.

She stopped briefly at the top of their property to let the stitch in her side relax, taking in the panoramic view from the château to Le Cengle. The sun inched toward the upper cliff of the mountain, where it would soon disappear. Once it dipped behind the high peak, the air would chill, and night would not be far behind. Her parents' worried faces appeared in her mind, lined with concern. She shook her head slightly, banishing the images. She must concentrate on the task at hand. And catch up with Pierre.

She exited through the upper gate in the rock wall surrounding the château property and then came to a sudden halt. The path before her split into two. Should she take the upper trail or continue straight ahead? Not for the first time, she wished she believed in prayer and in a God who would guide her.

A sudden gust of wind whooshed through the green oaks and pines surrounding her with their earthy, resinous scents. A spray of acorns showered the lower path. With the last direct rays of sunlight, Jeanne made her choice and hurried on her way.

CHAPTER 15
ROAD TO MONOBLET

Day 2
Thursday, 7 October 1683
Back road to Monoblet

With each step, the dusk thickened like fog around Pierre. The days were already growing short as winter approached. He estimated at least two more hours walking through the rocky hills and then the valley vineyards below before he'd reach Monoblet. He picked up his pace. The more distance covered before full dark, the better.

The twilight mist activated the herbal scents of the Cévenol *terroir*. The hints of wild thyme, bay, and sage, awakened his appetite. He'd left immediately upon Isaac's orders to find his brother and Etienne. There had been no time to grab any food. At least he'd thought to fill the small gourd he wore at his waist with water earlier in the day.

Trudging along the foothills, he chewed thoughts instead of food. So, Gabriel and Etienne hadn't joined Noguier. He wasn't quite sure what to make of it after all they'd said about fighting. Maybe joining Massador and Rafinesque was the more logical choice for them or at least for Etienne. It provided a way of taking action without blatantly disobeying his father.

A luminous half-moon rose and beamed across the valley in time to illuminate Pierre's descent. Across the *garrigue*, moon shadows flickered and danced among the scrubby bushes and taller trees—a magical night in any other circumstance. An eagle-owl's solitary hoots broke through the silent night, echoing Pierre's heart.

As he descended into the valley, rows of grapevines appeared, their winey fragrance stirring a deep longing in Pierre for the vineyards of

Château de Planque. He'd never been away from them for more than a day. His creations, his experimental wines, would all be lost?

He set his focus on the path ahead, on what was most important. From somewhere in the distance behind him, a branch snapped, piercing the silence. Pierre froze. Only a human or a sizable animal could create such a sound. A suppressed yelp filled the air, followed by complete silence. The hairs on his neck stood to attention.

Crouching for cover behind a tall *chataignier*, Pierre listened, every sense on high alert. Who else would be traveling through the night?

After several moments of quiet, footsteps continued, slowly crunching down the trail. Did the dragoons send spies of their own into the land?

Whoever it was stopped just past him. When they didn't move on, he slowly leaned his head out from behind the broad chestnut trunk. Pierre blinked a few times. It wasn't possible. Jeanne?

She turned towards him. Had he said her name out loud? And why did she survey the area, tilting her head as if listening to an inner voice?

With a deep breath, he stepped out into the path. "Jeanne?"

She jumped, whirled around, and looked him full in the face. "Oh! *Bonsoir*, Pierre."

"Jeanne!" He couldn't find words.

She stood silent, spine straight.

"What are you doing here?" Pierre whispered. His voice sounded detached like a phantom, something not quite real.

They stared at each other in the moonlight. Pierre didn't know what to say. And for once, Jeanne also appeared to be at a loss for words.

A soft wind swirled past them and rustled the few leaves still clinging to the vines, rousing Pierre to his senses. He took hold of Jeanne's arm and walked her quickly off the path, behind the chestnut tree. She pulled free from his firm but gentle grip.

"Jeanne, please. Why are you here? Did your father send you?" Even as he said it, he knew the truth.

She kept her eyes on the ground, toying with the spiked chestnut pods littering the path with her foot. Finally, she raised her head and met his searching gaze.

"No, Papa did not send me."

Pierre started to speak but stopped himself.

"I came on my own," she added, crossing her arms.

"You're on your way to find Etienne." It was a statement of fact. Jeanne lifted her chin, and his heart sank. He wanted to shake her, free her from whatever it was she wanted to gain by going after Etienne. Instead, he gripped a branch of the tree, channeling his frustration where it would do no harm. The tree shivered, and more spiky pods fell to the ground.

"Do you have any idea how dangerous it is for you to be out here, especially after dark? The dragoons…" He swallowed down the urge to shout.

Jeanne stood firm, her left eyebrow raised, reminding Pierre of her father.

After another minute of silence, Pierre spoke. "I should escort you home and get you to safety. But we're too far along, and it's too dangerous for you to go back by yourself."

"I've been fine this far on my own! I don't need your permission or protection. I'm going to Monoblet." Her words were quiet but brooked no argument.

Pierre studied her, then turned on his heel and strode down the path. Jeanne ran to catch up and then fell in beside him. As they trudged along in silence, he glanced at her. How could she be here, in the dark of the night, on the way to Monoblet? His gut clenched, and his jaw tightened. Yet mixed into this stew of emotions was a hint of admiration for her stubborn persistence.

CHAPTER 16
DAY IS DONE

Day 2
Thursday, 7 October 1683
Le Cengle mountain

The Lord's Army shivered collectively as the October sun sent out its final rays of warmth then disappeared behind the limestone crags of Le Cengle. The temperature dropped immediately, and the Huguenots asked themselves if it didn't seem much colder this year than last. Scores of swallows swooped and circled their twilight dance in the indigo sky. The second day on the mountain was drawing to a close.

Isaac stood at the edge of the terrace while his family once again spread out their woolen blanket bedrolls on the rocky ground. The whole family, except for Jeanne. Stress lining his face, he surveyed up and across the terraces for the twentieth time, hoping to see her familiar form approaching their camp. All around him, Huguenots prepared for another night in the open air, but there was no Jeanne in sight.

Jeanne disappearing without any word to them was utterly out of character. Something had shifted in her. Exactly what it was, he couldn't say.

He loved Jeanne's spunk, the way she threw her considerable energy into everything she undertook. She'd always been solidly dependable and completely responsible. But now, where had she gone, and for what reason? He let out a throaty sigh. Maybe she'd followed Pierre. Or did it have something to do with Etienne and his friends? He couldn't puzzle it out.

Should he go after her, as everything inside him wished to do? He'd held off, hoping she'd show up. Now, enough time had passed he doubted he could even find her. But shouldn't he at least try and protect his eldest daughter?

Gently tugging on his beard, he started walking towards the Lacombe camp to check in with André and then Guillaume. Their sons were also out in the growing darkness.

Isaac pressed through the crowds of camping Huguenots, like swimming upstream through rivers of anxious faces. The excitement and comfort of being together were wearing thin. Anxiety grew with each passing hour, as did the flow of never-ending questions directed at the elders. Where were the dragoons? Why hadn't they arrived already? Were they sure their plan would work? Nerves frayed thin, the constant suspense mounting like dry tinder ready to explode with the tiniest of sparks.

At the Lacombe camp, Isaac found all three of his fellow elders. He searched the faces of his friends. It was clear there was no new information.

Guillaume spoke first. "Let's go over this again. If Etienne and Gabriel were with Noguier, Pierre would've returned by now. He must be on his way to Monoblet, assuming they went there to join Massador and Rafinesque." He paused. "My best guess is that Jeanne followed him."

Isaac shook his head. "But it makes no sense; this is so unlike her."

"I asked Louise if she knew anything about Jeanne's whereabouts. She didn't seem that surprised. but she truly doesn't know anything about it," Guillaume said.

The men stood in silence, turning and pondering ideas and implications over in their heads.

"It doesn't seem wise to send any more of us out into the night," said André finally, resting his hand on his friend's shoulder. "If the dragoons choose to arrive now, it would only fare badly for those on the road."

"Which is exactly why Jeanne can't be alone out there." Isaac's voice trailed off.

He peered into the valley below, still hoping she would somehow appear. Finally, he turned his gaze to the men. "I can't wait anymore. I'm going after her. What if she's hurt?"

The elders said nothing, their faces full of understanding despite their concerns.

"I have to try and find her," Isaac stated.

No one tried to change his mind.

"Before you go, we have another pressing matter," said Louis. "I made the rounds this afternoon, checking on food supplies and general morale. Most families have eaten the last of their boiled chestnuts. Some have a few *saucissons* left, but all the bread is gone."

"I've heard the grumbling," André said. In a less tense moment, someone would have laughed and asked if it was in the form of words or growling stomachs.

Isaac nodded. "Many in the community didn't have enough food supplies ready to bring along. Plus, they thought we'd only be here for a day or two at the most."

"It's true. No one expected the dragoons would take so long to get here," said Guillaume.

"And, even if we gather together and share the remaining supplies, by tomorrow, there won't be enough to feed us all."

"I know. Some families have even started to talk about returning to town, to their homes."

"Some already have."

The elders stood in silence, listening for divine wisdom, seeking answers for the best course of action. The night closed in around them, and each man chilled deep within. Standing on the stone-strewn terrace, they shifted their feet as if searching for stability in their precarious situation.

"We'll keep it in prayer," said André. "Tomorrow may bring a solution." Placing his hand on Isaac's shoulder, he continued. "Godspeed, my brother. May his protection be with you and with all our children."

Isaac turned to go, then stopped abruptly. A tall figure strode up the main path. Isaac stiffened. It was Lord Aubanel, from the village of Cros, situated just below their mountain camp. The last time they had seen him was in the Bedos field three days ago. They'd heard that he'd stayed in town with Josué Noguier, helping prepare several hundred Huguenot men to fight the dragoons. So what on earth was he doing here?

"*Bonsoir.* Good evening." Aubanel greeted each elder in turn with a brief handshake. Despite having chosen different approaches to the impending invasion, they were still brothers in the faith.

Aubanel went straight to the point. "Governor Noailles sent me. He arrived in St. Hippolyte today from Montpellier." He paused, letting the surprising bit of information sink in. The King's governor of the entire Languedoc region had come to their small town.

"Governor Noailles has a proposal for you," Aubanel continued. He met each man's eyes before continuing. "If you return to your homes first thing tomorrow, *ahead* of the dragoons' arrival, he will extend a greater amnesty towards you all. He will grant more pardons."

The words hit Isaac like an unexpected punch to the gut. "Pardons? Amnesty? For what exactly? We've done nothing wrong."

"The governor made it quite clear there will be terrible consequences for all if you don't leave the mountain in the morning. Especially for the visiting pastors in St. Hippolyte these past months—La Roquette, Boyer, and the others." He paused and turned his focus on Louis Bedos. "As well as for those who hosted the worship services."

Each of the elders stood stock still while their minds whirled with implications. Governor Noailles planned to punish them for their move to the mountain!

Guillaume finally broke the silence. "If there are to be serious repercussions either way, why would we not stick to our original plan and stay here?"

Aubanel cleared his throat. "As I said, *if* the entire community returns to their homes in the morning, Noailles promises a greater measure of amnesty."

"And what exactly does it mean: 'a greater measure of amnesty'?" asked Guillaume. He had heard such promises from the King's officials in the limited court cases he had been allowed over the last few years and seen them all go unfulfilled.

"That's all the governor would say."

"Amnesty implies political offense. We are only taking a stand for our existing legal right to meet for worship," Guillaume insisted.

Aubanel shrugged slightly. "Governor Noailles would expand no further."

Silence followed as each man pondered the unexpected development.

After several minutes, Isaac turned to Aubanel. "What about *your* fighting men? Do you still plan to attack the dragoons when they arrive?"

"I've already promised Governor Noailles we'll stand down and return to our homes. I've ordered Noguier to oversee the withdrawal of our men as we speak."

Guillaume exchanged glances with the other men. "Come back at daybreak tomorrow, and we'll have our answer for the governor," he said.

Aubanel gave a curt nod and took his leave. Once he was gone, the elders continued to contemplate the enormity of the decision before them. Hold their position of passive resistance and suffer more significant consequences, or go back to their homes, separated from one another, and still be vulnerable to whatever the dragoons chose to inflict?

"I propose you sleep on it and make a decision first thing in the morning," said Isaac. "I'm going after Jeanne. If I haven't returned by dawn, go ahead with your decisions and any actions without me."

The elders agreed and parted ways, each lost in his own thoughts. Only one thing was clear. They were at a fork in the road from which there was no return.

CHAPTER 17
MONOBLET

Day 2, Thursday
7 October 1683
Monoblet

The flicker of candlelight shone through the windows of the *temple* in Monoblet, casting shadows out into the night. Usually, only on Christmas Eve would there be a service at this hour. Pierre and Jeanne glanced at each other, then moved towards it, like moths drawn to beams of light.

Pierre opened the back door and stepped inside, then motioned for Jeanne to follow. His height enabled him to see over the packed room to the front where Pastor La Roquette stood, doing his best to answer parishioners' rapid-fire questions. He strained to hear every word. Next to him, Jeanne stood on tiptoe, then jostled to see through the crowd, and finally gave up, crossing her arms with a noisy sigh.

"All we know is the dragoons arrived in Anduze two days ago and that they'll march through our village on their way to St. Hippolyte. This could happen at any time. We thought they would have done so by now. So, please, return to your homes and stay inside as much as possible until they've passed through."

A rough voice rang out. "Is it true our St. Hippolyte neighbors moved to the Le Cengle mountain and are calling themselves the Lord's Army?

"Yes, that is correct," replied the pastor.

"What do they intend?" shouted one.

"I heard they took guns!" called another.

The low murmurs escalated, then burst forth like a geyser, everyone loudly expressing their opinions at the same time.

Pastor La Roquette clapped his hands for silence. Once the villagers calmed down, he spoke again. "You all know that last month fifty churches in our region gathered in a General Assembly to discuss how to deal with the King's repressive edicts. You are also aware that the representatives from St. Hippolyte argued with great force for worship services to continue, all the while maintaining a profound respect for our monarch. Eventually, the rest of us agreed. In the same vein, they've now moved to the mountain in a stand of passive resistance."

Jeanne glanced up at Pierre; her eyes wide.

"We're definitely the most stubborn in a region of strong-willed people," whispered Pierre.

"Then why are they so surprised and upset by our move to Le Cengle?"

"It's one thing to continue to meet on Sunday mornings. But, moving almost four thousand people to a mountain is another. Especially one that overlooks the road where the dragoons will arrive."

A spark of hope dared to rise in Pierre as he watched her mull over this information. Calling themselves the Lord's Army and moving everyone to the mountain was enough of a bold statement, one that could easily backfire and bring dire consequences. It was clear to him that taking things to the next level by attacking the dragoons would only bring calamity. Would she begin to see this as well? Could her perspective shift? How he hoped and prayed she'd not continue to pursue fighting—and Etienne.

"Why are those from St. Hippolyte drawing all this attention to themselves?" cried an older woman.

"How do they think this will make any difference?" yelled a hard-edged farmer, cynicism laced through his voice.

"The St. Hippolyte Huguenots believe it's worth the risk," La Roquette replied. "They hope to show they stand for their rights, while remaining loyal to the King. Now, please return to your homes."

The people mumbled amongst themselves, then quieted. The pastor's voice rang out with a benediction:

"The Lord bless you and keep you;
the Lord make his face shine on you and be gracious to you;
the Lord turn his face toward you

and give you peace."[6]

Pierre and Jeanne withdrew into a back corner as the villagers filed out of the church. Those who noticed the pair scowled in their direction, hurrying past with their chins tucked down as if to protect themselves from the intruders. Were they recognized as from St. Hippolyte, or was it simply the parishioners' terror projected as anger?

Once the building emptied, Pierre and Jeanne moved into the light. They approached La Roquette as the last of his parishioners departed.

"*Bonsoir,* Pastor. I'm Pierre Lacombe, and this is Jeanne Tessier. The elders of St. Hippolyte sent us."

Jeanne shifted uneasily at the half-truth.

"I know who you are," La Roquette said, with warmth, coming towards them with his hand extended. "Of course, I know both of your fathers. So what brings you here at such a time as this?" He studied Jeanne, his eyes full of questions.

Pierre spoke up. "My brother Gabriel, and Etienne Gamond, are missing. It's no secret they wish to fight the dragoons. I've checked in town with Josué Noguier, but they weren't there. So they may be attempting to join Massador and Rafinesque."

"They wouldn't know where to go! No one knows their location except my wife and me."

"I'm not sure that would stop them from trying, sir."

La Roquette brushed his hand across his face, then gathered his cloak and hat. "Let's make haste to my house. You must need refreshment. Then I'll take you to the look-out point to see if they've managed to find our spies."

The trio walked silently through the village as it hunkered down in self-protection. *Volets* slammed shut in the hope the solid wooden shutters, adept at keeping out the night chill, would also protect them from the King's troops. The villagers barricaded their outbuildings and gave their animals extra feed. The atmosphere crackled with fear.

"I don't expect the dragoons to do anything more than pass through here," said La Roquette. "I've tried to explain this to my people. But I've also told them to prepare for any eventuality. It's hard to say *what* the soldiers will do. The dragoons are not exactly known for their manners, nor their mercy."

---

[6] Numbers 6:24-26 (NIV)

At the edge of town, they arrived at the lovely La Roquette *mas*. As La Roquette ushered them into the warmth of the main room, each one stopped in their tracks. There, at the dining table, sat Etienne and Gabriel.

"Well! What have we here?" La Roquette asked as he threw his cloak over a peg on the wall and posed his hat on another. "What happened to your foot, young man?"

Bruised blue-green and swollen, Gabriel's bare ankle rested, elevated, on the bench beside him. Etienne jumped to his feet. "*Bonsoir,* Pastor. We had a bit of misfortune with an exposed tree root."

"You had the misfortune of thinking you could take matters into your own hands," Pierre shot back. He sensed Jeanne stiffen beside him.

The two men stared at each other, lips pressed tight until Elisabeth broke the impasse. "Fortunately, their mishap occurred not too far from our village. Young Gamond said the elders sent them to join the spies."

At the startled expression on her husband's face, complemented by the scowl on Pierre's, the truth slowly dawned on her. Elisabeth glared at her visitors, with fire in her eyes, and words ready to give them a piece of her mind.

After a moment, she took a deep breath, smoothed her apron and turned to Jeanne and Pierre. "Please, sit down. I'll prepare something warm for you to drink."

Pierre's jaw clenched as Jeanne hurried to the seat closest to Etienne, who, in turn, studied her carefully. Pierre remained standing and then turned his focus to the fire.

Elisabeth threw a handful of dried *verveine* leaves into boiling water and the lemony herbal scent filled the room. When it had thoroughly steeped, she strained and then served them the fragrant *tisane,* the liquid warmth thawing the tension in the room by a degree. Elisabeth was known for her healing hospitality, and her husband sensed he could now broach the subject of what to do next.

"I've been thinking...," La Roquette and Pierre said at the same time. "Please, Pastor, go ahead."

La Roquette nodded, then studied Etienne and Gabriel. "Your parents must be very concerned about your disappearance. I should send you back to the mountain at once. First, however, there's the problem of the injured ankle."

"Sir? If I might?" Etienne asked.

"You might not! You left the mountain without consent, creating the problem before us," stated La Roquette with force. "You may, however, tell me how you managed to get Gabriel here after his injury."

"It happened not too far from your home. We made it here, slowly, with him using me as support."

The pastor stood and then paced the room's length several times, hands clasped behind his back. No one dared speak; the only sound was the hiss and pop of the fire as Pierre pushed and rearranged logs more times than necessary.

Finally, La Roquette turned towards them all. "A horse is needed to get him back home. Unfortunately, mine's injured, so I'll need to borrow one from a neighbor. But, I don't wish to disturb anyone at this late hour. Everyone has just secured their animals and homes for the night."

A burning log tumbled to the edge of the hearth, causing more than one person in the room to jump. Using the fire iron, Pierre shoved it back into place with force, sparks spraying wide up the chimney.

"We must wait until tomorrow morning," La Roquette continued. "Pierre and Gabriel will stay here with us tonight, and return to the mountain after sunrise, once I secure a horse. And, if by chance they're discovered by dragoons, the sprained ankle can serve as an excuse." He paused to look at each person seated around his table.

"What about Jeanne and Etienne?" Pierre asked, forcing his voice to sound neutral.

"I don't think it's wise for the four of you to go back together. You'd only draw more attention."

"Then, Pastor, what do you propose?" Pierre wished his words didn't carry such a harsh edge.

"Not that I like it, but the best solution is to send Jeanne and Etienne back tonight. It's now close to midnight, and it is unlikely the dragoons will arrive before daylight. Off the main road and under cover of night, they have a greater chance of getting back safely."

"But still in great danger!"

Jeanne rose to face Pierre. "I've already been on the road for several hours tonight, most of it alone, after dark. I'm not afraid!" Her chin lifted as she held his eyes.

The spark of hope that her perspective had shifted extinguished as he read the determination there. She hadn't even minded revealing she'd gone out tonight on her own. He turned back to the fire as another log crumbled and fell.

Jeanne returned to her seat. Pierre turned to La Roquette. "How can we possibly trust Etienne?"

The pastor dipped his head, then cleared his throat and faced Etienne. "After your escapade tonight, I have no reason to trust you. Unfortunately, I see no other choice. You and Jeanne must return to Le Cengle, quickly, before the dragoons arrive. For your safety, as well as to alleviate your parents' concerns."

Jeanne studied her *tisane*, avoiding the pastor's discerning gaze.

"Do you both promise you'll go back to the mountain tonight?" La Roquette asked

"Yes, sir," Jeanne and Etienne answered in unison.

"Then, go now, and may the Almighty bless and keep you safe from all harm."

Elisabeth stood and spoke out an additional prayer of protection and peace over them. She then handed Jeanne and Etienne each a gourd of fresh water and embraced them with three farewell *bisous*.

Pierre continued tending the fire, letting it absorb all his attention. Jeanne stopped next to him on her way out, but he couldn't bring himself to look at her, even when she started to say something. He poked and prodded and rearranged burning logs, staring at the heat and sparks they released as Jeanne followed Etienne out the door.

CHAPTER 18
IN THE LIGHT OF THE STARS

Day Three
Friday, 8 October 1683
Monoblet to St. Hippolyte

Tiny points of light shimmered in the night sky despite the moon's waxing brilliance. For Jeanne, they were the perfect adornment for the nighttime journey with Etienne by her side. Several hours were ahead of them—all alone. This turn of events was far better than anything she'd imagined.

With the warmth of the La Roquette home behind them and the hushed beauty of the *garrigue* all around, Jeanne breathed deep. Despite the coming terror and all the unknowns, everything seemed heightened, more fully alive, including herself.

After practicing several opening lines in her head, she spoke. "So, you and Gabriel planned to join Massador and Rafinesque at their lookout?"

"Yes."

They walked on in silence. The corner of her mouth tugged into a half-smile. He wasn't going to make this easy.

"And then what?"

Etienne glanced at her as he continued to forge ahead. She kept the pace.

"We planned to join the spies and stay with them until the dragoons were sighted," he said.

Jeanne nodded.

"Then, we'd have returned through the brush back into town. My friends and I spent many hours playing out here when we were young. We know the *garrigue* like the back of our hands."

Jeanne clamped her lips together to keep from bursting forth with questions. She sensed he'd retreat into short answers or, worse, silence if she spoke.

"Once in town, we'd have gone straight to Noguier's home, reported the news, and joined his men." Etienne closed back into his thoughts and they walked in silence.

Eventually, he said, "You know, it was partly because of you."

Jeanne blinked, and her heart skipped a beat…or two or three.

"Yes. When you came to the river and told me the elders had sent Massador and Rafinesque as spies. Even though I already knew, it got me thinking and led to this plan."

"It did?" she managed.

"At the time, I was frustrated in general, and truthfully, annoyed that you came to talk with me."

She tilted her head a little, waiting for him to continue.

"After Boyer's crazed antics, I had to make a clear decision. I still believe it's in our best interest and our duty to fight for our rights. Even if I lose my father's respect, even if I lose my life, above all, I trust God for the outcome—win or lose."

"I see," Jeanne replied. Since the villagers' comments in the Monoblet *temple*, she understood the dragoons could interpret even passive resistance as a threat. It wasn't as weak a gesture as she'd once thought. Nothing was as simple as it once seemed. Lifting her head to the shimmering stars, she drew a deep breath of silver-blue air.

"And, Jeanne, I finally accept the fact you want to fight. You were right. None of us have training or have ever engaged in battle. So we'll need every capable hand, trained or not, including you and any other women who wish to join."

Warmth spread through her chest, intertwined with sharp cold pricks of fear. It was one thing to contend for the right to fight, but quite another to be on the brink of taking action.

They started up the rocky path to the foothills leading back to the Château de Planque, green oaks and pines surrounding them, filling the air with their fragrance.

89

"Etienne, do you have a gun?" Jeanne asked as he held a branch out of her way.

"Non! My father has our family pistol, and he doesn't trust me anywhere near it." He booted a small boulder.

A good quarter of an hour went by in comfortable silence before they spoke again.

"Etienne, I have an idea."

"Go on."

"My grandfather fought in the wars of Rohan."

"So did mine," Etienne replied. "A perfect example of Protestants fighting for freedom."

"Yes. Well, anyway, *Grand-père* left his musket to my father. Papa cleans it faithfully, every Saturday." His slow smile helped her push through her last bit of inner resistance. "Even though that round of religious wars was unsuccessful, it's a prized family possession. Papa displays it on a shelf in our *grand salon.*"

Etienne stopped walking and turned to face her. "What are you saying?"

"I think we need to go to the château and get it, so that you're equipped to join Noguier's fighting men."

Etienne stared off into the distance and then straight back into her eyes. She prayed the moonlight concealed her flaming cheeks.

"So you still think I should join Noguier?" he asked. "What about our promise to Pastor La Roquette?"

An eagle-owl's cry reverberated through the hills. To Jeanne's ears, it was no longer a lonely sound but an expression of its purpose in life.

"As you said, we must fight for our rights," she stated. "Together, we'll go to the château and get the musket. Then, you can go on to Noguier, and I'll return to the mountain. We'll keep at least part of our promise, and I can cover for you."

"But I thought you wanted action. Are you sure you don't want to join Noguier too?" he asked.

"I do want to take action, and for now, this is how I can best help our cause. If I return, my family and the community will stop worrying about me, and I'll invent a story explaining where you are. With only one gun between us, it makes more sense that you go, for now anyway."

Etienne raked his fingers through his brown waves of hair. "All right then. If you're sure." He leaned closer, searching her face. "It's a good plan."

She could scarcely believe they'd arrived at this point, this moment. It seemed the world shifted infinitesimally, and the stars twinkled brighter.

As they continued on their way, Jeanne surveyed the perimeter of the valley, trying to drink it all in, trying to store away each minute in her memory—then tripped hard over a fallen oak branch. Etienne caught her by the arm and helped her to solid ground. Heat spiked through her body when he did not let go, even though the path smoothed out before them.

CHAPTER 19
LOOK OUT

Day Three
Friday, 8 October 1683
Monoblet

The early morning sunshine brought light but very little warmth. Pierre stood in La Roquette's garden, praying Jeanne had arrived safely in St. Hippolyte. A twinge of conviction rose in him; he heaved a sigh and added a request for Etienne's protection as well.

Rolling a small stone under his foot, Pierre contemplated the challenges ahead. He inhaled the frosty air and raised his head to the sky. Despite the chill, rays of the sun reached his face, a reminder he was not alone.

He rubbed his cold hands together, then stepped back inside the La Roquette home. Gabriel sat, just awake, staring intently out of the front window, his foot propped on a bench. Pierre mumbled *bonjour*. Gabriel replied, barely making eye contact.

Elisabeth rose from stoking the fire and greeted him with a sympathetic smile. Pierre responded to her warmth, especially as she appeared to take the conflict between the brothers in stride. Had she perceived more than he let on, even to himself, of his feelings concerning Jeanne? Pierre returned her smile but braced himself to focus on the urgent task at hand: Gabriel's safe return to St. Hippolyte.

As if on cue, La Roquette came through the front door. The pastor must have gone out before first light in search of the necessary horse.

"I went to the Vidalle farm next door to see if we could borrow one of their horses. I thought it best to go a while before dawn. The less the villagers know, the better. Any unusual activity only adds to their anxiety."

Pierre didn't voice another reason that came to mind for keeping what they were doing from the local inhabitants. One never knew who would provide information to the royal army in return for special protection or other favors. Although it only took an hour to walk between Monoblet and St. Hippolyte, each town existed as a small world of its own. As fellow Huguenots, they drew together from time to time, but a general distrust of "others" ran deep in French blood.

Elisabeth invited them to take a seat at the table where she'd prepared bowls of warm milk and slices of chestnut-flour bread, fresh from the oven, plus a small crock of lavender honey from the hives they kept on their property. La Roquette thanked God for their meal, then continued processing their dilemma. "Unfortunately, the Vidalles aren't able to help us. Fear has got the best of them." The pastor pressed his temples as he stared into his bowl. "Frankly, I don't think I can expect anything different from the rest of the village."

They all ate in silence, chewing their bread and searching for solutions. Finally, Pierre spoke. "I've been thinking. Massador and Rafinesque have two horses at their disposal, right?"

La Roquette steepled his fingers on his lips. "Yes, go on."

"What if we borrowed one of them? That way, we wouldn't involve any of your parishioners."

"What will our spies do when the dragoons appear with only one horse between them?"

"One would ride back as planned, and the other would return on foot, obviously with great care."

The pastor stroked his jaw with his thumb and forefinger. "It's certainly not ideal to leave Massador and Rafinesque with only one mount, but I do believe it's the best solution."

The men quickly finished the morning meal, then rose as one, the looming arrival of the dragoons pressing in like a slow-turning vise. Gabriel attempted a few steps, then sat back down with a growl of frustration. His foot was clearly not ready to support his weight.

Ignoring his brother, Pierre grabbed his cloak and followed La Roquette outside. Without further discussion, he followed the pastor swiftly down the road and into the forest. Pierre stretched his legs in long strides, glad to be on the move again. He welcomed the sting of the icy air as it filled his lungs and watched the cloud of his exhaled breath made visible in the shadowed forest.

Eventually, La Roquette slowed his pace and motioned for Pierre to do the same as they approached Massador and Rafinesque's lookout post, not wanting to startle the spies. Dried twigs crackled under their feet despite their soft tread and echoed through the stillness. Rounding the final corner, they found themselves staring down the barrel of Massador's pistol.

The pastor spoke calmly, his hands in the air. "Marc, it's me. Pastor La Roquette. And Pierre Lacombe."

Massador lowered his gun immediately, and Rafinesque appeared from behind a large boulder. Both spies gaped at the unexpected visitors.

"*Bonjour!* Sorry to startle you! We're here on urgent business. We've come to see about your horses," said La Roquette. "Pierre's brother is injured here in Monoblet, and we must get him back to St. Hippolyte before the dragoons arrive, Lord-willing. With your permission, we'd like to take one of your mounts to get him home, accompanied by Pierre."

Massador and Rafinesque exchanged glances.

"Then, when the dragoons arrive, one of you will ride the remaining horse to Le Cengle with the news, as planned," said La Roquette.

"And the other will go back on foot," finished Rafinesque, his bushy eyebrows pulled into a straight line over his piercing eyes.

La Roquette nodded. "We realize the risk, but we're out of options. The coming terror has rendered the villagers unwilling to part with any of their animals. Also, the fewer people who know about the comings and goings between here and St. Hippolyte, the better."

Massador stepped forward. "I'll do it. Once the dragoons arrive, I can go back on foot." Anticipating resistance from his companion, he continued, "Jacques, you're the better rider. It makes the most sense."

Rafinesque considered the younger man in silence.

"I apologize, but we must make haste," said La Roquette. "Are you in agreement?"

Massador laid his hand on his friend's arm. "I'll be careful."

Rafinesque finally gave a curt nod; his lips pressed tight.

The spies led the pastor and Pierre to the stone shepherd's hut sheltering the horses.

"Give us the slower of the two. Rafinesque, you should have the speed to get to the mountain with the message," said Pierre. Placing a hand on Massador's shoulder, he added, "Marc, thank you for your courage."

"It's nothing," said Massador, with a slight shrug. "God speed."

"And God be with you," returned Pierre and La Roquette in unison.

An hour later, the brothers were on their way back to Le Cengle, avoiding the main route as much as possible. With Gabriel on horseback and Pierre on foot, plus the need to avoid drawing attention, they traveled in silence. They had little to say to one another anyway.

Pierre surveyed their surroundings as they progressed, on high alert for any signs or sounds of the soldiers. A myriad of thoughts tumbled through his mind. Would it actually work to have Rafinesque warn the elders before the soldiers reached Le Cengle? Would their stand of passive resistance be misread anyway? Would they end up like their neighbors to the north, attacked and annihilated by the King's men?

He rubbed the back of his neck. In a way, the ankle sprain had been helpful. The injury slowed down his brother's pursuit to fight the dragoons, but not for long. Gabriel would never give up. In pain or not, he'd find a way. A glance up at his brother, sitting high on Massador's horse, confirmed his thoughts. Gabriel leaned forward towards his future, his shoulders set and his focus straight ahead.

Pierre sighed. Maybe he was done trying to protect his brother. Gabriel would very likely end up fighting. Perhaps they all would.

Drawing himself up, Pierre resolved to finish his assignment to get his brother safely to the camp. After that, they would undoubtedly each play their own part. Gabriel was born to fight, and he would no longer stand in his way.

CHAPTER 20
DRAGOONS ON THE MOVE

"Up and out! We must be on our way by mid-morning!" Colonel Arnault strode through his troops, accompanied by a trumpeter blasting the news. Men jumped to their feet, energy pumping through their veins. Finally, they were on their way!

General De Tessé appeared on horseback, trotting around the clusters of camped dragoons. "Ready your horses! Prepare yourselves! Our illustrious King Louis XIV has issued his mandate. We descend on St. Hippolyte de la Planquette now! We will arrest those who are armed. We will raze the homes of those who flee or resist submission. In short, we will 'inflict a terrifying desolation' as ordered by the war secretary of our King."

Arnault saluted his commander, taking care to hide his lingering frustration. General De Tessé's tryst had forced them to tarry three long days in Anduze. Not even the news that the Huguenots of St. Hippolyte had styled themselves the Lord's Army and moved onto a nearby mountain had stirred the general into action. He had lingered on in the embrace of his mistress while everyone else waited. Arnault was not impressed.

De Tessé barked out one more order before circling back through the camp. "Arnault's regiment in the front, followed by Montpézat's foot soldiers. Our army of twelve hundred will easily crush the rebel Protestants of the Cévennes."

The trumpeter continued his rousing call, ensuring every last man was on his feet. Groups of soldiers prepared food and horses for the journey. Their plan was to arrive in the town well before nightfall, which came early this time of year. However, with such a significant number of troops, more than half of them on foot, the journey would not be quick.

"*Enfin!* Finally we're released to get our hands on those heretics!" yelled Lieutenant Lefèvre, waving his cap, the long green side-tassel waving in the wind.

"We'll show those Huguenots who's in charge," spat Duboise. "I hope they do resist so we can show them the consequences!"

"Especially the women!" leered Rossel, his misaligned eye dancing wildly.

"Huzzah! Hoorah!" Sniggers and guffaws erupted as the soldiers raised the pewter tankards of the hard cider they drank while on the road.

Colonel Arnault stalked into their midst. "Focus on the task at hand, men! We'll fulfill our orders with the *dignity* worthy of our King!" He pivoted and strode away abruptly lest the image of Rossel rising off the Huguenot woman in the Dauphiné forest resurface.

The soldiers smoothed the smirks from their faces and carried on with the preparations. The colonel threw a fierce glance back over his shoulder, warning against any further ribald comments.

Arnault continued on foot through his regiment, hands clasped behind his back. A message had also arrived from Governor Noailles of the Languedoc region, which included the Cévennes. In it, the governor communicated his ultimatum to the Huguenots of St. Hippolyte: leave the mountain before the dragoons arrive and suffer "fewer repercussions. What exactly did that mean? Arnault frowned. He did not like gray areas.

The current strategy was to enact a "*dragonnade*," used effectively in the north. Groups of dragoons moved into Huguenot homes, took up residence, ate great quantities of food and drink, and applied pressure until the inhabitants converted to the King's faith. The colonel planned to carry out these orders to the letter. But, would Governor Noailles' promises of amnesty get in the way?

Arnault glanced around him. He intended to lead his men with strength and clarity. With four times the number of soldiers than the earlier campaigns, it was inevitable the Huguenots of St. Hippolyte would be subdued and converted in no time.

Against his wishes, the image of the violated Huguenot woman rose before him, her eyes filled with an other-worldly courage that haunted his dreams. In swift succession came other pictures: of the Dauphiné pastor, fearlessly leading his flock through the woods, running towards the dragoons, brandishing farm tools and antique muskets, and finally, of the trapped Huguenots singing Psalms as they burned to death in a barn.

Arnault's foot bobbled on the rocky ground. He steadied himself and stopped to take in the high-crested mountains surrounding Anduze. The Huguenots in this town hadn't caused any difficulty. But those in St. Hippolyte were known for their persistence, their resistance. What would the King's army encounter there? What was their best strategy to ensure total repression of the Protestant faith?

The colonel stopped at his tent to finish his own preparations. Inside, he gathered his shoulder-length hair behind his neck and secured it with a black silk ribbon. He then carefully set his magnificent black tri-cornered gold-trimmed hat on his head. He gazed at the lazy river through the open door of his tent, the great white feather adorning his hat waving gently in the breeze. The wait was over. They were dragoons, sent on this mission by the King, God's chosen representative on earth. His will would be done. Colonel Arnault stepped out of his tent, stood tall, more than ready for the task at hand.

CHAPTER 21
THIRD DAY

Day Three
Friday, 8 October 1683
Le Cengle mountain

The craggy cliffs of Le Cengle loomed protectively above the exhausted Huguenots of St. Hippolyte as the third day dawned on the mountain. Men, women, and even the children felt the cumulative effects of sleeping on cold, rocky ground. Muscles ached, bones creaked, and tempers frayed as exhaustion grew in mind, body, and soul.

Jeanne arrived at the foot of the mountain in the wee hours of the morning, well before sunrise. She considered making her way through the sleeping Huguenots in the dark but decided against it. It would be almost impossible to avoid stepping or tripping over someone and drawing unwanted attention to herself. Instead, she found a spot on the far edge of the lowest terrace and managed to sleep a bit, hidden away behind some scrubby bushes.

She woke with the sun and started up the mountain as daylight grew. With each step, her heart rate rose, and her pace slowed. She had a lot to explain and wasn't in any hurry to do so. Except to Louise, if she could manage it.

Limestone gravel crunched underfoot as she passed by bedraggled families rising and preparing themselves for the day. Would they know she had been out all night? Was it her imagination, or was everyone watching her? She pulled her woolen cloak tighter around her shoulders and picked up her pace.

With each step closer to her family's camp, her head constricted, then finally erupted into a full-blown headache. Maman saw her first; her shrill cry of pain and relief pierced Jeanne to the core. How she yearned to run from the suffering she had caused, but it was too late. The damage had been done.

Jeanne joined the family and, without a word, sat on a rock near the fire. Huddled in their blankets, her siblings stared at her as if she was someone they'd never seen before.

"Where's Papa?" Jeanne finally asked when the tension became as tough to deal with as the crust of bread Marion thrust into her hands.

"He's out looking for you," retorted Catherine, her voice edged and sharp.

A thousand cold sparks of guilt flashed through Jeanne. Papa was out somewhere searching for her, the danger increasing with every passing moment. Her choices had brought this about.

"Where were you?" asked Paul, gnawing on his stale bread.

"Paul! Do not speak with your mouth full. Anyway, enough about Jeanne. That's a discussion for when Papa returns." Maman's voice was surprisingly firm, possibly due to the normality of giving Paul a boundary.

Anne's amber eyes filled with curiosity. Out of all of them, Jeanne would have liked to confide in her little sister. But she didn't want to burden her with all she had experienced, with all that was to come.

No one moved from the fire. Winter was approaching; indeed, it seemed to be almost here. Everyone noticed it seemed much colder than usual, and all across the terraces, families huddled against the chill. Jeanne shivered and drew Anne close, glancing up just as André and Guillaume approached.

"Jeanne! You're back safely!" stated André, his voice full of relief.

"God be praised!" Guillaume proclaimed.

Maman stood, trembling head to foot, from more than the cold. "Any news of Isaac?"

The elders shook their heads, concern, and compassion written across their faces.

Maman sank back down onto her boulder.

Guillaume placed his hand on her shoulder. "We'll be sure you hear immediately when we have any news of him."

"We're also here on other business," André said. "Lord Aubanel brought us word yesterday evening from Governor Noailles. He demands we return to our homes before the dragoons arrive. If we do, there'll be fewer repercussions."

Jeanne stood abruptly. "Repercussions?"

"He didn't elaborate, but it's clear the governor isn't pleased with our attempt at passive resistance," Guillaume explained.

André glanced at Jeanne, then turned to Maman. "Before he left, Isaac gave us leave to make the decision in the morning. We've decided it's best to leave the mountain immediately and return to our homes. You are the first to know."

"We're backing down?" Jeanne asked, her eyebrows raised high. Would they give in so easily?

Guillaume tilted his head as if seeing her for the first time. "Believe me; we've prayed and sought guidance for a good part of the night on the matter."

"Our original plan to negotiate with the dragoons is no longer an option. The King's governor has deemed our move here an act of rebellion," added André.

"So now, we're just supposed to sit in our homes and let them overtake us?" Jeanne said, struggling to keep her voice respectful.

"Jeanne, we understand your frustration, but we've made what we believe is the best decision," said André. "Now, everyone else needs to know."

"One more thing," said Guillaume. "We'll talk later about where you went and why. But did it have anything to do with Etienne and Gabriel? Did you see them?"

"Or Pierre?" André asked.

Jeanne forced confidence into her voice. "Yes, I saw them. We all ended up at La Roquette's house." She avoided looking in her maman's direction.

"Where are they now?" demanded Guillaume.

"You were with Pierre?" his father repeated, craning his neck, searching the terraces. "Where is he now? Where are Etienne and Gabriel?"

Jeanne drew a deep breath before speaking. "Gabriel sprained his ankle, and Pierre stayed with him at La Roquette's house. They planned to find a horse and return to the mountain later this morning."

Her body felt like liquid, but she managed to keep her voice steady. "And Etienne?" asked his father.

"He also stayed to help."

"They sent you back *alone?*" André's voice rose. "That doesn't make sense."

Jeanne lifted her chin. "I travel fast and am small enough to hide well in the dark if necessary. So it wasn't a problem. I was–I *am* fine."

Guillaume studied her silently, his lips pressed together. Could he tell she was lying about Etienne?

Finally, he addressed the family. "Please pack up. We need to leave as soon as possible."

The Tessiers stood motionless, staring at the elders as they departed. The news then rippled from family to family, moving across the mountain like a shattering north wind. Almost immediately everyone burst into a frenzy of activity.

"You heard him. Let's get going. *Now!*" Marion flapped her arms as if corralling her chickens back into their coop for the night.

Jeanne snapped into action. "Catherine, grab those blankets and put them in the basket."

Her sister glared at her but did as she was told. Reestablishing their pattern of bossy big sister and the prickly younger sister somehow comforted them both.

Within an hour, a flood of Huguenots and their belongings flowed off the mountain. They tumbled down the hill, back the way they came, back to their homes. Each family would now face the dragoons and whatever atrocities they chose to inflict without the collective comfort of the community. Had they made their situation worse by forming the Lord's Army on the mountain? Possibly. Probably.

Jeanne walked alongside the family wagon, sensing the swirl of emotions emanating from the Huguenots as they scrambled to get home ahead of the dragoons. Anxiety had grown into terror as the world shifted around them. Men shouted orders and hurried their families down the mountain, children clung tight to their *mamans'* skirts, and the young adults walked on in somber silence. The sooner they were back in their homes, the better. Some of the women sobbed openly; others were stoic, moving resolutely towards whatever awaited them.

Jeanne longed to share all the developments, both her personal adventures and now this mass exodus from the mountain with Louise. She needed to process with her friend and hear her input. But in all the chaos, it was impossible to locate the Gamonds.

Disappointment filled Jeanne, heavy and dark, almost robbing her of breath with its strength. Her brow furrowed. Somewhere deep inside, beyond conscious knowledge, she must have placed hope in Papa's plan working. She massaged her temples. Why couldn't she land in one place, with one opinion, one route of action, and stay there? She was tired of being tossed and swayed by every new development.

Above all, Papa had trusted God to protect them. Where was God now? Fear and chaos swirled through the community. The dragoons would soon arrive, and they'd all be on their own to deal with them.

Suddenly, it came to her that if the Lord's Army faced repercussions for their stand of passive resistance, what would be the consequences for those who fought the King's soldiers? She shuddered at the awful possibilities.

Etienne had gone to join Noguier and his men with her strong encouragement. And her *grand-père's* musket. In the night, the two of them had managed to get into the château and get the gun. Etienne had then gone into town to find Noguier while Jeanne returned to Le Cengle.

As her family approached the bottom of the mountain, she brushed the back of her hand across her forehead and let out a noisy sigh. There was no one else to do the job. As soon as possible, she must steal away to warn the fighting men, especially Etienne.

CHAPTER 22
QUESTIONS

Day Three
Friday, 8 October 1683
Le Cengle Mountain

Louise trudged down the mountain beside her papa with her siblings in tow. She surveyed the throngs of Huguenots rushing by, hoping to spot the Tessier family. She'd heard that Jeanne had returned to the camp just as the elders decided to disband the Lord's Army. Before they all disappeared into their homes, she very much wanted to hear what Jeanne had been up to.

The last time Louise had seen her friend was right after Pastor Boyer's mad ravings at their mountain gathering. Etienne had stormed off, and she'd encouraged Jeanne to follow him. Her lip trembled. Since then, she'd learned that her brother, Gabriel *and* Jeanne had disappeared from the mountain. Had they gone together? Had they joined *Capitaine* Noguier in town? Why was Jeanne back but not Etienne or Gabriel?

Louise reached out, pulling her youngest brother close, and prayed silently for Etienne. She also prayed for Gabriel and for Pierre, who'd been sent to find them. She glanced through the crowds again, still unable to find Jeanne. More prayers flowed, this time for Jeanne and her papa, who was out searching for her. *Heavenly Father, please keep them all safe and bring them home before the dragoons appear. You are our shelter, our refuge, and we trust your promise to keep us from harm.*

Louise drew a deep breath of crisp air, watching the puff of visible vapor as she blew it out. Yes, God promised protection, but fighting the dragoons now seemed more unwise than ever. Where would Jeanne fit into it all? It was dangerous enough for Etienne and Gabriel and the other men, but for a woman? Louise shuddered as stories of atrocities committed by dragoons in the north came to mind. She quickened her pace, the desire mounting to be safely in the shelter of her home.

She craned her neck, looking for Jeanne as they reached the street below. Soon, the Gamond family would turn the corner towards their home, and any chance of finding Jeanne would be gone.

"Louise! Pay attention, please," Papa exclaimed as she stepped on his heel, causing his shoe to slide off the back of his foot.

"*Desolé*, Papa. I'm sorry," she said as they stopped. She kept one arm around her little brother and took her sister's hand as Papa bent to pull his shoe back on.

"You are very distracted, *ma chère*," he remarked as he stood up. He guided them to start moving again. "We must focus and return swiftly. The last thing we want is to be found *en masse* in the streets. Giving the dragoons any excuse...." He trailed away, leaving the unspeakable unsaid.

Louise nodded. "*Bien sûr,* Papa. Of course, we must." She held onto her siblings and kept pace with him. His keen-eyed glance in her direction told her he guessed, at least in part, that she was searching for Jeanne. Etienne and Gabriel were still missing, which was a worry to them all. But Jeanne's disappearance was less understandable, certainly for her papa. Did he think she knew more than she'd revealed? Itchy splotches rose on her neck. Was it her fault for encouraging Jeanne to follow Etienne?

The throng of Huguenots came to a sudden halt. Louise held tighter to her siblings.

"Follow me!" Papa said and forged ahead without explanation.

Louise instructed her brother to hang on tight to her arm while she held onto their sister with one hand and the back of Papa's coat with the other. She couldn't be sure if the crowd parted a bit out of respect for Papa or if his demeanor caused them to step back. Either way, they arrived rather swiftly at the cause of the commotion. Louise's eyes widened. Gabriel on horseback, being led by Pierre? It didn't make sense. Her heart sank. Where was Etienne?

CHAPTER 23
CAUGHT!

Day Three
Friday, 8 October 1683
Monoblet

Asea of emerald-coated dragoons, some astride horses, others on foot, thundered down the Route de Lasalle in the direction of St. Hippolyte de la Planquette. Even the birds stopped their usual daytime serenade as the torrent of soldiers inundated the valley road. From time to time, the officers cried out orders, further charging the atmosphere. Pent-up tension from lingering so long in Anduze unleashed in a roaring tidal wave of green coats and fierce faces. Today was the day! They were finally on their way to squash the stubborn Huguenots of St. Hippolyte!

"How *dare* they call themselves the Lord's Army? Ha! We'll show them who the *real* army is!" Lieutenant Lefèvre shouted, brandishing his musket high as a banner of war.

Jabbing his saber into the air, Rossel agreed. "We'll make a point of showing them who's really in charge!" The others guffawed, waving their weapons in agreement.

"If they don't get it, we'll have to give it to them straight!" said Pouget, thrusting his hips to indicate how he meant to subdue Huguenot women. The entire regiment burst out in lusty yells and lewd cheers.

"Huzzah!" "Huzzah!" "Huzzah!" they chimed in unison.

"We'll give it to them where it counts!"

Colonel Arnault's face darkened. He abruptly rotated his impressive amber steed and fell in alongside the gloating men. Their boasts trailed away.

"Eyes on the goal, men!" exhorted Arnault. "You know our orders! First, the Huguenots will submit to our authority, and then they will convert to the one true faith."

"General De Tessé insists we strike them hard and 'inflict a terrifying desolation,'" stated Lieutenant Lefèvre.

Stone-faced, Arnault stared at him and then at the others, each in turn without stopping their forward movement. "Yes, but our mandate is to accomplish this without an accompanying massacre. The Huguenots of St. Hippolyte number four thousand. The King's court has also warned us against a bloodbath."

Lefèvre failed to suppress a disgusted snort while Rossel flapped a hand as if shooing off an irritating mosquito.

"Enough!" retorted Arnault. "We are in the right, sent by God's representative on earth, our King. We'll establish control immediately and reserve more severe punishments for those who blatantly resist, and for those who carry arms."

Lefèvre and Duboise exchanged a smug glance as if this gave them further license in their quest to crush the Protestants.

Arnault observed them and pondered how he would keep them from going too far. It didn't help that General De Tessé had no qualms about doing whatever it took to ensure success.

Finally, under Arnault's intense glare, Lefèvre gave a curt nod, his jaw set, and the other men followed suit. Arnault glared at them for a minute more, then rode back to the head of the formation.

The sound of clattering hooves filled the air as the men marched onward, winding through the Cévenol mountains. Each soldier focused on the conquest at hand, entirely missing the valley's brilliant autumn splendor.

Rounding a corner, the tiny village of Monoblet came into view, where Arnault planned to stop and water the horses before the final descent into St. Hippolyte. Shouting the order down the line, he didn't notice the granite boulder rolling downhill until it was practically under his horse. His chestnut steed snorted and reared with a jerk that would have thrown off a lesser rider.

Cries and chaos broke out among the troops.

"Hey, Ho!"

"What was that?"

"It came from up there!"

"It's too large to have just fallen by itself!"

While several men threw out questions, Lefèvre and Duboise looked to Arnault, who gestured for them to go. They tore up the hill, racing towards the source of the boulder's trajectory.

Arnault charged up the path after them, arriving in time to see Lefèvre and Duboise on either side of a young man with both arms in the air, one trembling hand holding an ancient pistol. Wild-eyed in panic, his head flicked left and right like a cornered animal hoping to bolt. Finally, he stood stock-still, knowing his odds were impossible against three mounted soldiers.

"Stand back!" Arnault ordered his men. "You! State your name and your business here."

Silence was the only response. The man couldn't seem to find his voice.

"Answer me! I am Colonel Arnault, leader of General De Tessé's St Florentin regiment. Arnault directed his horse a few more steps towards the terrified man, towering over him, his face blazing with authority.

My, uh, my name is Marc Massador," he spluttered.

"*Why are you here?*" barked Colonel Arnault, wheeling his horse around the captive.

The impressive sight of the emerald-coated colonel, resplendent astride his mount, effectively silenced him once again.

"Seems to me he was spying on us from behind that boulder," said Lefèvre.

"He's armed!" said Duboise, stating the obvious. Both men circled Massador, moving their mounts closer as they spoke, spitting at the captured man in contempt.

"Enough!" cried Colonel Arnault. "Take him prisoner! Bind his hands and put him with the other Huguenot prisoner, the one we picked up near Lasalle. They'll walk behind your horses, attached by ropes so they can't escape. We'll take them to St. Hippolyte alive. They may be useful."

Lieutenant Lefèvre dismounted and followed the colonel's orders. "And, I'll take this," he said, yanking Massador's pistol from his hand. Under Arnault's observant eye, he couldn't do much more than bind the prisoner's hands a bit more tightly than necessary, trussing his arms high behind his back.

Tossing the length of rope to Duboise, the soldiers led Massador down the mountain like a sheep to the slaughter.

CHAPTER 24
HOME AGAIN

Day Three
Friday, 8 October 1683
Château de Planque
St. Hippolyte de la Planquette

The Tessier family, minus Papa, entered their rooms at the top of the château's grand staircase. Jeanne stood in the *grand salon*, taking it all in. Three days on the mountain seemed more like three years. So much had happened, and so much had changed, herself included, even the room around her appeared distant, out-of-reach, and not quite real.

Yet, everything remained just as they had left it—except for the space on the shelf where *Grand-père's* musket was usually on display. Jeanne bit her lip, eyes darting to Maman. When would one of the family notice its absence?

"Enfin! Finally!" Catherine cried. "I can't wait to sleep in my bed tonight, even with your cold feet!" she said, nudging Anne, who wandered around the room like a lost lamb.

Jeanne turned to her little sister. "Anne, why don't you come with me? Let's go down to the kitchen and help Marion prepare our midday meal."

Anne nodded and slid her hand in Jeanne's.

Using the servants' stairway, they started down the steps to the ground floor. Working on a practical task would be a good distraction for them both. Papa had yet to return; he was still out there somewhere searching for her. She could hardly bear to think about it.

"What will the dragoons do when they get here? Where will they go?" whispered Anne, her voice quivering despite her attempt to appear brave.

Jeanne stopped on the small landing halfway down to think a moment before answering. Her imagination filled with a picture of twelve hundred soldiers invading the town. Where *would* they go? Would they enact the infamous *dragonnades*, as they had done in other regions of France, moving in with Huguenot families to force conversions? She shut her eyes briefly, remembering the rumors of horrendous torture and harassment committed in Protestant homes.

Would Noguier's men, now including Etienne, go ahead with their plan to attack the dragoons? Jeanne's brow furrowed. She had to get to them, and soon. But it didn't seem like a good idea to get away just now and leave her family again. In Papa's absence, they counted on her more than ever to bring stability and keep everyone together.

"It's hard to say, Anne. We'll take it one step at a time," Jeanne stated, infusing her voice with more confidence than she possessed. "Papa will surely be back soon. He'll bring news and know what to do."

As they stepped into the dimly lit kitchen, heat blossomed up Jeanne's neck. Hours earlier, long before daylight, she'd used the outside servants' entrance just opposite her now, with Etienne by her side. Sneaking into the château with him in the dead of night now seemed like someone else's story.

Getting *Grand-père's* gun had been easy. Papa always kept it in the same place, on a shelf next to one of the *grand salon*'s fireplaces. Tears welled and stung. Papa would notice immediately the musket was gone. If only he were here.

Jeanne shook her head. This wouldn't do. She needed to be a reassuring presence for her little sister.

Marion welcomed their help. She usually had several day cooks come in and prepare the family's meals. Not today. All villagers were busy doing whatever they could think of to make themselves safe in their homes before the dragoon onslaught.

The housekeeper directed the sisters to dice the smoked ham to add to the soup she had started, then scurried off to the cellar. She returned with a crock of brine-preserved vegetables from the summer's harvest. She drained and then added them, along with the ham to the simmering water in the large iron pot hanging over the fire, then grabbed her long-

111

handled wooden spoon, and stirred it all together. The fragrance filled the room and brought back their fear-suppressed appetites.

Marion filled the gold-trimmed china soup terrine, a Tessier family heirloom, lifted it with care, and headed up to the *grand salon*. Unfortunately, there had not been enough time to bake fresh bread, which would have to wait for dinner. Jeanne and Anne followed, and once they entered the room the family slowly gathered around the large oak table.

No one moved to sit. The Tessiers glanced at one another, everyone avoiding looking at the head of the table where Papa's absence gaped like an open wound. Finally, they gave into Marion's insistence that they eat while it was still hot.

The family took their seats and, given the unusual circumstances, invited Marion to join them *à table*. They joined hands, bowed their heads, and Maman led them in thanking God for their food.

"Amen!" they said in hushed tones. Marion stood up and served the broth, handing each of them their bowl and a silver soup spoon. While the younger Tessiers tucked into their meal, Jeanne met Maman's eyes. Their mutual concern for Papa had dissipated Maman's lingering anger, but not Jeanne's guilt. She hadn't forgotten that her actions caused him to be out at such a time as this. But what on earth was taking him so long? The question hung in the air like an ominous shadow threatening to envelop them all.

Jeanne reached out and laid her hand on Maman's arm and was relieved her mother didn't pull away. Then, aware Anne was watching, she sat tall, and dipped into her steaming broth.

Halfway to her mouth, Jeanne froze, her spoon poised in midair. She tilted her head, listening hard. Marion's ladle crashed from her hand into the tureen, and a mini-explosion of soup spattered across the table. A distant rumble swelled and grew like a gathering storm. Maman suddenly pushed back from the table and stood. She leaned forward, listening, then walked stiffly to the window.

Jeanne found herself standing beside her mother, not remembering moving there. Maman opened the double windows with care and both women leaned out the slightest bit. To the right of the château, a giant dust storm roiled down from the Route de Lasalle, activated by hundreds of pounding horses' hooves. Even the solid, thick-walled château vibrated as the ground quaked and the surrounding trees trembled. A tangible presence of danger filled the air; the atmosphere darkened and thickened.

The younger Tessiers rushed to Maman and clung to her sides. Jeanne instinctively tried to pull them away from the window despite being on the second floor. Frozen by fear, they were unable to move. Rooted to their spots, they couldn't tear their eyes away from the multitude of dragoons bursting into view next to their home: the ferocious faces under green side-tassel caps, the brilliant emerald jackets, the knee-high black leather boots. Astride horses trained for war, the dragoons brandished weapons, some waving sabers, others holding muskets.

From a massive mount the color of ash, their leader called them to a halt before the Pont de Planque. As the road beside the château filled with dragoons, Jeanne's pounding heart competed with the crash of horse and soldier.

Without warning, Maman shrieked. Both hands flew to her mouth, and she staggered back a step. Jeanne followed her gaze and located the cause. The dragoons had taken prisoners.

Three Huguenot men, hands bound behind their backs, stood surrounded by soldiers. Like animals, each was tethered to a mounted dragoon. Jeanne didn't recognize the first man. She narrowed her eyes on the second, then gasped. Marc Massador! Her friend and the shepherd of the Château de Planque.

The third prisoner slowly lifted his head towards the window and fixed his piercing eyes on Jeanne. She wrapped her arms tight around herself as her knees threatened to give way.

PAPA!

CHAPTER 25
DRAGOONS IN THE CHÂTEAU DE PLANQUE

Day Three
Friday, 8 October 1683
Château de Planque

Tears rolled down Maman's cheeks, and Catherine sobbed, her face buried in her mother's shoulder. Jeanne pulled Anne and Paul close and strained to watch the shocking scene unfolding below.

Marion stood at one of the other tall windows of the *grand salon*, wringing her hands and moaning as she rocked from foot to foot. Down below, Martin stood statue-like at the entrance gate where he had been waiting and watching for his master's return.

One of the dragoon officers whipped his ash-colored horse around, then moved swiftly towards Papa and the other prisoners. Jeanne inhaled sharply. Everything about the man and his mount inspired awe. Jeanne trembled uncontrollably as if she were ill, and Anne pressed tighter against her side. Paul stared, his eyes wide open, his face drained pale.

The memory of Papa's voice reading Psalm 91 came to Jeanne, breaking through the fog of fear enveloping her mind, body, and soul.

"Whoever dwells in the shelter of the Most High will rest in the shadow of the Almighty.

I will say of the Lord,
'He is my refuge and my fortress, my God, in whom I trust.'"[7]

---

[7] Psalm 91:1-2 (NIV)

Jeanne lifted her eyes to the sky outside as if God himself had spoken to her from heaven. After a moment, she slowly shook her head. God wouldn't speak to her; it was doubtful he even watched over them. She stared down at Papa, bound and tied, and her soul cried out: *So, where is that refuge, and the safe fortress you promised, God? Where are you in all this?*

Jeanne sensed Anne shift and look up at her. Had she said the words out loud? Her little sister's arm tightened around her waist.

Below, the fearsome man who appeared to be in charge and another officer dismounted, then handed the reins of their horses to their *aides-de-camp*. The aids brought the horses around to Martin and mouthed a string of words Jeanne couldn't hear. Martin instinctively looked to Papa, who gave a quick nod. Martin's scowl deepened and he reluctantly led the aides and their horses towards the stables to the right of the château. The officers and several other dragoons strode towards the main entry's massive double-door.

"*Non! Pas possible!* It's not possible!" Jeanne cried. Four soldiers followed the officers, roughly escorting Papa, Massador, and the other prisoner. She gulped for air. The dragoons were coming inside!

Stunned, Maman and her siblings gaped, speechless at this horrific development happening right below their windows.

The ranking officer flung open the heavy entrance doors, crashing them against the inner walls. Dragoons and prisoners disappeared inside, and the Tessiers jolted into action. Everyone spoke at once.

"What should we do? They're coming in!"

"Maman, I hear their voices inside!"

"I'm scared!"

"Get *Grand-père's* gun!"

"It's not there!"

Marion ran back and forth from her window to the family, emitting small frightened animal sounds. Her usual bossiness had evaporated at the sight of the soldiers.

Jeanne took charge. "Catherine! Anne! Take Paul with you to our bedroom. Hide yourselves and *stay* there! Don't come out under *any* circumstance. Go!"

They did not need to be told twice. Catherine choked back a sob, grabbed Paul's hand. He wrestled free, but she seized it again, held it tight, and led him down the hallway. Chin trembling, Anne stood straight and walked steadily out of the room behind them.

"Marion, go downstairs to the kitchen, use the service staircase, and wait there," Jeanne ordered.

"*Non!* No! What if the soldiers find me?" Marion said, then glanced wildly around the room as if a way of escape might appear. "What if they go into the parlor? It leads to the kitchen."

"Marion! *Vas-y!* Go! There isn't time for this. Hide in the pantry."

She stared at Jeanne, then ducked her head and hurried off down the back servant stairway.

"Maman! Come, stand here with me." Jeanne stood next to the fireplace.

Mother and daughter barely had time to position themselves like sentries as the dragoons surged into the room. Jeanne folded her shaking hands at the front of her skirt, determined to appear calm. She stood tall and raised her head slightly. Maman did the same.

The two officers strode into the room as if they already owned the place. She bit her lip hard as both anger and fear surged within her.

After the officers came several more dragoons, two per prisoner. The captive she didn't recognize held his chin up, looking straight ahead. Massador, shy even in normal circumstances, stared only at the ground. Jeanne wished he'd raise his head, so she could impart some encouragement.

Papa entered next. Courage and love flowed from him, like a shining stream, reaching out and touching something deep inside her. He held Maman's gaze then hers. Jeanne felt it as an embrace.

Out of the corner of her eye, Jeanne observed the second-in-command watching them, an unreadable look on his face. He turned away, his brow furrowed.

The general's booming voice filled the room, jolting through Jeanne. Maman stiffened.

"I am General De Tessé, and commander of this army by the will of our King, His Royal Highness, Louis XIV." He turned to Papa. "Monsieur, this château, it is your home?"

"It is indeed, sir," replied Papa, his voice strong and clear.

The general gestured at the other officer. "Colonel Arnault informs me your name is Isaac Tessier. Is this correct?"

"Yes, sir."

Glancing at the women, he added, "You two are this man's wife and his daughter, I presume?"

116

"Yes…sir," Maman responded quietly.

The general turned his attention to the prisoners. "State your names and that of your towns!" He pointed to the stranger. "You first."

"Henri Soulier, from Lasalle, sir."

"And you?" he demanded.

"Marc Massador, from St. Hippolyte de la Planquette."

The general waved his walking stick like a scepter. "You both were arrested along Route de Lasalle for carrying arms and for the suspicious nature of your positions when our troops passed by."

Massador kept his head down, while Soulier's regard remained fixed on De Tessé.

"Sir, there's a good reason why I was there, where you stopped to water the horses and troops," said Soulier.

"You dare speak to me without permission?" interrupted De Tessé, his countenance blazing. "You are in no position to give excuses. We found you *armed,* near my troops, both of you," he finished, switching his glare from Soulier to Massador then back again.

Facing Colonel Arnault, the general continued issuing orders. "You will hold the prisoners here for the night, under the watch of your men."

The smirk stretched across the face of one of Arnault's men standing nearby was not lost on Jeanne, nor Papa, who met her gaze from across the room. Understanding passed between them: the dragoon with the lazy eye appeared particularly menacing.

For the first time since entering the château, Colonel Arnault spoke. "Sir, what about Monsieur Tessier? We apprehended him not far from here, unarmed. He claims to have been searching for something precious, something he'd lost in the forest."

Jeanne's stomach knotted, her head dipped. The floor swam before her and she prayed her burning face would go unnoticed by the dragoons.

The general paced the room several times, then pivoted toward Colonel Arnault. "Unarmed, you say?"

Arnault nodded. "Yes, sir."

De Tessé studied Papa, then announced, "He may stay with his family." Turning back to Arnault, he gave his orders. "Colonel, you and twenty of your men will lodge here in the château to keep watch on the family and the prisoners."

"Yes, sir."

"Direct the rest of the soldiers to move into homes throughout the town as planned. The surplus will camp in the fields next door leading down to the river."

The world seemed to tilt, spin, whirl, and then drop hard. The general's orders quickly overshadowed relief Papa would not be a prisoner. The *dragonnades* were starting. Where would it all lead? Cold fear snaked through Jeanne's chest, making it hard to breathe.

The rest of the army would be camping right outside in fields,which were, in fact, their vineyards. Pierre's domain. Pierre! She hadn't thought of him in hours. Had he returned yet with Gabriel? Had he learned of her deception, that Etienne hadn't returned to the mountain with her? Piercing through the living nightmare unfolding around her, this thought plucked at something deep within her, a discordant sound.

What about Noguier's fighters, now including Etienne? The dragoons must not find *any* of them with arms. Etienne was carrying her grandfather's gun, at her suggestion. She had to get to them, to warn them all. Of course, dragoons living in the château raised the risk considerably, but she determined not to let anything stop her.

CHAPTER 26
INVADED

General De Tessé continued issuing orders. "Colonel Arnault, place the prisoners under guard in the servants' quarters, each man in a separate room, with two of your men stationed outside each door."

Arnault motioned for Lieutenant Lefèvre, Duboise, and two others to follow him with the prisoners.

"Monsieur Tessier, you will show the colonel to your servants' rooms," the general announced.

Jeanne drew a small breath, relieved to see Papa lead them back out through the main *grand salon* doors to the exterior staircase and not to the inside service stairs—the ones at the end of the hall past their bedrooms. Lefèvre and Duboise yanked the prisoners along as they followed.

An awkward silence filled the *grand salon*. Maman and Jeanne were now alone with General De Tessé and the remaining dragoons. Jeanne fought to project calm despite the terror racing through her veins. The dragoon with the wandering eye made her especially uncomfortable, and his friend did not appear any better. She reached for her mother's hand.

She was determined to keep the existence of her sisters and little brother from these men. She wasn't sure how long she could steer them away from their bedrooms, just down the hall from where they now stood. Icy fear surged through Jeanne at the thought of dragoons anywhere near Catherine, Anne, or Paul. Unbidden, a prayer rose from her depths for her siblings' safety and that the dragoons wouldn't ask if there were other family members.

119

"Madame, do you have other children?" General De Tessé demanded.

Jeanne jumped. Everything in her screamed *NON!* What a fool she'd been to ask for God's intervention. He wasn't listening, nor did he seem at all interested in helping them.

Maman's hand tightened around Jeanne's. She met the general's eyes and answered his question. "Yes, sir."

Jeanne sucked in her breath.

"How many?"

"Three."

Slowly, Jeanne exhaled, deflated.

"And servants?"

"We employ several servants, but at present, only two live in the château with us."

"Where are they now?"

"I'm not sure. I imagine the man who tends our horses and wagons is in the carriage house. The housekeeper's in the kitchen."

The words hung in the air while De Tessé contemplated this information. The salacious look passing between the dragoons strengthened Jeanne's instincts about these men.

"Where are the children?" prodded De Tessé.

Maman paused, then spoke, her voice steady. "They're in the bedroom down the hall."

Jeanne admired her mother's honesty but couldn't help wishing she'd invented some other explanation. Surely God would forgive such a lie, wouldn't he? Not that it mattered to her, but for Maman, it did. Jeanne had to admit she had never seen her mother so composed, so courageous, as if telling the truth activated an inner strength in her.

De Tessé gave orders to the wild-eyed soldier. "Rossel, go and fetch the children and bring them here. You! Accompany him," he finished, pointing at Pouget.

Bile rose in Jeanne's throat at Rossel's sickening leer.

"I'll show you the way," she stated, stepping forward.

"As will I," said Maman. Neither woman waited for the general's permission as they walked across the *grand salon* and through the door leading to the bedrooms. The soldiers followed, practically stepping on their heels, like hunting dogs closing in on their prey.

Jeanne and Maman walked as slowly as possible down the hallway. They reached the children's bedroom door and stopped. Jeanne tried to think of a way to stall the dragoons a bit longer, seeking a reason to delay them laying their lustful eyes on her sisters and brother.

"Rossel! Pouget! What's happening here?" demanded Colonel Arnault. He strode down the hall from the inside servants' staircase with Papa right behind him.

"Sir! General De Tessé ordered us to locate the children of the house."

Colonel Arnault paused a minute and then glanced back at Papa before responding. "Return to the main room. Tell the general that I'll assess the situation of the children and report to him when I've finished."

Rossel opened his mouth, then clamped it shut under Colonel Arnault's icy stare. With a mumbled, "Yes, sir!" Rossel headed back down the hall towards the *grand salon* with Pouget at his heels.

Once his men were out of sight, Colonel Arnault asked Papa to open the door. Papa hesitated, then opened the door and stepped into the room.

"Papa!" cried Catherine, rushing towards him.

At the sound of her sister's voice, Jeanne cut in front of Colonel Arnault and followed Papa into the bedroom. Anne and Paul jumped up from their huddle behind the bed, relief flooding their faces, then just as rapidly draining away at the sight of the tall green-coated dragoon.

Arnault closed the door behind him, regarding each child in turn. Silence filled the room for several long minutes.

Finally, the colonel spoke, mainly addressing Papa. 'Be assured; I have no intention of letting my men cross boundaries they should not."

The Tessier family glanced at one another. The dragoons were known for their cruel violence. So what did this mean exactly? Was this a form of God's protection? Jeanne batted away the thought like a pesky fly.

"We're in St. Hippolyte to restore order and to convert you to the religion of our God-ordained King," said Arnault.

Papa's eyes narrowed. "We've done nothing wrong. Nothing outside the law."

The colonel met his eyes. "You and your fellow Huguenots continued to meet and worship openly, even when the King issued restrictions."

121

"Our right to exist as Protestants is still guaranteed under the Edict of Nantes, as it has been for more than eighty-five years. Meeting together for worship is at the very foundation of our faith."

"But, the King calls us to the one *true* Catholic faith, as well as one law and one king."

"And, we *are* loyal to the King! In that, we have never wavered. On the contrary, we have sought to obey the law as it stands. Yes, we worship God in a different form than the King, but that does not imply any disrespect to him or his faith."

Arnault reflected for a moment. "Did not someone in your community insult the priest five years ago, not offering him proper respect as he passed by?"

Papa shook his head. "The truth is quite a different story. After the morning service, we came out of our *temple* when the priest passed by, carrying materials for the last rites for a dying parishioner. Despite the crowded street, we respectfully made room for his passage. But, the priest singled out one of our men, who acted no differently than the rest of us. Something about him perturbed the priest."

"I am not familiar with all the details of the event," Arnault commented.

"They're important! The priest became enraged with our man and pulled him out of the crowd and onto the steps. Then, in front of everyone, he slapped him twice, hard across his face."

Jeanne's hands curled into fists until her nails dug into her palms. With her family, she had pressed back against the front of the *temple* and had seen the whole thing unfold. Only thirteen years old at the time, she had been frightened but also furious at the injustice. The Huguenot in question hadn't done anything wrong!

Papa continued. "As you probably know, this grew into a legal affair which dragged on for almost three years."

Colonel Arnault gave a curt nod.

"The resulting penalty was the destruction of our *temple,* which we had to carry out with our own hands. We did so in full compliance, again to demonstrate our loyalty and obedience to the King."

The colonel stared out the window.

"But did you not, even then, continue to meet for worship?" asked Arnault, rounding back to Papa, his voice sharp.

"Yes, we did, as is legally our right under the Edict of Nantes. At first, we met on the rubble of the temple. Later, we met in neighboring villages. When their buildings grew too small for us all, we were forbidden to enlarge them. So, we worshiped again in our own town, in a large field belonging to one of our community."

"Yet, when you heard the King had sent an army of dragoons your way, you moved to a mountain, calling yourselves the Lord's Army."

"Our intentions were only for self-protection and to take a stand of *passive* resistance to maintain our rights. We planned to explain all this when you arrived."

The bedroom door suddenly burst open. Jeanne swiveled around and Maman let out a startled cry. Rossel and Pouget stalked into the room.

"Colonel Arnault, sir. The general requests you to appear immediately in the *grand salon*. You are to bring the entire family with you," stated Rossel, ogling the Tessier women with his one good eye.

A dark shadow crossed Colonel Arnault's face. He motioned Rossel and Pouget to go out first. Once the pair were a safe distance down the hall, he led the family out. Jeanne put her arm around Anne's shoulders, and Catherine took Paul's hand as they followed their parents out of the room.

With everyone in the *grand salon*, General De Tessé motioned towards the double entrance doors on the opposite side of the room. Rossel and Pouget sprang into action, opened them, and ushered in a young Huguenot man. The general scowled at the lanky prisoner, whose deep brown eyes regarded him with composure.

"Do you know this man?" he barked at the Tessiers. "My soldiers found him in the vineyards next door."

"Pierre!" cried Catherine.

CHAPTER 27
CHEZ LACOMBE

Day Four
Saturday, 9 October 1683
Quartier de Planque

The sun rose as always, but nothing else in St. Hippolyte remained the same. All over town, husbands and wives watched over sleeping children, whispering in corners, out of earshot of the dragoons now living inside their homes. It was a whole new world, one they had never encountered before, one with no road maps or guidelines.

Within hours of the Huguenots returning home, the King's dragoons had swept into town. The majority of the soldiers had now moved into Huguenot homes and began consuming massive quantities of food and drink, sleeping in their beds, taunting their "hosts," and completely disrupting their lives. The horrors of the *dragonnades* had begun.

Not all the soldiers fit into homes. The overflow camped in the château's vineyards next to the river Vidourle, with no apparent care for the damage done. The access to water made it an ideal location for the men and their horses. Also, it placed them directly out front of the Lacombe home.

Throughout the evening, André and Isabeau sat in stunned silence. Dragoons surrounded and filled their home. The family had huddled around the fireplace in the kitchen, a circle of strength in the midst of their enemies.

As dawn approached, André and Isabeau kept watch over their sleeping daughters, grateful the girls were unaware of the terror, at least for a little while. Also, that they didn't yet know both their brothers were missing.

The family's relief at Pierre and Gabriel's safe return to the mountain was short-lived. The brothers had arrived just as the last wave of Huguenots rushed back to town, hurrying to get to their homes before the dragoons showed up. In all the chaos, Gabriel had disappeared. It wasn't hard for André and Isabeau to guess where he'd gone. That he managed to get away on his twisted ankle only proved his determination to join Noguier and his fighters.

To make it worse, Pierre was now missing as well. Earlier, André had considered sending him after Gabriel but without knowing the dragoons' next move, had decided to wait. In any case, Pierre had explained he wouldn't stand in Gabriel's way. If his brother was determined to fight, so be it. André and Isabeau were not of the same opinion but hadn't forced the issue.

Sometime in the late afternoon, Pierre had stepped out for a quick check of the vineyards. While he was away, the dragoons infiltrated their house and fields. They hadn't seen him since.

The first rays of daylight seeped through the window.

"The sun is rising," murmured Isabeau, "as it always does."

"Our whole world has shifted, making the ordinary strange," André said.

The image of the dragoons passed out in the family's beds rose in Isabeau's mind. Revulsion pulsed through her. "Ten dragoons in here, hundreds more camped right outside. They've implied we're not to go anywhere without permission. How are we supposed to live like this?"

André reached for Isabeau's hands. "Our God never changes. He is *with* us, and he is *for* us."

She basked in the warmth of her husband's hands and his never-wavering faith, which in turn bolstered her own.

"When shall we tell the girls about Pierre and Gabriel?" Isabeau whispered.

"Let's hold off saying anything until we have something concrete to tell them," André replied in a low voice.

Isabeau nodded as she rose from the table to begin preparation for the breakfast bread. How many loaves would it take to fill the ravenous dragoons when they woke? How long would they have to keep feeding them before supplies ran out altogether?

Andre stood. "While the dragoons sleep, I'm going next door to the château to see what I can find out."

Isabeau stopped kneading bread, her eyebrows raised high. "Is that wise if the officers are indeed inside?"

"I *must* have word of Pierre. I suspect he's there, taken by the soldiers from the vineyards or nearby."

Isabeau thought for a moment, then agreed. "We shouldn't sit here if there's any chance we can help him."

André lifted his woolen jacket from its hook. "Tell the dragoons I've gone to check the animals at the château and to procure more food. Hopefully, that will deter them from coming after me. I actually will check on the animals if I'm able to get to them."

"What about Gabriel?"

"After I discover what's going on at the château, I'll go to Noguier's home and, if he's there, try to persuade him to desist from this foolish fighting idea."

"Didn't you say Lord Aubanel told Noguier to disperse his men?"

"Yes, but it doesn't mean Noguier obeyed his orders. I believe he and at least some of his men are determined to fight, no matter the consequences."

Isabeau and André held each other's gaze. Gabriel would surely be numbered among the remnant of fighters.

Isabeau's brow furrowed. "Not knowing becomes more unbearable with each passing minute. I wish you didn't have to take the risk and go out there, but if you can help either one in any way, well, then you must go." She swallowed hard and lifted her chin. "Go with God! Please, be careful!"

André drew her close, kissed the top of her head, and departed before emotions rose and rocked the resolve of either one of them.

CHAPTER 28
GABRIEL IN ACTION

Day Three
Friday, 8 October 1683
St. Hippolyte de la Planquette

Gabriel stood directly behind Josué Noguier as the *Capitaine* turned the wrought iron door knob, then grabbed hold of the large ring above it and slowly pulled open his high and heavy front door. Noguier carefully stuck his head out and glanced right and left, up and down the rue Blanquerie. Finally, he gave a quick nod; the coast was clear. No dragoons in sight. At least not yet.

Earlier, word had come through Noguier's scouts that the soldiers had indeed arrived in town. This was the moment for which they'd been waiting and preparing. They needed to move now. The top of the rue Blanquerie connected with the town's central square, and the lower end of the street opened into the area used for seasonal *foires,* where farmers and artisans came from throughout the Cévennes to sell their wares. There was no doubt the soldiers would soon find and invade the stately Noguier home.

The *Capitaine* stepped out into the street, motioning for Gabriel to stay close behind. The two men moved swift and silent down the rue Blanquerie to an alley, then onto one of the main access roads into St. Hippolyte. Gabriel's every sense was on high alert. He felt fully alive, maybe for the first time ever. With his finger poised on the trigger of his father's musket, he was ready for action.

Pain pulsed and shot up his calf with each step. He ignored the twisted ankle, determined nothing would keep him from participating. Finally! He was on his way to fight the dragoons.

Noguier led the way through town, darting from doorways to side streets. Passing by one Huguenot home after another, random childhood memories flashed through Gabriel's mind. They were a tight-knit community; he knew each and every family. He'd played many times in these same alleys and gardens, and was aware of every nook and cranny. As they moved along, his mother's face, etched with concern, rose in his mind's eye. He shook his head, banishing such thoughts. There was no time for regrets; he must concentrate on the task ahead.

It had been easy to decide to steal away from his family not long after Pierre and he had returned to the mountain. He'd simply slid off his horse and melted into the crowds. The chaos of the Huguenots scrambling to get home before the dragoons arrived provided him with the perfect cover. But, in reality, he'd made his choice since hearing of the dragoons impending invasion. He couldn't imagine *not* fighting for their rights.

Noguier had welcomed him into his army at the end of the morning––to his great relief. If the *Capitaine* had turned him away, he wasn't sure what he would have done.

After spending time with Noguier, Gabriel was more convinced than ever God was on their side. If Psalm 91 promised ten thousand would fall before the righteous, their band of men shouldn't have any trouble subduing twelve hundred dragoons for the Almighty. Their cause was just.

Yes, the dragoons had slaughtered their fellow Huguenots in the Dauphiné. But they'd been led by their pastor like wild beasts into the forest, straight at the soldiers. Traveling merchants had brought word that the Huguenots—to everyone's surprise—had held the soldiers at bay for several hours before perishing in the smoke and flames. But, in St. Hippolyte, they were better organized, had a wiser strategy, plus *Capitaine* Noguier.

Some of the other fighters in Noguier's home informed Gabriel of Lord Aubanel's visit with orders for them to desist and how Noguier did not back down. The *Capitaine* had never wavered in his mission to fight for their rights. Many of the men chose to return home and avoid repercussions, but a number remained ready to follow his lead. Gabriel felt a surge of pride to be part of the loyal remnant.

Not long after Gabriel's appearance, Noguier had deployed several scouts around town. Word came back that the dragoons had finally arrived and were dispersing into homes. The *Capitaine* ordered the fifty with him to leave, before the dragoons installed themselves. Noguier sent the same message to his men who lodged in their own houses. They were all to quit their homes, then hide in places only locals would know, until the soldiers completed their infiltration of Huguenot homes. Later, under cover of night, they'd rendezvous up on Le Cengle mountain behind the old *lavoir*.

In groups of two or three, the men snuck out of Noguier's house, but the *Capitaine* had insisted Gabriel stick by his side. Was it because of his injured ankle, or did the *Capitaine* like him? There were similarities between them: both brash, out-spoken, and unwavering in their opinions. Maybe he'd finally found someone who understood him.

Noguier and Gabriel turned left at the end of the alley then made their way up the main road into town, the Route d'Alès. Although the dragoons had arrived on the other side of St. Hippolyte, on the Route de Lasalle, they were by now moving in groups into every Huguenot home, along every street. Noguier and Gabriel tried to time their movements when the coast looked clear. After dragoons almost discovered them for the second time, they hid for several hours in a covered passageway.

By nightfall, the streets were quiet. The only sounds filling the air were those filtering out of nearby houses, of dragoons sounding more raucous by the minute as they ate and drank their way through the Huguenots' provisions. When all finally seemed quiet, Noguier and Gabriel carefully ventured out, then continued their path towards Le Cengle.

Finally, they arrived at the foot of the mountain. Gabriel breathed a sigh of relief. His injury hadn't held back the *Capitaine* from making it to this point. Plus, he was now in even more familiar territory; he knew these brush-covered hills by heart. Happy hours of invented games played here with Pierre would come in handy.

Gabriel and Noguier progressed up the mountain, from boulder to boulder, lest any stray dragoons from the street below happened to look up. They crouched low, waiting before moving again. Gabriel inhaled the familiar scents of thyme and wild mint filling the air, triggering memories of a time when he and Pierre were in accord. He chose to ignore the tightness in his chest. This was no time for sentiment.

Noguier gave the signal to move. Gabriel stood quickly. A burst of pain flared from his ankle and radiated up his leg. His foot wobbled on the crumbly mountainside, releasing a spray of rocks.

"Gabriel, pay attention!" Noguier whispered with force.

Gabriel pulled himself together, nodded at his *Capitaine*.

Noguier held his finger to his lips. Then, slowly, they continued to pick their way across the mountain. Although most of the dragoons were by now in homes, a contingent of soldiers camped in the château's vineyards, not far from this end of Le Cengle mountain. Although the proximity to the dragoon-filled vineyards made it risky, Noguier had chosen the spot for a good reason; they were on the high ground, with a strategic advantage when the time came to attack.

They approached the rendezvous point, a rock retaining wall sitting high above the old *lavoir*. The outline of other Huguenot fighters huddled behind the boulders grew visible.

As they drew near, Noguier identified himself and Gabriel to the hidden fighters. One of the men jumped to his feet and stepped out of the shadows.

"Etienne!" Gabriel cried. "You're here!"

"Gabriel! And you!"

Immediately, Noguier yanked them both down behind the wall. All the fighters present held their breath, listening hard for any sign of dragoons responding to the outburst.

"When will you learn? We must *not* draw attention to ourselves. The element of surprise is essential," Noguier hissed, a spray of spittle landing on Gabriel's face.

"Sorry, *Capitaine*. I didn't expect to find Etienne here. I last saw him in Monoblet a couple of nights ago," Gabriel said, his voice low.

"Your ankle, you're walking on it!" said Etienne.

Gabriel grinned. "I wouldn't miss this for anything! But how are you here?

"After Monoblet, I joined Noguier before dawn this morning. He sent me out on training exercises in the Bedos field."

"The *Capitaine* made me rest my ankle in his home during the day."

"He sent me to stay at Jean Bedos' home until we received word to evacuate before the dragoons moved in," Etienne said.

Noguier drew a sharp line with his hand. "*None* of that's important now. Focus only on following my orders. Keep your mouths shut!"

Gabriel and Etienne obeyed, their lips clamped tight. More words weren't necessary as they sat shoulder to shoulder on the cold ground. Despite all the twists, turns, and opposition from their fathers, they had both finally managed to join Noguier's fighters.

In spite of the drop in temperature and the pre-battle energy pumping through their veins, they eventually nodded off. Even the arrival of the rest of Noguier's men didn't rouse Gabriel and Etienne from a deep slumber.

CHAPTER 29
INTO THE CHÂTEAU

Day Four
Saturday, 9 October 1683
Château de Planque

The beautiful day, with blue skies and trees blazing autumnal shades, all went unnoticed by André as he rapidly crossed the Route de Lasalle separating his house from the Château de Planque. The very same road the dragoons had roared down less than twenty-four hours earlier.

André slipped into the street-side servants' entrance into the kitchen. Seeing no one around, he quickly shut the door, just as Marion came at him brandishing a large iron pot.

"Marion! *Attend!* Wait, it's me, André!" he cried, both hands raised.

"What…oh!" With a ragged breath, Marion lowered the heavy pot. "Monsieur André! What are you doing here?"

"Pierre? Is he here?"

Marion's shoulders sagged. "Yes, he's here. The dragoons took him; they did. In the vineyards yesterday afternoon."

"Where is he now?"

The housekeeper's face contorted and her ample chest heaved.

"Marion, please tell me what they've done with my son!"

"Monsieur Pierre's with the other prisoners in the servant's quarters."

André leaned back against the wall. Marion's news confirmed his suspicion thatPierre was in the château. Butto learn that the dragoons had taken Pierre prisoner hit him like a hammer. He shut his eyes, reminding himself to be thankful that at least Pierre was still alive.

"And the Tessier family?" he asked after several moments.

"They all spent the night in the children's room. I slept here in the pantry, behind the sacks of flour, trying to keep out of sight. Some of them dragoons have that gleam in their eye as if they'd like to eat you, or worse."

André's voice was sharp. "Have they tried anything? Hurt any of you?"

"No, not yet. Colonel Arnault sees to that. It's his men who look like trouble, but he's trying to keep them in line."

"How many soldiers are there?"

"There's Colonel Arnault, he's not too bad, and twenty of his men. At first, the general of the whole lot of them was here. De Tessé is his name. He's a nasty man, that one! All those ribbons and the way he struts around like *he* owns the château! A voice like a rooster, squawking and bossing everyone in sight. You can tell he don't care one whit what his soldiers do to us." Marion trembled head to toe. "Finally, he left on to other business and put Colonel Arnault in charge here. He and his men slept in the master and mistress' bedroom. I saw 'em retreat in there after I came to clear their dinner plates."

"What about the prisoners? Have the dragoons caused them any harm?"

"I haven't seen 'em since the soldiers put 'em in us servants' rooms." Indignation momentarily replaced her terror.

André pressed his fingers to his forehead, trying not to imagine the worst.

"Have you brought breakfast up?" he asked.

"Not yet. I'm preparing it now."

"I have an idea. Take the food up to the *grand salon*. Say nothing about my presence here, except to give a signal to Monsieur Isaac. Tell him the kitchen chimney that Monsieur *Gamond* cleaned recently appears to be blocked again."

"But it isn't!" Marion retorted.

"That's the point. Hopefully, Monsieur Isaac will understand it's some kind of a message, as our lawyer friend Guillaume Gamond is not exactly in the business of fixing chimneys."

"What if they don't let him come with me or send down one of their men?"

"Insist only Monsieur Isaac knows how to fix it because it's relatively complicated. If that doesn't work and they send a soldier with you, do the following: when you enter the kitchen, announce loud and clear, *"Right this way, sir."*

Marion bit her lip, nerves getting the better of her. André rested his hand on her shoulder. "You can do it! Go now! Quickly!"

Shouted orders and the clatter of hooves in the road outside stopped the housekeeper cold. André put a finger to his lips as the double front doors of the Château de Planque burst open, smashing like cannonballs into the limestone walls of the entry foyer. Marion yelped then clapped both hands over her mouth.

"Shhhh!" said André firmly. He gently pushed her back into the pantry hiding place. "Stay here. *Don't move!*"

"What...? Where are you going?"

"I must know what's happening." He left before she could say another word.

André exited the kitchen into the reception parlor. Commanding voices reached him from the foyer on the other side.

"*Bonjour,* General De Tessé."

"*Bonjour,* Colonel Arnault. I present to you Governor Noailles of the Languedoc region. He will oversee the prisoners' trial."

André imagined the colonel saluting or bowing, or whatever it was one did before a King's governor.

"Bonjour et *bienvenue* Governor. Welcome to the Château de Planque!"

André cringed at the ensuing laughter, certainly over the irony of a colonel of the King's army welcoming the King's governor into a Huguenot home.

"The prisoners?" asked Noailles. "What's their status?"

"They await trial in the *grand salon* just above us."

"Take me to them immediately!"

Once the sound of soldiers' boots on the entry staircase died away, André hurried back through the kitchen and up the servants' stairs. Then, pressing his ear against the service door to the *grand salon,* he tried to discern what was going on inside.

"You say you apprehended these two men with arms?" demanded Governor Noailles.

"Yes, sir," responded General De Tessé. "This one, Henri Soulier, was found near Saint-Félix de Pallières."

"Where are you from, Henri Soulier?" the governor asked.

"The town of Lasalle, sir."

"What were you doing in Saint-Félix? That must be a good two hours journey on foot from Lasalle."

"I'd gone to visit a sick friend."

"A sick friend?" Noailles continued, eyebrows raised. "With a gun?"

Soulier responded firmly, "Yes, sir."

"Explain yourself. Now!"

"I planned to hunt a rabbit or some other small creature to bring to his family. He's been ill for weeks. They're near starvation."

"You planned to hunt, you say?"

"Yes, sir."

"Did you catch anything?"

"No, sir. The soldiers apprehended me before I was able to do so."

Silence followed. André imagined the governor assessing the poor man. Crack! What must have been the governor's tall walking stick, fashionable among men of his stature, struck the floor like a gavel. "I've heard enough."

"And this one? Where did you find him?" André's blood raced at the tenor of the governor's voice.

General De Tessé answered him. "Colonel Arnault tells me they found this one on a small hill near Monoblet, overlooking the route from Anduze, a perfect place to view our approach."

"He was detected how?"

Colonel Arnault spoke up. "As we passed by, a large stone rolled down the road in our path. When my men investigated the cause, they found him—alone and armed."

"What's your name?"

"Marc Massador," came the mumbled reply.

"Speak up, man! Look at me!"

"Marc Massador."

André's heart sank at the thought of the timid shepherd being held captive and interrogated by these fierce men.

"Well, Marc Massador. What reason can you give me for being in such a place at such a time and *armed*?"

Silence.

"Why were you on that hill with a gun? *Answer me now!*"

"I was hunting."

Noailles humphed. "You also were hunting?"

135

André couldn't make out Massador's response.

The walking stick crashed onto the floor with such force that even the solid stone walls seemed to shake.

After a moment, Governor Noailles spoke again.

"And you! State your name and town!"

Cold fear rippled through André at the sound of the third prisoner's voice.

"Pierre Lacombe, sir, of St. Hippolyte de la Planquette."

CHAPTER 30
SHOT!

Day Four
Saturday, 9 October 1683
Le Cengle mountain, above the old lavoir

apitaine Noguier examined their surroundings through the inky vestiges of the night as it faded into the early morning light. He sat back on his heels, considering the movement of the King's troops. The soldiers who had camped in the vineyards overnight were packing up and moving out! Several squadrons had gathered on the bridge, spilling into the road below, preparing for what appeared to be a departure.

Noguier counted his men; only half were there. It was most likely they had been unable to get away from their homes when the *dragonnade* began. Twenty-five men would have to do. The natural odds had never been in their favor. Truly only God could bring them victory, and it would take a miracle.

Glancing over his men, he found Gabriel Lacombe awake. Despite himself, he liked that one. Impetuous, yes. But Gabriel's passion, conviction, and fearlessness were traits one couldn't teach. If they had more time, he would have developed the natural leadership latent in the young man.

As if on cue, Gabriel scooted closer. "Let's go down the side of the mountain to the Route de Cros and come at them on this end of the bridge," he whispered.

The *Capitaine* studied him. "There's no time to do that and maintain an element of surprise. Plus, they'll just keep coming at us from the château side. If other dragoons join them from the homes along the road, we'll be surrounded."

"We were always going to be outnumbered."

"Which is why I'm discerning our best strategy."

The rest of the *Capitaine's* men awoke as the energy around them increased. Suddenly, Jean Bedos and Etienne inched closer to Gabriel, nudging him hard and pointing wildly to the road below.

Gabriel alerted Noguier. "Sir! Dragoons have left the road directly below and are coming up the mountain. They're advancing towards us!"

Without waiting for a reply, Gabriel bolted from behind the rock wall. He slid out of Noguier's reach and started down the hill as the *Capitaine* shout-whispered "*NON!*"

Jean Bedos responded quickly and rounded down in front of Gabriel, cutting him. "*Capitaine* says no!" he grabbed Gabriel by the arm and hauled him back behind the rock wall.

"They're coming this way," protested Gabriel.

"Don't be a fool," said Noguier. "Wait for orders! Understood?"

Noguier glared at him until he acquiesced.

"Once the soldiers are right below us, and *I* give the order..." He threw a pointed look at Gabriel. "*Then,* and only then, we sweep down upon them. We must use the element of surprise in our favor."

The Huguenots readied their guns, poised for action, eyes fixed on Noguier. Each second passed like an hour. Noguier sensed the tension mounting in his men but determined to choose the most advantageous moment to reveal their presence.

Several minutes passed as the fighters crouched, poised for action, not daring to breathe. Finally, a hawk flew overhead, and Noguier sensed it was time.

"Now!" Noguier commanded, dropping his raised hand, leading out the charge.

Gabriel burst out from their hiding place like a cannonball, Etienne and the others right on his heels.

One of the green-coated dragoons responded immediately, raised his gun, and fired. The rest of the soldiers followed, releasing a hail of bullets, while Gabriel shot back, downing his first dragoon.

Kneeling to reload his arm, Gabriel raised his head as an emerald blur rushed at him. Etienne appeared from the side and aimed at the dragoon. The shot went off in a small explosion of smoke. Misfire! Etienne yowled in pain and dropped his weapon.

Jean Bedos ran interference and took out the dragoon, just as the soldier got off a shot.

Gabriel cried out and crumpled to the ground clutching his left shoulder.

Noguier and the others held off the dragoons as Bedos managed to pull Gabriel behind the rock wall. A hail of bullets flew in their direction as the rest of the dragoon contingent ran towards their hiding place.

Noguier motioned for his men to scatter into the hills as fast as possible. Every last one of them was born and bred Çevenol and knew every rock, bush, tree, and crevice on the mountain. In a matter of seconds, they disappeared as the dragoons climbed up the hill. Several soldiers peeled off after them.

Alone with Gabriel, Noguier had less than a few minutes before the remaining soldiers discovered them. He needed to find cover and do it fast.

"*Capitaine!* Hide us! There's a small cave above, behind that rocky ledge." Gabriel raised his head a fraction and pointed before dropping back to the ground with a groan.

Noguier wrapped his arm around him, bearing the brunt of his weight. The pain of moving appeared to clear Gabriel's senses, and they scrambled up over the ridge. Amid more shots by the dragoons, they crawled into the cave without being hit. The low-ceilinged cave barely fit the two of them, plus a large boulder.

"Here, roll this into the mouth," Gabriel rasped. "I hid here from Pierre when we were children." He then curled onto his right side.

Noguier fitted the boulder into the cave's mouth only a minute before the soldiers drew near. The dragoons stopped within meters of the cave.

"Where'd they go?"

"They couldn't have just disappeared into thin air."

"How many were there?"

"There were at least two dozen, maybe more!"

Gabriel and Noguier barely breathed as the dragoons tramped around the rocky hill hunting for Huguenots, hunting for them. After what seemed like an eternity of listening to the soldiers shouting threats and shots fired, the dragoons' footsteps and voices finally faded away.

When silence reigned for a reasonable length of time, Noguier carefully rolled the stone open a crack, enough to let in some fresh air and light. A few rays of bright sunshine trickled in, and both men gulped in the welcome oxygen. With the light, Noguier saw that blood covered the front of Gabriel's shirt. He feared the worst.

"Do you know where you're hit?" Noguier asked.

"Shoulder...?" Gabriel fought to stay conscious. The fear and sharp pain that fueled their flight had now worn off.

Noguier slowly lifted Gabriel's shirt. A bullet had indeed gone straight into his left shoulder and out the other side.

"It went clean through, but thankfully missed your heart! Divine protection, I'd say. But we need to stop the bleeding. *Now.*"

Noguier untied his formerly white neck scarf and wrapped it under Gabriel's arm and around the shoulder the best he could. He bound it as tightly as possible, wishing the tie was a bit longer.

"I'm no doctor, but this will have to do for now. Hold your hand on the wound. Press hard."

Gabriel tried, but the pain was too much. His hand fell away, and his face became an even paler shade of gray.

"Gabriel! You *must* do this! You're still losing blood!" Taking the young man's hand, he pushed it firmly against the wound, holding his own over it for extra pressure. "Look at me, Gabriel! *Gabriel!*" Noguier took hold of his chin with his free hand, shaking it slightly until Gabriel managed to make eye contact.

"All right, that's better. I'm going to get supplies and help. Once I'm out of the cave, I'll roll the stone back in place. I'll leave a tiny sliver open for air, but close it with your foot if you hear anyone. Do you understand?"

Gabriel blinked, trying to maintain focus.

"Keep your hand pressed hard on the wound. Do you hear me? You must do so!"

Noguier watched the young man muster enough strength to meet his gaze.

"Yes, sir," Gabriel replied, his voice faint.

The *Capitaine* prayed protection over them both and slipped out of the cave.

CHAPTER 31
CHÂTEAU TRIAL

Day Four
Saturday, 9 October 1683
Château de Planque

Jeanne studied Pierre's face as the dragoon guards brought the prisoners into the *grand salon.* Despite spending the night in the servants' quarters, under guard with the other captives, he appeared calm and steady, not much different from how he was on any given day. Jeanne was anything but calm. Jangly and jumpy, she found it hard to stay still. Smoothing her skirt with her hands, she tried to press some peace into her body. These dragoons would *not* see her anxiety!

A glimpse of autumn's vibrant colors through the high *salon* windows brought a measure of peace. The thought crossed her mind that there must be something good about the Creator of such beauty. He couldn't be all bad, even if he was distant, or worse, didn't care.

"*You!*" roared Governor Noailles, his ferocious glare fixed on Pierre. Papa and Maman pulled the younger children closer. Jeanne reached for Catherine's hand and was relieved her sister didn't yank it away. They needed each other now more than ever.

"State your name and town!"

"Pierre Lacombe, sir, of St. Hippolyte de la Planquette."

Turning to Arnault, the governor asked, "Where was he taken? Was he armed?"

"My men found him in the vineyards attached to this château. And no, he was not armed."

Noailles turned to Pierre. "What were you doing in the vineyards?

"I was checking the state of the vines," Pierre said, his voice calm and firm. Jeanne marveled at his composure.

"What business have you in the château's vineyards?"

"I'm employed by Monsieur Tessier."

"To do what?"

"I am the vine master and winemaker."

"The *vendanges* have passed; the grapes have been harvested."

"Yes, but the vines need to be prepared for the resting stage until we prune them in early winter. I also help manage the affairs of the château," said Pierre.

"Your age?"

"Twenty-two."

"Isn't that rather young to be the estate manager?" asked Noailles, his focus now on Papa. "I find that hard to believe."

Neither man answered his question. Noailles rapped his walking stick hard on the floor several times, glaring at Papa. "Answer me! You say he *manages* this château? At age twenty-two?"

The servant's entrance door flung open. Jeanne sucked in her breath as Lefèvre and Duboise thrust André into the room. What on earth was he doing here? A glance at Pierre told her he was equally shocked.

Several soldiers stepped forward, hands on the hilts of their sabers. Lefèvre and Duboise grabbed André's arms again and twisted them hard behind his back while Rossel and Pouget performed a quick search for weapons and came up empty-handed.

"What is the meaning of this?" Noailles demanded.

"Sir, we found him outside the door, listening," said Lefèvre.

"*Bring him closer!*" Noailles thundered. Lefèvre and Duboise shoved André to within a few feet of the governor.

"What is the meaning of this? I say! Who are you?" he barked as he paced and pounded his walking stick in repetition. Jeanne's head squeezed tighter with each crash.

"I'm André Lacombe, sir. *I* am the manager of this estate. My son Pierre tends the vineyards and makes the wine, as he said. He also assists me in running the place under the overall supervision, of course, of Monsieur Tessier."

Governor Noailles studied André, then slowly observed Papa and Pierre. All three Huguenot men stood firm, not a hint of fear on their faces. Their oft-repeated motto: "On our knees before God, on our feet

142

before men," came to Jeanne's mind. Here was a picture of just that. Knowing these men, they were praying and trusting their God.

Papa spoke up. "Sir, it's true. These men are in my employ. They manage the affairs of the Château de Planque with my oversight."

Noailles did not interject, so he continued. "They are utterly trustworthy men. Both of them are faithful in all they do and, I can assure you, loyal to the King." Papa met the governor's eyes.

Silence weighed heavy in the room. Maman's lips moved in silent prayer. Even Catherine mumbled a desperate plea for God's help.

The governor paced, then stopped to confer with General De Tessé and Colonel Arnault. Finally, he thumped his stick on the floor and swiveled to address the Huguenot men.

"Heretics! You are all members of the 'Pretend Reformed Religion,' correct?" It was a rhetorical question; the answer was obvious. Few in St. Hippolyte and the surrounding region were not Protestant "pretenders," as the King and his authorities called them. The prisoners remained still, except Massador, who rocked from foot to foot, then raised his head briefly before slumping and sagging under the weight of it all.

Jeanne longed to comfort her shepherd friend. Over the years, they had spent hours together, inventing humorous stories for each other, mainly about the silly sheep while he carried out his duties. If only she could recount one to him now.

The governor's stick crashed onto the floor again. "You were all apprehended under suspicious circumstances near the royal army. Moreover, two of you carried guns, which can be construed as a treasonous action against the King," he stated.

Jeanne inhaled sharply. What was he saying?

"However, the King, in his mercy, wants the errant sheep back in the fold of the one true religion. If you agree to recant, to turn away from this pretend 'reformed' heresy and give your allegiance to the King and his rightful, legitimate church, leniency could be accorded."

The air seemed to siphon out of the room like an atmospheric shift before a storm. Concrete pressure to deny the faith had begun.

Jeanne tried to imagine what their lives would be like if they became Catholic. Would they go to mass and be forced to get rid of their Bibles, with only the priest allowed to read and interpret the scriptures? Would

143

they have to do penance, or worse, pay money for the removal of their sins?

Even in her state of unbelief, Jeanne couldn't imagine that way of life. It was not just a preference in how they worshipped; their core values were unalterably different. Each Protestant man, woman, and child had direct access to God through the Bible and in prayer. As a result, personal responsibility was highly prized and an integral part of their identity. No matter that she and God weren't on good terms, she wasn't about to give up her freedom.

For the Huguenots, to let go of their Protestant faith meant denying God altogether. But, what would be the consequences if they did not? How far were the dragoons willing to go?

"*Take the prisoners back to their rooms!*" barked Noailles. "We'll give them some time to think on it. And Monsieur Lacombe as well," he added, pointing at André.

Governor Noailles and General De Tessé motioned for Arnault to join them. They spoke in hushed tones, then moved to the dining table like three judges convening to pass sentences.

The Tessier family huddled awkwardly at the other end of the room. For now, the officers seemed to have forgotten them and Papa observed the dragoons with his eyes narrowed, strategizing how to navigate it all.

General De Tessé raised his head. "Where's that servant woman? She never brought our *petit-déjeuner*. Tell her we'll now take our midday meal earlier."

"I'll give her the orders," Jeanne spoke up. She needed an excuse to get out of the room and get to Etienne. He must get rid of *Grand-père's* musket!

"Go then!" commanded De Tessé, dismissing her with a flick of his wrist. With a nod to her parents, her back straight, Jeanne walked out of the *grand salon.*

144

CHAPTER 32
VERDICT

Day Four
Saturday, 9 October 1683
Château de Planque

Down in the kitchen, all was quiet. Even the mice, who perpetually fought for their rights to sustenance, had gone into hiding.

"Marion," she called softly. "It's me, Jeanne."

Rustling noises came from the pantry as the housekeeper emerged between substantial sacks of flour, a wheat-colored smear across her cheek.

"I'm so glad to see you!" Marion whispered, flinging herself into Jeanne's arms. "What's happening up there? Monsieur André didn't come back."

Jeanne quickly filled her in. Both women stood immobile, holding onto each other's forearms for strength.

One glance around the kitchen revealed Marion had not started preparations for breakfast nor the midday meal. The women who came in daily to help had not shown up, which was not surprising. Dragoons now occupied Huguenot homes and were most likely patrolling the streets.

"Let's get started," Jeanne said, grabbing one of the cooking aprons from its peg, glad Maman had insisted she learn the basics of meal preparation. Today it would come in handy; Marion would never have the meal ready without her help. She sighed, her lips pursed. Getting away to warn Etienne would have to wait.

Marion blinked a few times, then bustled about, gathering wheat flour, yeast and salt into smaller pottery containers. She thrust them on the wooden work table and told Jeanne to get going on the bread dough. The housekeeper then scurried off to the larder beyond the pantry and soon returned clutching a smoked ham hock from the last slaughter and a crock of shelled and roasted chestnuts. She lit a fire under the heavy iron pot which had previously been filled with water. While waiting for it to boil, she headed out to the *potager* to see if there were any late vegetables to add to the soup.

Marion returned with an armful of leeks and washed them in the stone sink with its pipe running through the wall to drain the water into the street outside. Jeanne was relieved the servants had filled all the tall kitchen pitchers with water the last time they'd been there. One less thing for the two women to do now. Also, as the well was in the center courtyard, it allowed them to stay inside and away from wandering dragoons. Thankfully, the soldiers avoided the kitchen, at least for now.

Once the water in the iron pot rose to a boil, she added the leeks along with the chestnuts and gave it all a stir with her long-handled wooden spoon. She glanced at Jeanne and both women shrugged. They could only hope their daily fare for this time of year did not raise criticism or complaints from the dragoon officers used to the fancier food of northern France. Jeanne didn't care one bit if they liked it or not, but it seemed best to avoid raising their ire.

Jeanne finished the dough, punching it with vigor, a small catharsis for the stone-like dread lying in the pit of her stomach. Questions rotated through her mind as she folded and kneaded the yeast throughout the mixture multiple times. What had happened since Etienne had joined Noguier's men? Her idea for him to take *Grand-père's* musket had seemed inspired at the time. Now, if the dragoons apprehended him, he'd face a trial with life-threatening consequences. She could barely stand to think about it.

Would any of them recant, renouncing their Protestant faith? She couldn't fathom any of the St. Hippolyte Huguenots doing such a thing. But never before had they been put to the test like this. If it came down to life or death, was it really that wrong to give in and join the King's faith?

Pierre's steady brown eyes, full of peace, came to mind. Even under the pressure of the governor's questioning, he emanated strength as solid as the earth. Jeanne breathed deeply, folding the dough a final time, then dividing it into separate loaves.

Massador had barely made it through the trial. Nervous energy alternating with stark terror had flowed out of him. She wasn't sure he could stand much more strain.

Then there was the man from Lasalle. She didn't know his character, but he seemed unfazed and fairly sure of himself.

And André! He had come to find his son but was now a prisoner as well. Jeanne chewed on the corner of her lip. Where would this end?

Marion took the dough from Jeanne and set the rounds to rise in a warm corner by the broad kitchen fireplace. Doing routine tasks had settled the housekeeper, and she began singing as she worked.

"For he will command his angels concerning you to guard you in all your ways;
they will lift you up in their hands
so that you will not strike your foot against a stone."[8]

Jeanne accidentally bit her lip hard. With all they were facing, the thought that God kept them from harm was more far-fetched than ever. How she wished it were true! Every hour the situation grew more dire, with no end in sight. Grabbing the long-handled wooden spoon, she stirred the soup vigorously.

Yet as Marion continued to sing, her irritation ebbed. Not that she believed in what the psalmist expressed, but it brought comfort nonetheless. For the housekeeper's sake, she joined her in the chorus.

"Whoever dwells in the shelter of the Most High
will rest in the shadow of the Almighty.
I will say of the Lord,
'He is my refuge and my fortress, my God, in whom I trust.'"[9]

Jeanne leaned over the iron pot, taking care to keep her skirts from the open flame, inhaling the comforting aroma. She stirred the broth, slowing her pace. Something tiny shifted inside her, something she couldn't name. It made her think of the rising warmth of embers glowing in a cold room. It was not unwelcome.

The bread rose quickly in its warm nook. Marion slid the loaves into the brick oven in one corner of the kitchen fireplace, then added more wood to the fire. Both women pulled chairs close to the warmth, enjoying a bit of rest and quiet while the bread baked.

---

[8] Psalm 91:11-12 (NIV)
[9] Psalm 91:1-2 (NIV)

Once the bread was ready, Jeanne and Marion loaded and carried wooden trays laden with the midday meal up the servant staircase. They moved slowly, keeping the chestnut soup from splashing over the sides of the porcelain tureen that had belonged to Jeanne's great-grandmother. Neither wanted to give any of the dragoon officers reason to complain or worse.

Jeanne and Marion entered the *grand salon,* setting their trays on the sideboard. Jeanne glanced over at Papa and Maman, still standing awkwardly in the corner next to the farthest window. Anne and Paul sat on the floor, fidgety with hunger, while Catherine stared out the window as if she longed to be far, far away.

After serving the governor, the officers, and the rest of the soldiers, Jeanne and Marion returned to the kitchen, then brought up the family's meal. Mounting stress robbed them of any real appetite, but the adults sat on the window bench, trying to eat a little. A smile tugged at the corners of Jeanne's mouth. Her siblings didn't seem to have any problem eating as they all tucked right into the meal.

Governor Noailles and the dragoon officers continued a low-voiced discussion at one end of the dining table as they ate. Jeanne guessed they were deciding the fate of the prisoners but couldn't make out what they were saying. She watched Papa, who leaned towards the soldiers' conversation. Their eyes met, and with one eyebrow raised, he looked pointedly at the foot she tapped, unaware. She stopped, her own eyebrows raised in a silent question. How long would this take? Papa's slight shrug was not unexpected. None of them knew.

As each hour passed, her anxiety grew. She needed to get away and warn Etienne before it was too late.

Finally, unable to sit still a minute longer, Jeanne motioned to Marion, who had joined them for lunch. They both rose to stack the family's empty bowls and plates. With a return trip to the kitchen, she'd try to slip out to the Gamonds.

Without warning, Noailles cracked his ever-present stick on the floor and stood abruptly. Jeanne flinched, struggling to hold onto the dishes. The rest of the Tessiers jumped to their feet. Papa placed a reassuring arm around Maman as she inched a bit farther in front of Catherine, Anne, and Paul, instinctively putting herself between the dragoons and her children.

"*Bring the prisoners down!*"the governor ordered.

148

Colonel Arnault nodded and moved immediately across the room towards the door leading out to the family hallway and the interior servant staircase. He avoided eye contact with the family as he passed by. The tall grandfather clock Maman inherited from her *Grand-mère* ticked loudly in the silence.

In a short while, Arnault reappeared with the four prisoners and their guards. The colonel directed the Huguenot men: Massador, Soulier, André, and Pierre to form a line before Noailles. Their dragoon guards remained close behind.

The governor began. "Pretenders! You two, step forward now!"

Soulier advanced, head held high. One of the guards pushed Massador forward. He stumbled towards the governor, staring at the ground.

"I, Governor Noailles, am appointed by His Majesty, the King, to govern the region of Languedoc. Therefore, by the authority vested in me, I sit in judgment of you, members of the 'Pretend Reformed Religion.' He regarded each prisoner in turn. Then, striking his baton on the floor, he continued, "It is a treasonous offense to be in proximity to the King's soldiers while armed. Henri Soulier, you were found in possession of a musket near the dragoons at Saint Félix de Pallières. I, therefore, sentence you to death by hanging."

Jeanne gasped. The tray of dishes fumbled in her hands, a bowl toppling to the floor, shattering into what looked like a hundred pieces and earning her a fierce glare from Noailles.

Stoic, Soulier received the news without reaction, only gazing towards heaven as if agreeing to his fate with an unseen presence.

The governor carried on. "Should you wish to recant and convert to the one true religion of the King, we will pardon you."

Soulier looked full in the governor's face. "*Non*, sir, I will not renounce my God."

"Then your fate is sealed. You will hang in one hour's time."

Jeanne couldn't breathe as Noailles turned his attention to her friend.

"Marc Massador, the King's dragoons found you at a lookout point above the road to Monoblet as the royal army marched below. You were armed and in the proximity of dragoons." The governor paused for effect. "You are also sentenced to death by hanging."

Massador swayed slightly and shot a glance around the room without focusing on anyone or anything.

The governor stepped towards the shepherd. "Should you choose to recant, your sentence would commute to the payment of a fine. What say you?"

Mumbling something no one could hear, Massador shook his head.

"*Speak up!*" Noailles commanded.

"*Non*, I do not recant," whispered Massador.

Jeanne flushed hot then cold. Was it really so bad to recant—and live?

"Then you also will be executed in one hour's time," the governor announced with a final baton crash reverberating across the wood floor. Even the solid rock walls of the château seemed to tremble at the sound.

At this, Massador crumpled in a dead faint. Jeanne leaned against the wall, her knees weak. Where are you, God? How is this protecting us?

Lieutenant Lefèvre gave Massador a swift kick with his heavy boot to no avail. He had passed out cold. Duboise grabbed a water goblet left on the table and threw its contents on the prisoner's face. Spluttering, disoriented, Massador regained consciousness as his captors dragged him to his feet and shoved him back in line.

Maman wept quietly into her hands; her children huddled close. Papa stood firm, and his arms stretched out to enfold his family while striving to make eye contact with the shepherd. Jeanne shut her eyes. Even if Massador were able to focus on him, it wouldn't be enough.

The governor ordered the guards to return all prisoners to the third floor. He'd not mentioned André or Pierre. What did it mean? Jeanne glanced across to Pierre and found his gaze already on her. For a moment, all else receded. They were connected in the present but also a realm far beyond—a flash of peace amid the chaos.

Then the dragoon guards yanked Pierre away, forcing him to follow his father and the condemned men they led out of the room. Finally, the door slammed shut, leaving a palpable void. Her chest squeezed tight. She fought for air, panic rising as if she was trapped in a cave with no way out.

Like a lifeline, she remembered there was something to do. Etienne and Noguier's army still needed to be warned. These dragoons would not render her inactive. She breathed a tiny bit easier. Jeanne narrowed her eyes at the dragoon officers and then began to comfort her siblings.

CHAPTER 33
DRAGOONS BRINGING FIRE

Day Four
Saturday, 9 October 1683
St. Hippolyte de la Planquette

*C*apitaine Noguier crouched low as he emerged from the cave, hand over his brow at the bright flash of daylight. He inched the boulder back into place, leaving a narrow crack as planned for fresh air for Gabriel.

He crept from bush to tree, making his way down the hill, praying as he went for young Lacombe and for all his men scattered after the skirmish with the dragoons. Were any of the others wounded? This was not the successful outcome he'd imagined.

Once at ground level, he waited behind a massive boulder before venturing farther, checking for dragoons in all directions—none were in sight.

His pulse raced with each step as he wove his way through town using tiny lanes and hidden passageways. He prayed the dragoons had not yet discovered these out-of-sight places.

Finally, he headed towards his home, where he had a stash of medical supplies and food rations. Plus, down around the corner, on the Grande Rue, lived a doctor he trusted.

Noguier emerged at the end of an alley leading to *centre ville* just as a cluster of dragoons appeared at the far end. He ducked into a deep entryway, pressed himself tight against the door, keeping one hand on his musket. Had he been seen? If he was apprehended, they might recognize him from the earlier clash. He offered up a prayer of protection.

151

No shouts or cries materialized. Noguier dared to peek around the corner of his hiding place. The soldiers stood in a heated discussion, at times gesturing towards the far end of town, in the direction of the Bedos family home and fields. For the hundredth time, Noguier wished he knew what they planned to do.

Finally the dragoons moved on and Noguier cautiously stepped out making his way to his street. He jumped over a low wall between two homes at the top of the road and continued through the gardens. Since his land extended behind several of the houses on the rue Blanquerie, he quickly arrived at the edge of his property.

Noguier carefully rose from behind a large bush and peered over the rock wall into his garden, rapidly sinking back undercover. At least twenty dragoons lounged and milled around his land. From his rapid survey over the wall, he'd seen the doctor's garden beyond his own. It, too, was filled with soldiers. There was no question of him getting anywhere near either home.

Sweat beaded and dripped from his forehead. He swiped it away, mentally formulating a new strategy. Gabriel's mother possessed healing skills extending far beyond midwifery. Although fetching her meant crossing back through town to the Lacombe house, he couldn't see another way. Short of a surgeon, she was Gabriel's best chance for recovery. Also, the Lacombes had a right to know their son was wounded.

Slowly, Noguier stole his way back through the gardens and then the town. He finally arrived at the limestone arch leading onto the Planque bridge on the town side, the Lacombe house in his sight across the river. While keeping out of view, the *Capitaine* assessed the situation. Several hundred dragoons milled about the Planque vineyards on either side of the bridge. Soldiers filled the land leading up to the Lacombe home on the left and the Château de Planque to the right.

Without warning, the château's massive double entry doors flew open, and two pairs of dragoons strode out, talking as if they owned the place. Noguier's brow compressed. What was going on inside the most significant home in town?

With no other choice available, he took off up the side road towards the village of Cros. From there, he'd circle around to the back of the Lacombe house.

After what seemed like an eternity, Noguier arrived at the Lacombe's rear garden, mercifully clear of dragoons. However, a glance through the window revealed there were soldiers inside the house. Now what? Crouching, he made his way to the low rock wall surrounding the well. He slid down, hiding and waiting for one of the Lacombes to step outside.

Over an hour later, the back door opened. Isabeau! Noguier waited as she crossed the garden to draw water from the well.

Not wanting to startle her, he whispered softly, "Isabeau! It's me, Josué Noguier!"

She froze, water bucket mid-air.

"Don't stop! Keep moving!"

She composed herself with a deep breath and dipped the bucket.

"I have news of Gabriel."

For a split second, she stopped again, then forced herself to go on. "Is he...?"

"He's alive but wounded."

Isabeau gasped then steadied herself against the well.

"He's been shot through the shoulder."

"Where is he now?"

"Hidden in a cave above the old *lavoir*. Could you come with me to clean, dress his wound, and bring him food and water?"

"Of course! But André is not here. He's out searching for Pierre and Gabriel."

Isabeau started filling a second bucket. "Give me a minute. I'll tell the dragoons I need to check on a pregnant woman due to give birth. My housekeeper and her brother live with us. They can watch over my daughters."

"Good plan. I'll leave now and wait for you just behind the old *lavoir*. Then, if I'm not there or if dragoons are about, go to the town end of the Planque bridge and meet behind the large fig tree on the right bank. You'll have to take the long way around; there are still dragoons in the vineyards out front."

She nodded once, lifted the full water bucket, then disappeared back into the house.

Quite a while later, Isabeau found Noguier at their rendezvous point. No dragoons patrolled the area, so they started their careful climb up the mountain.

Suddenly, shouts drifted over the rooftops. Noguier and Isabeau ducked behind a thick juniper bush. After a few minutes, Noguier leaned out, scanning the horizon. A burgeoning column of smoke rose from the southern end of town, where the Bedos family lived. The *Capitaine* pulled back and reported what he'd seen to Isabeau. They both sat stunned, contemplating what was burning. Could it be the Bedos' family home and fields?

Noguier and Isabeau slowly continued up to Gabriel's cave. Once there, Noguier called softly to the wounded young man. "Gabriel, it's me, *Capitaine* Noguier—and your mother." There was no answer. The rock did not move. Noguier gently nudged the boulder with his foot to create an opening. Isabeau couldn't wait one second longer. She pushed herself through and crawled into the small space to be near her son.

"He's passed out but breathing," she reported to Noguier, who crouched outside to give her space to work. Isabeau set about cleaning the wound, then gently packed healing herbs onto the open area. Noguier winced at the young man's groans but mercifully, he did not wake. The *Capitaine* watched Isabeau finish by winding clean linen tightly over and under Gabriel's shoulder to staunch the bleeding. She whispered a prayer for his complete healing, thanking God for sparing his life. Smoothing back his hair, she kissed her son's forehead.

A few moments later, Isabeau stuck her head out the opening and gulped the fresh air. "He needs to rest in a safe place. Help me take him to our home. We'll hide him in Pierre's *cave à vin.*"

Tempted to joke about exchanging one cave for another, Noguier thought the better of it. Shading his eyes with his hand, he surveyed the mountain and road below for dragoons. Carrying the dead weight of the unconscious, muscled young man posed an enormous challenge. Moving him down a rocky hill, then the long way round to the Lacombe home, while avoiding dragoons seemed impossible. But the desperation on Isabeau's face communicated the need to get Gabriel under her roof, where she'd care for him properly.

"All right, let's try to move him. We must act quickly while the dragoons are occupied with whatever it is they're doing on the southern end of town," Noguier said.

Isabeau immediately wriggled out of the cave, then Noguier squeezed in and took Gabriel carefully under the arms. As she lifted her son's feet, Noguier gave the signal. Gabriel groaned as they hoisted him up but did not wake.

"Wait!" she whispered, her voice urgent. "Back in the cave! Dragoons!"

Out of necessity, all three stuffed themselves into the cave. Noguier quickly fitted the stone across the opening. The soldiers shouted on the road below. Isabeau placed her hand gently over Gabriel's mouth to cover his moans.

"They came out of nowhere," she mumbled as the sounds of the dragoons faded.

"I know. At least they make a racket wherever they go, plus their bright green coats make them easy to spot."

Noguier moved the boulder aside and crawled out to see if the coast was clear. "The street is empty, for now," he reported.

He leaned back into the cave, and the pair stared at each other.

Isabeau's eyebrows knit together. "It's too high a risk to try to move him now. We can barely carry him and can't hide him quickly enough once we're away from here."

The *Capitaine* nodded. They decided it was best for her to stay with Gabriel while Noguier returned to their home to explain her absence to her family. At the Lacombe house, he'd gather food and clean bandages, at least enough to hold them over until they figured out a way to get him home safely.

Promising to return as soon as possible, Noguier slipped out of the cave.

Curious about the smoke still billowing over the far end of town, he crept his way once again through alleys and gardens. Eventually, he arrived at *l'Argentesse*, St. Hippolyte's second and smaller river. The rains hadn't been sufficient to replenish its waters, and he swiftly crossed the rocky bed, praying to escape detection.

Once on the other bank, he darted from one doorway to another and through two more alleys, the smoke growing thicker as he approached its source.

Around the corner of the last small lane, a blast of heat assaulted him, his eyelashes curled. He struggled to draw breath. Above him, a wall of fire, yellow white-hot, blazed high into the sky. He pressed himself tight into a small crevice between two houses. Even wedged in the frigid air between the rough rock walls, the world seemed to be melting around him. The Bedos family home and fields were ablaze, surrounded by cheering dragoons. The spot that had been their meeting place these past months, where they'd continued to gather despite the King's restrictions, was up in flames.

Noguier reached down for his neck scarf to cover his nose against the smoke, forgetting he'd tied it around Gabriel's wound. Tucking his nose into his gritty shirt, he gasped for air. What would become of the Bedos family? Where were Louis, his brother Jean, and their families now?

Life as they knew it had changed irrevocably. Certainly there was no safe way to move Gabriel out of the cave now.

One more time, he started his surreptitious journey across town. It was up to him to come up with a new plan to ensure young Lacombe's safety.

CHAPTER 34
VERDICT

Day Four
Saturday, 9 October 1683
Château de Planque
St. Hippolyte de la Planquette

Jeanne rested next to Catherine on the wooden bench, leaning back against the wall next to the window. Although the fireplace burned strong near her corner, she shivered, unable to feel any warmth. She wrapped her woolen shawl more tightly around her shoulders, pulling it high to cover her neck as well, and began to relax into its warmth. She had barely been off her feet all morning while busy helping Marion prepare and serve the meal. It was a relief to sit for a while. Slowly, her muscles relaxed, the weighty pull towards sleep enveloped her body. Jerking herself upright, she fought against it. Although General De Tessé had ordered the family to stay in the room, she intended to remain alert and watch for the opportunity to get away to warn Etienne.

Through heavy eyelids, she observed the officers still deep in discussion while Papa remained standing guard between family and soldiers.

Suddenly cold, she is trapped, no way out. She gropes in the darkness without success. The shadow of death approaches, leeching every last visage of warmth, of life. She gasps, her lungs clawing for air...

Jeanne woke with a start, almost causing the bench to topple. Cold sweat prickled across her body. Catherine scowled at her and hunched back towards the window. The normality of receiving one of her sister's grumpy glares brought her a tiny trickle of relief.

157

Jeanne looked out the window. The late afternoon sun hung low in the sky; she must have been asleep more than a few minutes. Across the room, Papa now stood with Governor Noailles and General De Tessé. The two officers explained something to him while Colonel Arnault listened. Maman joined Jeanne on the bench with raised eyebrows and a slight shrug. She didn't know what they were talking about, either.

Papa joined them a few minutes later. Mother and daughter stood to hear what he had to say. It was not unusual for Papa to take his time to think before speaking, but this time his silence lasted longer than usual. Jeanne's throat constricted at the deep sorrow etched across his face, tinged with a hardness she'd never seen before.

"Papa? What is it? Is it about André and Pierre? Us?" She choked the words out, wanting the answer, and dreading it at the same time.

Papa drew his palm across his face before answering. "Governor Noailles will extend mercy to the Lacombes as they weren't armed, as an example to others to not carry guns."

Jeanne glanced at her mother, then whispered, "That's good, right?" Everything on Papa's face said otherwise.

"The dragoons say they'll spare them, but they must convert to Catholicism or face severe consequences." Tears filled her father's eyes. With a deep groan, Maman lay her forehead on his chest as if she couldn't hold her head up a minute longer.

"*What* consequences?" Jeanne asked, hating that her lip trembled.

"They didn't clarify, but the dragoons have installed themselves in Huguenot homes all over St. Hippolyte. Five to forty dragoons per house, depending on its size."

"Installed? You mean they intend to stay?" Jeanne's whisper twisted out. "For how long?" She gazed at the table where the officers were still conferring. Dragoons *living* with them indefinitely?

A slight nod was Papa's only answer. His shoulders slumped and tensed alternately. Finally, he drew her into a tight embrace next to her silent, trembling maman. If only she could stay forever in the circle of her father's love. But this new development was beyond even him. She closed her eyes. At least the last of the distance between them since she'd run away had evaporated. There were far more crucial issues at stake here: their faith, their safety, indeed their lives.

158

"One more thing," Papa spoke in a voice so low Jeanne barely heard him. "We're all...." He paused, a muscle twitched in his jaw. "We are all required to view the executions from these windows."

Jeanne pulled away abruptly. "What! *All* of us? The children! *Non!*" It was inhuman, impossible, and beyond cruel. Maman stiffened then threw her daughter a sharp look with a finger to her lips. They certainly did not want to draw the dragoons' attention nor wake the sleeping children.

Jeanne glared at the soldiers across the room and willed herself not to scream or rage at them. It wouldn't change anything but only make things worse if that were possible. She dropped down hard on the bench and joined her sister in staring out of the window, envious of the swallows circling and swooping. Higher up on the cold mountain currents, an eagle floated, barely flapping its wings. *How I wish I were there, high above, far away from this nightmare. Where are you, God? Don't you see what's happening to us down here?*

Jeanne massaged her temples. Why am I talking to God? He doesn't seem concerned with keeping us safe. Maybe it was in their hands alone, after all. Maybe Massador and Soulier should become Catholic to save their lives. Perhaps they *all* should. It seemed the only way out, the only way to avoid persecution and death. She wrapped her arms around her body, holding herself together. Pressure increased into a substantial and encasing entity. There were no good options. Even Papa didn't know what to do.

She stood and moved closer to the window. Her thoughts wandered to Etienne. One question followed another in a torrent of anxiety. Where was he now? Out with Noguier's men? Was he in danger, or worse, had he already been taken by the dragoons? What would he choose if allowed to live only by changing his religion?

Deep down, she knew the answer. Etienne would *never* recant. He had been willing to fight and even die for the right to live their faith. She had joined his side, agreeing with him out of her own need to take action, and if she was honest, out of her desperate need to win his trust and affection. All of that was worthless and now left her empty and cold inside. Was it not better to live, even if it meant becoming Catholic?

Passive resistance had worked back in July when the Huguenots of St. Hippolyte had met in the Bedos' field for worship. But, clearly, this time, it hadn't. And the plan to fight the dragoons utterly failed also.

159

Etienne and the other Huguenot fighters were in grave danger; they also could be executed for treason if caught with arms. Not to mention the sheer number of ruthless dragoons made the whole idea seem like the last stand for their faith, ending in certain death. She now understood the only way for the Huguenots to overcome the royal soldiers was if God performed a miracle. But she knew better than to count on God to care or intervene.

Jeanne's gaze lingered on the towering ginkgo tree on the corner of the field across from the château. Spectacularly arrayed in delicate lime-green fan-shaped leaves, it created a jarring contrast to her current ordeal. Usually, the tree, in all its splendor, filled her with delight. Today, only dread-filled thoughts moved through her with the imminent executions and the dragoons forcing the children to watch. Jeanne shuddered as a wave of nausea wrenched her stomach, bile rising in her throat.

Governor Noailles' booming voice jerked her back into the room. "Colonel Arnault! The hour approaches. Take your men here and prepare the execution. It will take place before the sun sets."

The colonel stood to go, indicating for Lieutenant Lefèvre and several other soldiers to follow him. Jeanne stared at them as they left the room, seeing but unwilling to accept what was about to happen.

A short time later, Governor Noailles ordered Rossel to fetch the prisoners and their guards. The time had come. Rossel left rapidly, a sick glee evident in his entire demeanor, his lopsided leer, and his roving eye.

Within a quarter of an hour they all assembled in the *grand salon*. The four prisoners stood with their hands bound behind their backs, and heads held high–except Massador, who trembled like a fall leaf caught in a storm. Jeanne wished she could do something, *anything* to console or encourage the shepherd with a sensitive soul. It was unbearable to watch his anguish. For anyone this would be an ordeal, but it was torture for the solitude-loving young man.

Pressing her clammy hands against her apron, she studied each prisoner in turn. She came to Pierre. He was waiting, already observing her. Shame prickled through her scalp. Besides the brief connection at the end of his trial, their last interaction was on the road to Monoblet, when she insisted on fighting these dragoons. Yet, instead of recrimination, she found his usual calm gaze. It was as though he saw to the depths of her soul, which simultaneously pleased and terrified her.

160

Jeanne also sensed something she couldn't identify or take the time to understand. Her face flushed. Despite the terror at what was about to take place, a strange sort of hope appeared. Warmth filled her, despite the cold shards of fear still lodged in her chest. Everything seemed to open and then close before her: life and death, hope and fear, longing and loss. Overwhelmed, she pushed it all away—for now.

She startled at the crack of Governor Noailles' baton. *I really hate that thing. And him. Plus the whole lot of dragoons.*

"Take the prisoners below to the ginkgo tree across the street," the governor ordered Colonel Arnault. "All *four* of them!"

CHAPTER 35
LIFE AND DEATH

Day Four
Saturday, 9 October 1683
Château de Planque
St. Hippolyte de la Planquette

Jeanne gasped; her hand flew to her mouth. André and Pierre too? Utter helplessness engulfed her as the colonel and the dragoon guards wrenched the prisoners forward and marched them out of the room.

Governor Noailles continued his orders. "Monsieur Tessier, you and your family remain here by the front windows. You will view the executions from there."

Papa stepped towards the governor. "Sir, *s'il vous plaît,* may the children be spared this? I beg you!"

Noailles crashed the floor with his stick. "The whole family will observe what we do with traitors, especially with those we apprehended with arms." He pointed at Anne and Paul, where they clung to each other on the floor. "Even those two."

With shaking hands, Maman and Jeanne helped the young ones stand while Governor Noailles turned crisply and headed towards the door. At the last minute, he added, "I'll send one of my men back to guard you. Do not suppose you can get out of this in any way."

Stationed as ordered at the windows, the huddled Tessiers observed Governor Noailles emerge from the entry door below then join Colonel Arnault and General De Tessé. Jeanne let out a sharp cry as they led the four captives to the gallows hastily constructed on her beloved ginkgo tree. Recoiling at the sight of the noose hanging from the branch under whose shade she had passed many happy hours, everything in her wanted

162

to scream *NON!* She squeezed her eyes shut. She couldn't believe this was happening, at her home, with fellow Huguenot believers. Adding injury onto unbearable pain, the dragoons had chosen one of her favorite spots.

Where are you now, God? Didn't you promise we could trust you and count on your protection? Doesn't the psalm say you would be our refuge, our fortress?

Nothing had worked, not the elder's plans nor their faith in God. They were definitely *not* safe, and all ideas of fighting these hardened soldiers now seemed absurd. She opened her eyes, taking in the nightmare unfolding around her.

Her focus landed on Pierre, who was staring up to the window—at her. Her heart thumped hard. Was he saying goodbye? What were the dragoons going to do with the Lacombe men?

Behind Pierre, Governor Noailles pointed to one of the soldiers and motioned for him to return to the *grand salon*. The dragoon saluted and started towards the front door. Papa shook his head, mouthing *non*! He turned to her and their eyes connected. They were sending the lecherous one up to guard them!

"Suzanne, children!" Papa spoke in a rush. "Quickly! Listen to me. They're sending Rossel up to guard us. I trust him even less than the others. *Only* I will interact with him. Understood?" Pale faces nodded. "No matter what he says or does, he will only go through me," Papa finished just as Rossel barged through the *grand salon* doors. Everyone jumped to attention. Papa stepped forward to face the soldier, putting himself between the dragoon and his family.

"Open the windows!" ordered Rossel, peering around Papa, ogling the women of the family like horseflesh for sale. No one moved.

"You heard me. Open the windows. Orders of Governor Noailles!"

Papa opened the window closest to his family, his body rigid, anger pulsating from every pore. Maman and the children pressed in close to the window, trapped between the horror unfolding outside and this monster within.

Rossel moved over to the second set of windows and flung them open. Approaching the family, he continued to check out Jeanne and Catherine from head to toe, as if he were making a choice. Before he got a word out, Papa cut him off.

"I will stand with you, sir, at this window. The women and children will view from the other one." Startled at Papa's boldness, Rossel hesitated and tried to resist. He appeared unable to speak, reminding Jeanne of the lions in biblical Daniel's den. Rossel's mouth seemed strangely shut. Confused, he gave in and followed Papa to the window. Maman and Jeanne quickly shielded the other children.

Commanding voices floated up to the windows from the street below. Governor Noailles stood off to one side, his baton propped on the ground like a King's scepter. He had evidently handed the proceedings over to General De Tessé.

"Henri Soulier, of Lasalle," called the general. "Step forward."

Soulier obeyed with extraordinary composure. His head tilted slightly as he stared beyond the soldiers, past the rope looped over a sturdy branch of the ginkgo tree. To Jeanne, he appeared to have already said goodbye to this world and was anticipating the next. Peace emanated from his very being. He seemed to see above and beyond the horror of the temporal events unfolding around him.

"Monsieur Soulier! You must recant. If you leave the "pretend reformed religion" and its heretical tenets behind you, and if you convert to the one true faith, that of our King Louis XIV, God's representative on earth, you will be spared death by hanging." General De Tessé paused, then asked. "What say you?"

Soulier didn't answer right away. Jeanne couldn't decide if the stillness of the air and the profound silence were due to the gravity of the situation or if everything was so extreme she was simply numb to it all. Taking his time, Soulier surveyed the assembled dragoon guards and officers gathered at the foot of the tree, finishing with a serene gaze heavenward.

General De Tessé grew impatient. "Mr. Soulier! You must recant! Change religions, and then you shall have your life!"

"Yes, sir, I know I must change, but it will be a change from this land of misery to the kingdom of heaven, where a blessed eternal life awaits me."

A low-pitched growl escaped De Tessé's lips.

"This is your last chance, Monsieur Soulier!"

"Sir, there is no other option before me than the honor of following my Lord Jesus Christ."

"So be it. Bring the prisoner forth," the general commanded.

Jeanne shuddered as Lefèvre and Duboise led him to the noose hanging from the ginkgo tree, her beautiful place of refuge. Soulier's composure never wavered, even as he climbed onto the wooden barrel raising him to the level of the rope. He radiated calm as they lowered the noose over his head, then tightened it around his neck. She wasn't sure, but it appeared his lips were moving in silent prayer or perhaps reciting one of their beloved psalms. Jeanne stared in wonder at his face, glowing like the brightest sun, while tears fell like scalding rain down her own.

Once he was in position, General De Tessé gave the order. Lefèvre kicked the barrel out from under Soulier's feet. As he twitched and jerked, his body fighting for life, Jeanne snapped her eyes shut, determined her last image of Soulier to be his shining visage.

Several minutes later, she sensed it was over and tentatively opened her eyes in time to see the soldiers take down Soulier's body and set it off on the side of the road. Massador swayed at the sight. It was now his turn.

General De Tessé motioned for the guards to bring him forward. "Monsieur Massador, of St. Hippolyte, you have witnessed the death of your fellow Huguenot. You may escape this fate if you renounce the heretical 'pretend reformed faith.' Recant and live!"

Massador buckled and slumped down onto one knee. The guards rapidly jerked him back up to a standing position.

"What say you?" De Tessé demanded. Massador failed to answer. Lefèvre grabbed a fistful of his hair and yanked his head up. "Answer the general!"

His eyes bulged in his ashen face, and Jeanne feared he might drop dead on the spot. He tried to speak but choked on his words. Finally, on the second attempt, he found his voice. Looking around wildly at nothing in particular, he mumbled, "I recant."

De Tessé stepped forward. "What did you say? Speak up! Louder!"

"I recant," Massador repeated the words, misery marking every fiber of his being.

Jeanne took a step back. Massador's words hit her like a blow, shocking her almost as much as his choice to recant. Given their circumstances, she'd thought letting go of their Protestant faith might be the best thing to do. But, after watching Soulier die and his brilliant, peaceful strength, she was no longer sure.

"Well, well! Here is one who sees to reason!" exclaimed De Tessé, delighted to have their first convert. He walked over to confer with Governor Noailles before taking the next step.

Suddenly, Pierre called out in a loud voice. "Massador! Brother! Take courage! Stand by your faith in the Lord Jesus! You must not recant!"

With a nod from De Tessé, Lefèvre struck Pierre across the face—twice, hard.

Jeanne struggled to breathe. What was happening? She longed to yell at Pierre to stop drawing attention to himself. Instead, she clamped both hands over her mouth and bit her lip until it bled.

Massador lifted his head and slowly fixed his gaze on Pierre.

Pierre locked eyes with him and continued, "You now face the ultimate trial! Don't turn your back on God! Be courageous! You will soon be in his glorious presence forever."

Immediately, he received two more slaps across the face. Lefèvre then yanked him back, away from the action.

The exhortation roused Massador from his fog of fear. Light began to fill his eyes, like sunlight rising from behind a mountain. He drew a deep breath, his shoulders settling as he exhaled. Several seconds passed in a silence so complete, so outside of time it seemed to contain all of eternity. Finally, Massador blinked slowly, then placed his attention on General De Tessé.

"I spoke in error. I do *not* recant. I will not turn away from my faith in Jesus Christ." His voice held a tiny tremor but also a solidity leaving no question as to his decision.

General De Tessé clapped his hands hard, then shook his fist at the young man.

"How can this be? Do you not know your mind? Come back to reason, to the one true faith, and save your life!" Furious his convert had slipped through his hands, De Tessé continued his lecture until Governor Noailles struck the ground with his baton three times.

"Enough!" cried the governor. "Execute him."

Jeanne marveled at the change in Massador's countenance. The crippling fear was gone, replaced with firm resolve. His face was pale as the ice at the edge of the river in winter, yet he stepped up onto the barrel with a steady foot. Massador trained his eyes on Pierre, and Jeanne was overwhelmed by the depth of understanding the two men exchanged. She leaned forward, farther out the window, needing to absorb every detail of what was happening below.

With a final nod at Pierre, Massador lifted his chin, and his face tilted heavenward, focused on the world to come.

Lieutenant Lefèvre shoved his head down hard to get it into the noose. De Tessé bellowed out the signal, his voice full of anger. Duboise kicked the barrel, separating Massador from his life on this earth.

Jeanne watched, eyes wide open, until the end. She recoiled as Massador swayed and twitched until he fell silent but did not let herself turn away. It was the least she could do to honor him and acknowledge his courageous choice.

Afterwards, Colonel Arnault insisted on taking down Massador's body and laid it with care on the ground next to Soulier. He stood over the two Huguenots, head bowed, with his right hand on his chest. Was he praying for the "lost" souls? Indignation flared in Jeanne. Massador belonged to their community, the very one now being persecuted and killed by Colonel Arnault and the dragoons. She wanted to run downstairs and shove him away from the fallen men, to scream he had no right to be anywhere near the men he'd just murdered.

Catherine and Anne wept, their heads buried in Maman's shoulders. Paul was as white as snow, but rage surged across his face. His eyes carried a hard sheen, his innocence lost. Jeanne's fists clenched. It was awful to see her family's pain, and she hated feeling trapped and helpless, like the small animals she sometimes secretly set free from her father's snares on the hillside behind the château.

Why had God not protected Massador and Soulier from death? Even as furious thoughts took form in her mind, something stopped her. Understanding gently crept up, like the slow rise of the river, imperceptible at first but suddenly flooding the banks. She could continue to doubt God, even hating him for allowing all this to happen despite their tenacious faithfulness. Or, she could start down a brand new path.

What she had seen in Soulier and Massador as they bravely died for their God was undeniable. The profound, palpable peace emanating from them made no sense, given the circumstances. They both exhibited extraordinary strength. Witnessing their deaths had shifted something in her as surely as the river displaced rocks in its flow. Belief in their heavenly Father was so real, so substantial, that in the end, they were willing to let go of this life to follow him to the ultimate destiny.

Jeanne had heard the tenets of the faith her whole life. But she'd never fully believed them, even before her baby sister died. Certainly not in the extremely tangible way lived out in front of her today.

Maybe God's protection over them was more significant, more vast than just keeping them safe moment by moment. Everything was different now, with her perspective stretched and enlarged to include eternity. Understanding dawned on her that God's presence had been with them throughout the ordeal, as an actual shelter, a fortress of the soul. She had seen it on Soulier and then on Massador at the end. Weren't those two now in the safest place of all? For all eternity?

Sensing someone watching her, Jeanne scanned the scene of the executions. Once again, she found Pierre observing her with his characteristic intensity—plus something else. An emotion filled his face, something she couldn't quite put her finger on. Heat rose in her cheeks, but Jeanne did not look away. It appeared he understood, in some form, what was happening inside her. He tipped his head slightly, the faintest hint of a smile tugging at the corners of his mouth.

If only they could go for a walk and discuss all this. But General De Tessé had not yet made clear Pierre's fate. He was still a prisoner. A pain shot through Jeanne's chest. What did the dragoons have in mind? Would they require Pierre and his father to recant or die?

CHAPTER 36
TEARS OF GOLD

Day Five
Sunday, 10 October 1683
St. Hippolyte de la Planquette

Sunlight streamed through tiny cracks in the wooden *volets*. Jeanne stirred and slowly opened her eyes to a new day. The rhythmic breathing of her sleeping sisters enticed her to linger a few more minutes. Exhaustion weighed on her like a dense fog, seeping into bones and joints. Usually, she enjoyed rising before everyone else, soaking in the early morning quiet. And since today was Sunday, they normally would attend the worship service. But normal had entirely disappeared these past five days.

Jeanne rolled over onto her back and stared up at the crack in the ceiling, mentally flashing through images of the three days camping on the mountain as the Lord's Army, the abrupt return home, the dragoons arriving, prisoners and trials, fear and faith mixed all together. Emotion rose as she pictured Massador's final minutes, and hot tears coursed down her cheeks, born out of grief mixed with a strange sort of release. She would never be the same.

Watching Soulier and Massador die had been brutal. The tormented cries of her siblings throughout the night wrenched her nerves, adding further layers of grief and stoking her anger at the injustice of it all.

Yet she marveled as the seeds of faith growing in her soul transformed even these emotions. They did not overwhelm or unmoor her. Deep within, undergirding everything else, the essential missing piece was now in place. How freeing it was to trust God! The profound peace he imparted both sustained and strengthened her, even though

169

their situation remained the same. If anything, their circumstances were now worse than ever.

Jeanne shut her eyes as the final scenes from last night came to mind. After the executions, a messenger had arrived on horseback for General De Tessé. He immediately gave orders, and a dozen dragoons rushed to the vineyards, mounted their horses, and sped away. The attention then turned to the Lacombe men. Her heart pounded even now, remembering. The Tessiers stood at the open windows on the second floor of the château, watching and waiting as the officers decided Pierre and André's fate. Governor Noailles had earlier promised mercy, then appeared to change his mind, enraged at Pierre convincing Massador not to convert. Colonel Arnault had whispered something to De Tessé, who then consulted with Governor Noailles.

Her body clenched tight, remembering those excruciating moments last night. She found it hard to process the myriad of thoughts and feelings swirling through her this morning. Needing to move, she rose from the bed, placing her feet solidly on the floor.

Finally, Colonel Arnault had convinced Noailles and De Tessé that "conversions" to the Catholic faith set a better example and would ultimately please the King. Governor Noailles then upheld his promise of mercy to the Lacombe men.

The Tessiers collectively heaved a massive sigh of relief from the *grand salon* windows as the dragoons released André and Pierre, then ordered them to return home. Yet, for all of the Huguenots, the future was still wholly unknown. It remained unclear how long they had to decide to convert and what were the repercussions if they did not.

Also, the dragoons were staying in their homes indefinitely. At least twenty more moved in after the hangings. Jeanne closed her eyes as a wave of dizziness engulfed her. The world spun out of control, impossible to imagine. Those horrible men, those dragoons, eating, drinking, sleeping, and living with them? A cold wave of terror snaked through her core.

"Fear not!"

Jeanne spun around yet knew in an instant it was her heavenly Father communicating. She couldn't have described exactly why, except to say it was spiritual and recognizable at the same time.

"Fear not! I am with you always."

Her anxiety drained away. Fear lost the power to incapacitate her.

She dressed slowly for the day, then stepped into her leather shoes, knowing her soul stood on new ground. Even if the situation was dire, she was experiencing the protection of the deepest kind.

Opening the bedroom door with care, Jeanne leaned out slightly and checked the small hallway. No soldiers in sight, she tiptoed the length of the corridor and entered the *grand salon,* praying her parents were there, alone.

Since Colonel Arnault and his aides, Lefèvre and Duboise, had moved into the large bedroom, her parents were forced to sleep elsewhere. Papa and Maman slept in Jeanne's bed for the past two nights, and she'd squeezed in with her sisters. But this morning her parents had risen before her. She breathed a prayer of thanks to God they now sat in their upholstered chairs in the empty *grand salon.*

"*Bonjour,* Jeanne," Papa said in a low voice. Dark circles smudged beneath his eyes.

"*Bonjour,* Papa, Maman."

They exchanged *bisous,* lingering a bit with each one. Everything had changed.Everything was full of meaning.

Jeanne pulled another chair close to her parents and took a seat. "Papa, Maman, I need to tell you something."

Papa's one eyebrow raised.

"You may have noticed *Grand-père's* gun is no longer here," Jeanne began.

Maman turned sharply towards the display shelf, then back to Jeanne. Papa nodded; both eyebrows now pushed high. "Go on."

"The night I was away," she drew a deep breath. "It was my idea to get the musket for Etienne, so he'd be armed to join Noguier's men."

After a pause, Papa spoke. "So, Etienne didn't stay with Pierre and Gabriel as you said? He came back to town with you?"

Blood rose to her cheeks, but she forced herself to meet his eyes.

"Yes." She gathered her breath. "I am so sorry I lied to you. And stole from you." Speaking the words out loud lifted a burden she hadn't known was there.

Papa and Maman met her eyes and said in unison, "We forgive you, Jeanne."

"Thank you," she whispered.

Papa took their hands and bowed his head. "Heavenly Father, thank you for the grace we stand in because of Jesus' sacrifice. You have freely forgiven us of every wrong-doing and blessed us with the ability to forgive others. Through Jesus' death, you brought life to those who believe—abundant *life* now and for all eternity."

Tears welled and spilled as Jeanne absorbed this truth for the first time in her life. Warmth surrounded and filled her with peace.

Papa continued. "Father, you know all things, and we trust you'll not abandon us. Protect our family and the Huguenot community. Please, give us your wisdom and strength."

Colonel Arnault entered the room and stopped short. He started to turn away, then appeared to change his mind. Standing stock-still, he waited while they finished their prayer. Catholics mainly recited prayers, led by the priest, who alone had direct access to God. Would Arnault punish them for the "heresy" of daring to talk to God as if he were right there in the room?

Out of the corner of her eye, Jeanne watched him watch them. Papa finished and the Tessiers all joined in the final amen. The colonel started to make the sign of the cross: forehead, shoulder, shoulder, then stopped. His lips pursed, his brow furrowed. It was clear the Huguenots confused him.

"Monsieur Tessier," he announced. "I've been thinking about how to make this cohabitation work for us all."

Papa stood and gave him his full attention. There were now forty soldiers living in the château and plans needed to be made.

Arnault continued. "We will use the *grand salon* for meetings and dining. Your servants will bring our meals here, as has already been done."

Papa gave a curt nod, knowing he didn't have any choice in the matter.

"Also, I propose that your entire family continues to sleep in the children's bedroom and that you eat in there as well," said Arnault.

Papa remained silent, his piercing eyes studying the colonel. After a moment Arnault added in a quiet voice, "I wish to keep my men from mixing with your children as much as possible."

"Isn't the point of you being here to make us uncomfortable? To apply pressure to convert us from our faith to yours?" Papa replied.

Arnault's chin pulled back. "While that is the goal, I am a man of faith. I am also a father, with children of my own."

Each man regarded the other.

Finally, Papa nodded. "Then, I thank you for your consideration. My wife and I will stay with the children. We'll dine in there as well."

Arnault gave a slight bow of his head and turned to organize the soldiers arriving in the *grand salon*. Papa, Maman, and Jeanne exited the room. In the hallway, Jeanne stopped her parents and whispered, "I must get to Etienne and warn him to hide *Grand-père's* gun. Maybe he's already done so, but I'm responsible for him having it. I must warn him of the consequences if the dragoons discover he is armed."

Maman took a step back. Papa paused, tugging on his beard, then kissed her forehead. In a louder voice, he suggested she go down and assist Marion with the morning meal. Jeanne met his eyes, gratitude filling her for the understanding that passed between them.

Downstairs, Jeanne entered the kitchen slowly. "Marion, it's me," she called in a low voice. The housekeeper emerged from her pantry nest. "Did you sleep well?" Jeanne asked.

"Not exactly, but better down here than anywhere near those men. I shudder to think of all them soldiers in the rooms upstairs! I'll stay down here, thank you very much."

"I understand." Jeanne said. "Marion, I need to find out what's happening with the Gamond family and the others in our community." Jeanne decided to keep it simple and not go into the part about the gun. The housekeeper's anxiety level was already quite high.

Despite her stress, Marion couldn't hide the glint of amusement dancing across her face. "Yes, I'm sure you are concerned about everyone equally."

"Well, yes, I am. Louise, the children, Etienne, I'm concerned about all of them," Jeanne stated as firmly as possible, which did not stop the heat filling her cheeks. Honestly, did everyone know about her feelings for Etienne? Was she that transparent?

"Even if you slip away, is it safe out there?" Marion asked, glancing at the outside door.

Jeanne's forehead wrinkled as she shrugged slightly. She had no idea what was going on in the rest of the town. Were the Huguenots allowed to move about freely or not? Were all the dragoons in homes, or did some patrol the streets? She certainly didn't want to face a group of soldiers out there alone.

Both women thought in silence.

"Martin!" they both said in unison, then chuckled a little. It felt good to laugh, to relieve a bit of the pervading tension that was now part of their daily lives.

"We can ask him to 'spy out the land' then report back to us. At his age, he's less likely to be seen as a threat if stopped by the dragoons," said Jeanne.

"The dragoons don't seem to be paying much attention to him. He's been keeping himself out of sight."

"He can make up some need for the horses, something that he must get in town or from a neighbor."

"He can also check on the other château workers and insist that they serve here today. I can't continue to feed all these soldiers by myself, even with your help."

With that, Jeanne took off to convey the message to Martin, carefully crossing the central courtyard, peering right and left for stray dragoons. She wasn't even sure if moving freely around her own home was permitted or safe.

She arrived undetected at the carriage house and stable. She found Martin in his workshop where he had been sleeping since the dragoons arrival. He readily agreed to the plan, glad to do something useful and especially to go out beyond the confines of the château.

While Jeanne waited, Martin prepared a wooden hand-cart to support his claim of retrieving feed for the dragoon officers' horses. He gave the signal when ready and Jeanne opened the stable doors. She peered out into the street.

She clapped her hand over her mouth. "Oh!"

Her beloved ginkgo tree! Yesterday, it had been an instrument of death, and she'd worried its glory would be forever eclipsed by the grisly scene. But now! She stared, not quite able to take in what she was seeing.

Overnight, every single leaf had turned a brilliant gold and now gently rained down, like tears drifting and floating in the autumn breeze, cleansing and creating a dazzling swirl of luminous color. It was as if creation wept with them while transforming the pain into breathtaking beauty.

Jeanne longed to go outside, to stand under the showers of golden leaves, to let them pour down all around her, to throw her arms open wide and twirl and soak in the wonder of it all. But drawing attention to herself or to Martin's *sortie* wasn't wise. From her safe place just inside

174

the stable door, she drank it all in. Despite the deaths, despite the terror of dragoons living in her home, this glittering splendor poured out like a healing balm. It brought life into the depths of her soul.

Her heavenly Father was with her and would never abandon her. Jeanne slowly shut the heavy door. She didn't know how to get through what lay ahead of them but knowing she was not alone changed everything. The same powerful presence of God she had seen on Massador and Soulier as they died was also here with her, and that made all the difference.

CHAPTER 37
CAVE BOUND

Day Five
Sunday, 10 October 1683
St. Hippolyte de la Planquette

Time trickled away like the water seeping down the cave wall. Isabeau didn't know how long it had been since Noguier had left to fetch help and supplies for her wounded son. Despite her effort to stay awake through the night, exhaustion had won the battle.

Isabeau had done everything possible to keep Gabriel warm and comfortable in the damp chill while they waited for Noguier. She offered up a prayer of thanks that he slept most of the time.

Judging by her hunger pains, they had missed several meals. She was used to fasting or eating very little during long births, but Gabriel needed food to heal.

Aware of the danger, Isabeau slid open the boulder that sealed them into the safety of the cave. Even a few inches were enough to reveal the sun low in the western sky. She guessed at least twenty-four hours had passed since Noguier left.

Fresh air and light filtered through, and Isabeau gratefully breathed it in. Gabriel stirred behind her as she peeked carefully around the stone, out onto the hill and the street below.

Done scouting, she pulled the boulder almost into place, leaving a crevice open. She found Gabriel awake. He tried to return her smile, but a spasm of pain twisted it into a grimace.

"Stay still, son. You're not yet out of the woods."

"I'm not even out of the cave!" His attempt at humor was a good sign.

Isabeau brushed her hand across his forehead. "You don't have a fever, which means no infection. But we're out of water and food, and you need both."

"Noguier didn't come back?" Gabriel mumbled.

Isabeau shook her head and put the supply basket over her arm.

"I won't be long, I promise."

As she reached for the boulder, Gabriel clasped her arm. "Maman! Be careful! The dragoons..."

"Save your energy, son. Rest and heal. Have faith!"

With that, she was gone.

Isabeau hated leaving him, but there was no other choice. She reassured herself that she'd return as swiftly as possible or send someone to care for Gabriel and get him home. How it would all work out, she didn't know. She could only hope and pray.

Carefully making her way through the town, Isabeau ducked into nooks and various small spaces to avoid patrolling dragoons. A bit breathless, she arrived home and pushed open the front door, expecting to find her daughters and hoping to find André and Pierre. Isabeau pulled back. More dragoons!

When she left, there were ten installed in their home. Now at least twenty dragoons filled her front room, sitting, talking to each other, eating her family's food, and drinking their wine. The soldiers stopped to appraise her head to toe, then casually went back to their conversation. Her eyes narrowed. How dare they make her feel like a stranger in her own home.

Isabeau searched the rest of the *salon*. André and Pierre were there! They stood at the far side of the room, waiting for her to notice them. Their eyes met and joy flowed between them despite enemies in the way. From across the room, André conveyed warmth and reassurance. With a slight upward glance, he reminded her of where their faith lay. She breathed a prayer of thanks for her husband and eldest son's safe return. Beyond them, her daughters sat in the corner playing some invented game with a string.

"Maman!" Her eldest daughter, Thérèse, stood and started towards her. "You're home! Finally! Where's Gab..."

Pierre swiftly moved in front of his sister, cutting her off.

177

"Welcome home, Maman," Pierre said in a loud voice, drowning out his sister's question. "How was the birth? Have the Marolles welcomed their newest child?" he continued.

It only took Isabeau a second to catch on to his improvised scenario, which provided an explanation for her overnight absence. "Oh, yes. I mean, no, it was a false alarm."

Some of the dragoons listened intently, while keeping their attention on her daughters. A shudder rippled through her body. "Françoise had contractions for hours. They were strong, like real birth pains, but they didn't progress."

The soldiers stiffened. Their suddenly pale faces gave Isabeau a spark of pleasure—and an idea. "The birth canal started to open but didn't widen past four centimeters. Nor has her water broken. The mucous plug is still intact. No bloody show."

That did the trick. The dragoons had no desire to hear such things and swiftly recommenced their loud conversations, eating their way through the Lacombe's food. If the situation weren't so dire, Isabeau would have laughed out loud.

Unfazed by birth talk, Pierre steered her around the dragoons. Then, giving each daughter three *bisous,* she whispered fiercely in their ears. "You absolutely must *not* ask about Gabriel! Not a word is to be spoken about him at all. Yes, he is alive! But for his safety, you must pretend he does not exist."

Isabeau assessed the room and situation. Her experience as a midwife enabled her to gauge people and circumstances accurately and rapidly. While most of the dragoons were preoccupied with consuming enormous quantities of food and wine, one in particular never stopped eyeing Thérèse. The hair on her neck bristled. Pierre placed a hand on her arm. His eyes told her that he was aware and not about to let the soldier out of his sight.

Assured that Pierre watched over the girls, she announced to her husband, "André! I need to get water from the well, and I'd like you to help me."

He understood immediately and moved to her side.

"Send your daughter instead!" the leering soldier called out. He winked at his comrade and ogled Thérèse. Almost thirteen, on the verge of womanhood, she was beautiful both inside and out. Not that the soldiers cared anything about her character. She blushed, bewildered by the attention.

"Soldier!" barked a lieutenant, who appeared responsible for the platoon. "It's not for you to give orders."

"Yes, sir!" Disappointed but not deterred, he elbowed his friend, indicating he would get back to his goal later when the officer was distracted.

André and Isabeau slipped through the back door.

"What happened to Gabriel? Where is he?"

Isabeau quickly shared Gabriel's situation while André pulled up the heavy buckets of water to fill the large two-handled ceramic jar.

"Thank our Lord God you are both home safely. What happened with you and Pierre?"

André rapidly related the main points of their incarceration in the château and the hangings, including Pierre's bold and brave words to Massador.

Tears filled Isabeau's eyes, a mixture of grief and pride, welling, releasing. "And then, the dragoons let you and Pierre go, just like that?"

André set the water jar on the ground and took her hands. "The officers allowed us to go as we did not carry arms. But with a catch. They stated we must recant our faith. I think they're still working out how to enforce that amongst themselves."

Isabeau sat down hard on the edge of the well. It was a lot to take in. This threat now overshadowed her relief for God's protection over André and Pierre. None of them would deny their faith. What consequences would they be forced to endure?

Fighting to keep her voice low and calm, Isabeau said, "First things first. Our most urgent problem right now is Gabriel. He needs food, water, and clean bandages. And a decent place to recover..." she trailed off.

André rested his hand on her shoulder, its strength and warmth reminding her that they were not alone. Their heavenly Father was with them through it all. His guidance and protection remained, and they could trust him no matter what was going on.

Isabeau sat in silence, then stood and faced her husband. "This is what we'll do," she began. "We'll use Françoise Marolle's impending labor as a reason for me to leave. I'll tell them she must be checked on frequently as her time is near. Let's pray there's a delay of enough days so I can get food and tend to Gabriel as many times as are needed."

"All right. If the soldiers insist on accompanying you to the Marolle home, you must, of course, actually go there."

"In truth, I *do* need to check on her, although she's not actually in labor, not that I know of anyway."

"If the dragoons go with you, then ask Emmanuel Marolle to take supplies to Gabriel. You can bring what's needed in your bag, saying it's for the birth process. I don't think they'll ask too many questions about that."

"But," Isabeau's throat grew tight. "We can't bring him home, not with all these dragoons here. Can you think of another way we can get him somewhere safe to heal?"

André glanced towards the house, filled with dragoons. "Not right now. I'll keep praying and thinking about it. I'll ask Pierre; he may already have an idea in mind."

"We should go back in before the soldiers get suspicious."

Isabeau and André leaned against one another, whispering prayers for wisdom and safety. God was their fortress and their rock. He gave them the strength and courage needed for their family. They stood tall, carrying the water jar between them, ready to face what lay ahead.

CHAPTER 38
NEW REALITIES

Day Five
Sunday, 10 October 1683
St. Hippolyte de la Planquette

Tiny beads of sweat broke out across Jeanne's forehead, and a dusty streak of flour marked where she'd brushed a runaway strand of hair back into place. She stopped kneading the bread dough to take a deep breath and calm her mind. Martin had been gone for several hours. Waiting for information about what was going on with the Gamonds grew harder by the minute. Not to mention what was happening throughout the château. Dragoons were everywhere—on the stairs and in the courtyard, milling around like they owned the place. Jeanne punched, stretched, and smacked the sticky dough far longer than necessary.

Late midday, Jeanne and Marion took the soldiers their meal. Lefèvre poked at a boiled chestnut suspiciously, complaining that they were not beasts of the forest who ate foraged nutmeats. Jeanne's jaw clenched, and she bit her lip to prevent herself from blurting rash words. How dare they complain? At the rate they were eating, the food would soon run out. Then what?

Jeanne ignored their banter, determined not to be cowed into apologizing to them. They were, after all, invaders, unwanted "guests." They could take it or leave it. Or better yet, just leave.

The dragoons soon finished eating, and Jeanne helped Marion gather up the plates and bowls. For once, Jeanne was glad of the linen bonnet Huguenot women wore indoors and out. Usually, she preferred the freedom of no head covering, but with it pulled far forward around her face, she felt a little more hidden from the lusty dragoons.

Jeanne and Marion worked quickly, kept their heads down, and tried to keep their bodies out of the soldiers' reach—unsuccessfully. Raucous laughter burst out as Rossel placed his hand on Marion's backside, then slid it farther down her leg and back up again, ending in a pinch and a hearty slap. The housekeeper yelped and jumped away, jostling her tray. Dishes crashed to the floor, causing more hilarity from the soldiers.

Papa burst from the bedroom and strode across the *grand salon*. He towered protectively over the women as they picked up broken crockery and scraps of food. Rossel jumped to his feet in front of Papa, ready and willing to take it to the next level. Lefèvre joined him, as did several others. Silence fell over the room as each side calculated their next move.

Jeanne stood with her tray and moved between Papa and Rossel, looking from man to man, not sure what to do next. Thankfully, Colonel Arnault entered the room and all motion stopped. The colonel barked orders at his men to calm down and back off, and instructed Papa to return to the children's room. Taking advantage of the distraction, she nudged Marion and led the way out of the *grand salon.*

Back in the kitchen, Marion sank onto the sacks of flour. She covered her face with her apron and sobbed. Jeanne knelt beside her, stroking her back. It had only been two days of living with dragoons, and already they were exhausted with all the food preparation, especially without the usual outside help. The almost unbearable stress of having lecherous men all around them, crossing boundaries in word and deed, threatened to push them over the edge.

Jeanne prayed silently. *Father God, please comfort Marion, show me how to help her. I know you're here with us. Protect us from these men. Give us wisdom on how to live through this.*

The idea came immediately, *coax Marion to engage in routine kitchen tasks.*

"Come, Marion. Let's get these dishes done and start preparing for the evening meal."

Gently but firmly, she helped the housekeeper to her feet. Together they set about bringing order to the kitchen. Marion wouldn't soon forget the abuse she'd experienced, but directing her energy into work appeared to restore some of her equilibrium.

As they finished up, Jeanne's patience in waiting for Martin's return ran out. Seeing that Marion needed rest, she made her decision.

"I've no idea what's keeping Martin, but I'm not waiting any longer. Stay down here, out of sight. I'm going to the Gamond family on my own."

Marion nodded. Since her ordeal, she hadn't said a word. Jeanne led the housekeeper into the pantry, situated her comfortably amongst the flour sacks, then slipped out the servants' entrance onto the side street.

Inhaling the fresh outside air invigorated Jeanne in body, soul, and spirit. She searched right and left, up and down the Route de Lasalle alongside the château. No dragoons. *Thank you, heavenly Father.*

Without looking back, she moved down the road to the front right corner of the château. As fast as possible, she crossed the street out front, then pushed through the tall wrought-iron gate that led down stone stairs to their vineyard. Praying no dragoon appeared in the road or happened to look out their front windows, she hurried into the rows of vines, which offered a bit of cover if she hunched low. Midway through, at the edge of the water mill, she ducked into the stone hut where Pierre stored his workers' tools. Was it her imagination, or did his scent linger here? She shook her head a bit. How could she think of such a thing while trying to evade dragoons?

With a deep inhale, Jeanne darted out and through the vines down to the rivers' edge. All senses on high alert, she crossed the river below the bridge, jumping from stone to stone. Out of breath, feet wet despite her best efforts, she finally reached the far side of the Planque bridge undetected.

Jeanne waited behind a large fig tree to be sure all was clear; no sudden cries of dragoons or the marching of boots. Silence reigned. She hurried past the end of the row of houses that lined the river, crossed a small street, and entered a large garden. All the hours spent playing *cache-cache* with Louise and their friends were coming in handy today. Jeanne knew the neighborhood inside out including all the best hiding spots.

From a small alley on the far side of the garden, someone approached. It sounded like at least one person plus something on wooden wheels rumbling towards her. Ducking behind a tall stone water cistern, often her favorite hiding place during childhood play, she crouched and waited. This was no game.

As it drew closer, she held her breath. Once it passed by, she dared to peer out from behind the cistern. Martin! He was finally returning from his errand, with hay for the horses loaded in his hand-cart. Whether as pretext or necessity, Jeanne smiled at his ingenuity, relieved he was on his way back to the château.

Jeanne continued her clandestine journey towards the Gamond home. Within minutes she stood at the servants' entrance. Gently, she pushed the door open, then stepped inside the dark hallway. Cold radiated off the tiled floor, adding a further chill to her wet feet. She waited for her eyes to adjust. Blood pounded in her ears, partly from the quick travels, partly from fear of discovery. And, if she were honest, mainly from the excitement of finally taking some action.

She moved down the hall, then stepped into the kitchen, hoping the dragoons avoided that room as they did at the château. Silently closing the door, she turned to find two surprised faces staring at her—Louise and Etienne!

"Jeanne! What are you doing here?" Louise practically leaped across the kitchen to embrace her friend.

"I had to know what was going on. I had to see you. *Both*." Jeanne decided to hold nothing back.

Etienne, arms clasped behind his back, met her eyes and held them. "What has happened since we parted? I have to say I'm greatly relieved to see you here."

Louise beamed. "As am I! I searched for you as we left the mountain but of course, in all the chaos, couldn't find you. Etienne has filled me in on...on your adventures, at least up until you returned to the camp."

Etienne smiled at his sister, then turned to Jeanne. "After leaving you at the foot of the mountain—two days ago now—which seems hard to believe, I headed to the Bedos' fields to search for Noguier and his men. They were there and welcomed me to join them in their drills."

"Please sit down, Jeanne," Louise interjected, gesturing at a chair by the fire. "So far, the dragoons stay upstairs and leave the kitchen alone."

All three settled around the unpolished oak table.

Etienne continued. "At mid-morning, Lord Aubanel came to us with the news of Governor Noailles' promised amnesty *if* the Lord's Army returned to their homes before the dragoons' arrival. He informed us that the elders had decided to comply, which of course, you know."

Jeanne and Louise exchanged glances, nodding.

"Aubanel urged us to go home. To abandon the idea of fighting the dragoons. Pastor Boyer had joined Noguier's men, but he barely tried to counter Aubanel's arguments." Etienne's face darkened. "Anyway, since his ravings on the mountain, he's lost all influence."

The fire hissed and popped, causing both women to jump. Louise reached for Jeanne's hand, "Having dragoons in our home makes us all on edge. How many are there in the château?"

"Around forty, including a Colonel Arnault. Governor Noailles and General De Tessé were also with us during the past two days, from the dragoons' arrival until this morning."

Louise's hand tightened around Jeanne's. "And the hangings?"

"You've heard then! Marc Massador and a man from Lasalle. They even forced us to watch." Jeanne blinked hard as stinging tears threatened to spill over.

"Oh, Jeanne! How awful for you all!" Louise's eyes carried a depth of compassion that comforted Jeanne but also made her want to lay her head down and weep, which she determined not to do. Especially in front of Etienne.

"It was," Jeanne replied, hating that her voice shook despite her efforts. Then, without warning, or even by prayer, a calm settled upon her. Why did it matter if Etienne saw her emotion? She'd put far too much store in what he thought, and now that seemed like the least important thing in the world. Beyond struggling to figure out living in this new reality, something deeper had changed.

Jeanne shut her eyes. "But at the same time, it was, and I don't mean this disrespectfully, but somehow it was also incredible, miraculous." She opened her eyes. "I'll tell you about it sometime, but first, Etienne, please go ahead and finish."

She couldn't help but notice the surprise in Etienne's eyes. Whether it was her brief description, hinting at what had transpired at Massador's death or her directness, she wasn't sure. Either way, she was closer to being her true self than she'd ever been around him, and it felt good.

"After Aubanel left, there was a heated discussion. Finally, over three-quarters of the men abandoned us. I stayed and spent the night in the Bedos' home, determined to stick to the plan to fight." Etienne stared into the fire.

"The following morning, yesterday, we rose early. Then, in groups of two or three, we made our way to the hill above your vineyards, where

185

the dragoons camped that first night. Finally, we all met up with Noguier on the hill above the old *lavoir.*"

A burning log rolled to the front of the fireplace. Etienne stood, grabbed the fire iron, and began prodding it back into place with his left hand.

Jeanne stared at his right hand and forearm, bandaged in strips of white cloth. "Oh my goodness! What happened to you?"

Etienne hesitated. Eyebrows high, she tilted her head, waiting.

"We engaged the dragoons, or rather they came at us, I pulled the trigger on the musket. Well, then it created a small explosion out the side of the gun."

The words rang in her ear, and heat filled her cheeks. She gaped at Etienne, then at Louise, who as always, wordlessly conveyed compassion.

Jeanne jumped up and took a step towards Etienne. "I'm so, so sorry…." Her voice trailed off. "I had no idea *Grand-père's* musket didn't function properly. How badly are you hurt?"

Etienne put his good hand on her arm. "It's not that bad. You didn't know it was dangerous. I don't hold you responsible."

A myriad of feelings swirled through Jeanne. She searched his face and her own rapidly beating heart. Of course, she hadn't known *Grand-père's* gun didn't work correctly. Papa never actually used the musket, only cleaning it weekly and keeping it on display. Still, it had been her idea. Instead of protecting Etienne, it could have killed him.

Looking deeply into his eyes, she found no trace of bitterness, only warmth and kindness. Tension released from her shoulders as she returned to her seat. Peace filled her soul. But that was all.

Jeanne studied Etienne as he shifted burning logs in the fireplace, increasing the heat of the room. She observed him and tried to figure out what had changed. Handsome as ever, she was grateful they'd grown closer. But something was different. Was it him, or was it her? Probably both of them. Her brows knit together as she sought to understand her feelings for him.

Etienne finished tending the fire as a grandfather clock chimed on the floor above, bringing Jeanne back to present realities. She rose to her feet. "I'd best be getting back. I promised Marion I'd help serve the evening meal."

"Before you go, Jeanne, there's one more thing." Etienne glanced at Louise. "The dragoons razed the Bedos family home and fields. It's burnt to the ground, and nothing will grow on their land for some time."

Shaking her head as if to rid it of the bad news, she whispered, "*Non!* That can't be true!"

Etienne's lips pressed into a thin line.

Jeanne stared at him. "And the Bedos family? What happened to them?"

"One of our servants brought the news that Louis and Jean fled. There's a rumor that the dragoons seek to arrest them for hosting our meetings these past several months. We don't know the fate of the rest of the family."

"But...." She stopped, pulling her thoughts together. "Governor Noailles promised amnesty if we left the mountain ahead of the dragoons' arrival!"

Etienne shrugged, spreading his hands wide. Jeanne winced at the reminder of his wound. "We only know the governor will publish the King's decision soon."

Jeanne couldn't take it all in. The King's soldiers had destroyed the Bedos home and lands, and the family was scattered. More consequences from the King were coming soon. It was unthinkable, and not one of the three knew what to say.

Louise stood and wrapped her arms around her friend, bringing Jeanne back to the here and now. It was time to go; she'd already stayed longer than planned. She hated to leave the cozy warmth of the Gamond kitchen. Despite the horrible news, being able to talk everything over with friends had been beneficial to her soul. They had to do it again, and soon.

"Louise, promise me you'll come to visit in the next few days. You can cut through the garden on the street facing the river, where we used to hide, and then through the vineyards to the château. Stop in Pierre's stone hut on the way if needed. We have to stay connected!"

Besides processing everything happening around them, she wanted to tell Louise more about her new faith and discuss her shifting feelings for Etienne. Also, where Pierre fit in it all.

Louise agreed, and the friends said goodbye. The three *bisous,* for "Father, Son, and Holy Spirit," felt like a benediction. Jeanne stepped out of the kitchen door to make her way home.

CHAPTER 39
DRAGONNADES

Day Five
Sunday, 10 October 1683
Chez Gamond
St. Hippolyte de la Planquette

Etienne reached his arm across Louise's shoulders after Jeanne left. Surprised, she studied his profile. Although he cared for her deeply, he wasn't often physically affectionate. He'd changed since his encounter with the dragoons.

Silently, they found their places at the end of the kitchen table close to the hearth. What now? How did one proceed with life when enemy soldiers occupied your home?

"The cook will be down soon to finish dinner preparations," said Louise.

Etienne stared at the fire. "I won't eat another meal upstairs with those soldiers around. We'll have the family dine here in the kitchen."

"Do you think Papa will agree to that?" Louise braced herself; she certainly didn't want any more conflict in their home. It was difficult enough having it filled with dragoons.

Etienne started to press the matter but backed down, as alarm spread across his sister's face. "We'll ask him what he thinks. But I don't think there's a better solution, do you?"

Louise shook her head. It was awful eating in the corner of their *grand salon*. "I think Papa will most likely agree. Watching the dragoons consume his best wine like water angers him, as it should. But I don't want any of his irritation to make things worse than they are already." She didn't need to add that the same could be said about her brother.

"Also, it's safer to keep our young brothers and sister out of their way as much as possible," Etienne added.

Etienne stood and began pacing the length of the fireplace and back like a caged animal. Louise understood the frustration at being reduced to hiding out in their own home. While Etienne had become more introspective since the dragoons' arrival and all that followed, he was still a man of action. Waiting or fitting in with other people's agendas didn't suit his temperament, especially when it was the King's soldiers pressuring them to renounce their faith.

"Etienne, why don't you go outside for a short walk. I know it's possibly dangerous, but Jeanne made it here safely, and you know all the back ways. If stopped, make up an excuse that you're going for supplies, firewood, or something like that."

Etienne stopped and considered her proposal.

"Go, gather information on how the other Huguenot families are doing. Find out what's happened to Josué Noguier, Gabriel Lacombe, and the Marolle family. Françoise's baby's due anytime now. If you go now and make it quick, you'll be back by dinner. I'll keep Papa and the children distracted."

Etienne didn't need further encouragement. He pulled on his coat and was out the door in less than a minute. The shadow of a smile crossed Louise's face. She was pleased that her brother had gone out, even if it was risky. He needed to move, to do something useful. And hopefully it would release some of his built-up tension before it spilled over and made a mess with Papa, or worse, with the dragoons.

Careful to avoid the soldiers, Louise headed up the servant staircase and joined her siblings. Papa sat reading in the corner of the bedroom they now all shared. Speaking softly, she proposed that they dine downstairs. He bristled, then gave in, seeing the wisdom of the plan.

At dinnertime, they all went down into the kitchen, just as Etienne came through the door.

"*Son!*" Shock rendered Guillaume's voice louder than intended. Where have you been?"

Louise put her finger to her lips, glancing up at the ceiling, reminding them of the "guests" eating supper on the floor above. "Papa, it was my idea. I thought he needed to get out of the house, have a change of scenery. I also thought he'd bring us information on what's happening out there with our friends." Before her father could respond, she turned to Etienne. "So, what did you find out?"

"Do you know how dangerous that was?" Guillaume exclaimed. "The *last* thing we want is to draw attention to ourselves, especially to you, as a young man of fighting age."

"Papa," Etienne spoke firmly but with respect. "I'm aware of the issues. But it was informative to see how things are going for our community. And, quite honestly, I needed to get out of here for a bit."

Louise motioned for them all to take a seat at the kitchen table. After Guillaume gave thanks for their meal, she served up their chestnut soup, passed around fresh bread, and then tried again. "So, Etienne, what *did* you find out?"

Glancing at his father, who focused solely on his bowl of soup, Etienne forged ahead. "First, I went across the river to the *moulin à huile*, to the Marolles home."

Guillaume's spoon clattered to his bowl. "*You crossed the river?* The Planque bridge can be seen from the château! And we've heard that dragoon officers installed themselves in there!"

The younger children stopped eating and stared. Louise's heart sank and she prayed the conflict would not escalate. Could these two men who she loved most in the world ever make their peace?

Etienne replied calmly. "Papa, I'm here. I'm safe. Let me tell you what I found out."

Guillaume shot him a stern look and returned to his soup.

With a glance at Louise, Etienne continued. "Françoise has not yet had the baby. Isabeau was there checking on her. Dragoons live in both of their homes as well. They are *everywhere*. Just as in the northern regions, they're enacting the *dragonnades*. Anyway, so far they're leaving Isabeau alone as they don't want anything to do with birth and all that it involves."

Despite the gravity of their situation, Louise couldn't help a tiny tight smile. It seemed they all were figuring out how to work around the ubiquitous soldiers.

Etienne threw her a pointed look, then continued. "I also learned that André and Pierre were held in the Château de Planque overnight and put on trial with the other prisoners."

Louise met his eyes. Jeanne had shared this information with them earlier. With a slight nod, she conveyed her understanding. He didn't want that visit mentioned in their father's presence. Papa was barely keeping calm as it was.

"Anything else, Etienne?" she asked.

"Yes. The dragoons hung shepherd Marc Massador and a man from Lasalle in front of the château yesterday. André and Pierre Lacombe were apprehended then allowed to go free. But, they, and indeed we *all*, are under threat of dire consequences if we don't recant—soon."

Guillaume shook his head, heavy with sadness. "So the rumors of what transpired at the château are true. Oh, how I've prayed it was not so."

The only other time in her life Louise had heard her father speak with such intense sadness was at her mother's death. Her eyes blurred as all the grief rose, blended, and spilled over.

Finally, Guillaume asked, "Have they given any clarity on what those repercussions are?"

"No, they haven't. Just like the dragoons in our home, they eat and drink enormous amounts and threaten to destroy furniture and buildings if we don't convert. They terribly harass the women and children. Other than that, we don't yet know what will happen if we continue to hang on to our beliefs."

Guillaume thought for a few moments. "It appears they don't know quite how to make nearly four thousand people turn from their beliefs. Perhaps we have them in a bit of a quandary."

"And perhaps our heavenly Father is using that to protect us," Louise added.

"Agreed. Although the fact that dragoons are installed indefinitely in every Huguenot home in St. Hippolyte exerts an almost unbearable pressure." Etienne looked his father in the eye.

Guillaume dabbed at the corners of his mouth with his cloth napkin. "Yes, son, it certainly does."

Louise blinked and slowly exhaled. She'd longed for this, for the two of them to have a healthy, respectful conversation. With all the horror going on around them, at least one change was for the better.

"There's more," said Etienne.

Louise and her father sat back in their chairs, waiting.

191

"First, some good news. After the dragoons apprehended Massador, Rafinesque fled Monoblet undetected. His safe arrival in St. Hippolyte coincided with our exodus from the mountain, so he returned home directly."

"That *is* good news," Guillaume conceded. "Thanks be to God." He studied his son, waiting for the rest.

Etienne took a deep breath. "Gabriel was shot in the skirmish with the dragoons. He's alive but wounded in the shoulder. Noguier hid him in a cave above the old *lavoir*."

"The same encounter that left you wounded?" Guillaume leaned forward, eyes fierce.

Etienne paused, then met his father's intense gaze. "Yes, sir."

The room was quiet, save the crackling fire. Louise had tended to Etienne's hand, and together they'd hidden his injury from Papa. She should've known that nothing escaped his notice or understanding.

"How is Gabriel now?" Louise asked, genuinely concerned, but also to redirect the conversation.

Guillaume stared at her, then motioned for Etienne to continue.

"Isabeau manages to bring him food and clean bandages daily while out on her midwifery rounds. As I said, the dragoons steer clear of anything to do with birth. The Lacombes are desperate to get him out of the cave, but they're not sure how, or where to take him. Dragoons roam the streets and are in every single home."

Louise's chest ached and tears welled. Father and son regarded each other, searching for solutions in the face of the other.

Eventually, Guillaume reached for his wine. "Is there anything else, son?"

Etienne nodded. "As you know, the Bedos' home is gone, their fields ruined. Louis and Jean have fled to Switzerland."

Guillaume stared at his wine glass as he set it down. "When Claude Brousson first came to us from Toulouse and brought the idea of passive resistance, he talked of his extended family in Switzerland. He told us that if our plans failed and the King retaliated, he'd flee from France and go to Switzerland, in the Geneva area."

"I don't know about Brousson, but apparently, that's where the Bedos brothers intend to go. The rest of the family has fled to relatives in Sauve, at least for now. Thankfully for them, the dragoons already swept through that town and went on their way."

"So, it's all happening." Guillaume sighed heavily, every line in his face deepening. "We've enjoyed peace and great prosperity for almost one hundred years. The Edict of Nantes remains the law of the land! Yet, Huguenots must flee the country to save their lives." He stared into the distance as if trying to discern what the future held.

"Where will they stop, Papa?" Etienne leaned across the table. "They've hung prisoners, ruined the Bedos lands, and Gabriel's wounded and stuck in a cave. Every Huguenot home in town has dragoons living with them. They're rapidly consuming our goods and pressuring us to convert by their presence, with more violence likely to come. I...I don't think I can live this way. I can't bear it." Etienne got up and began pushing logs around the fireplace.

Louise and her father exchanged glances. Etienne wouldn't live peaceably with the soldiers in their home for very long. A gnawing pain grew around Louise's heart. Where would this all end?

Guillaume excused his younger children to go and play in the corner of the kitchen while he finished the discussion with Etienne and Louise. "This afternoon, I overheard the dragoons upstairs discussing Governor Noailles publishing his decision, the amnesty he promised us if we came down from the mountain. It should clarify the repercussions of our having formed the Lord's Army and of Noguier's men fighting some of the dragoons." Guillaume narrowed his eyes at Etienne, who quickly lowered his wounded hand into his lap.

"But Governor Noailles said we'd have *fewer* reprisals if we left the mountain before the dragoons arrived, which we...." Etienne paused. "Which *you* did."

"Yes, but we won't know the exact consequences until the governor makes the King's verdict public this Wednesday, in three days' time."

Silently, they each processed the potential implications. Passive resistance had failed. Fighting had failed. What now?

Guillaume spoke first. "Until Wednesday, and even after that, no one leaves this house without my knowledge or permission. Understood?"

Louise and Etienne each managed a quiet "Yes, sir."

"Once we know the contents of the King's decision, we'll make plans on how to deal with all this," Guillaume concluded as he rose from the table.

Etienne continued to stoke the fire while Louise slowly gathered the dinner dishes. There was nothing more to say for now. But Louise knew her brother. His tense shoulders and fierce prodding of the burning logs told her that he was formulating plans of his own.

CHAPTER 40
JUDGMENT DAY

Day Eight
Wednesday, 13 October 1683
Château de Planque
St. Hippolyte de la Planquette

Jeanne dropped her book on her lap. It was impossible to concentrate. She stared out the bedroom window at the empty ginkgo tree, longing for freedom. Freedom to move safely around her home and go outside for fresh air when she wished. Freedom from fear. Basic things. She promised herself that she'd never again take such simple things for granted whenever this ended.

Even stepping out of the bedroom was fraught with tension. If Colonel Arnault wasn't around, Rossel and Pouget loitered in the hallway, attempting to catch a glimpse of the Tessier women. Papa rarely slept. He remained always on guard, ensuring the dragoons didn't get anywhere near his family.

Antsy, Jeanne stood up and stretched. Papa paced the width of the room near the door, pulling on his beard, thinking. The dragoons had now been living with them for six days. It seemed infinitely longer. Maman tried to keep the younger children occupied, no easy task after days cooped up inside the château. She continued lessons as always, using the top of Jeanne's trunk as a desk when it wasn't in use as their make-shift dining table. They all needed a good dose of exercise and fresh air, like the chickens that usually ran free-range on their property, except during the night when they were caged for protection from predators. Jeanne grimaced. Our predators now *live* in our home.

Colonel Arnault held daily talks, trying to convince them to convert. It was futile. The Tessiers would never renounce their faith, no matter the consequences, which remained unclear.

Jeanne felt suspended in time, trapped, stagnant. She almost didn't care anymore if things got worse. If only something moved or changed, anything to break out of the strange cycle of terror and boredom stretching out endlessly before them.

Jeanne crossed the room to where her father paced. "Papa, do you think Governor Noailles will publish the decision of the King today as planned?"

"Unless there's an unforeseen delay, yes."

"What do you think it will say? We did as he said and returned home ahead of the dragoons' arrival."

"He stated there would be *fewer* consequences if we did so."

Jeanne's brow furrowed. What did that mean? Would it apply to everyone or a certain few?

Her thoughts wandered back to the mountain. The elders had decided to send them home while she'd been out on the road overnight, first with Pierre, then with Etienne. All that seemed like another lifetime, which it was in so many ways.

Doors banged open down the hall. The Tessiers froze in place. After a moment, Papa moved to the bedroom door. "Wait here. I'll see what's going on."

Jeanne sank into the chair next to her mother.

Within minutes Papa returned and announced that they were to assemble in the *grand salon.*

"The verdict has come from the governor?" asked Jeanne.

He gave her a curt nod while Maman, shoulders rigid, gathered the children. They followed Papa to the main room, bunching tight to avoid contact with the soldiers streaming past them. Every current inhabitant of the château flowed into the *grand salon.* The Tessiers instinctively crammed themselves close to the hallway door that led to their bedroom, closest to a way of escape.

Colonel Arnault called for order. Standing directly across the room from the Tessier family, the colonel unrolled the scroll delivered to him earlier. Jeanne sucked in her breath as he read out the verdict.

"Amnesty is accorded to the followers of the Pretend Reformed Religion of St. Hippolyte, those called Huguenots, as promised for their swift return to their homes on the 8th October 1683, before the arrival of the King's Royal Army."

Jeanne glanced at Papa, eyes wide.

"However, our glorious King Louis XIV declares that this amnesty does not extend to ministers of said faith. The following thirteen pastors are condemned to capital punishment by the law of the King for preaching, pastoring, and aiding the Huguenots of St. Hippolyte."

Papa took a step forward; Maman placed a warning hand on his arm. Colonel Arnault continued in his powerful baritone. "...Pastor Boyer, Pastor La Roquette."

Jeanne found it hard to focus. Their world was already spinning out of control and now was turned inside out. The death penalty! For pastors! Papa's face, set like stone, with his eyes on fire, confirmed that he had not seen this coming.

Arnault's voice droned on, listing pastors who had come to serve their community over the past few years. Thirteen in all. Jeanne's core seemed to hollow out a bit more with each name, leaving her cold and empty inside. *Where are you now, God? Why are you letting this happen to those who chose to minister to us?*

"In addition, the following are also condemned to death."

Jeanne's hand flew to her mouth. More?

"*Capitaine* Josué Noguier, for organizing men to fight the King's soldiers. Louis and Jean Bedos, for the repeated use of their family home and fields as an illegal place of meeting for the Huguenots."

After visiting Etienne and Louise, Jeanne shared with her parents that Louis and Jean Bedos had fled. There was a tiny bit of comfort knowing they were hopefully beyond the dragoons' reach. But what about La Roquette and the others?

Colonel Arnault continued. "In addition, it is forbidden for pastors in this region to reside within twenty-four kilometers of their *temples*. Furthermore, the parishioners of Lasalle, Cros, Colognac, and Monoblet must demolish their *temples*. Failure to do so will result in fines of three thousand *francs*."

Stunned, the Tessier family remained in their corner, unsure what to do, while Colonel Arnault began issuing orders to his men, dispatching them to round up the condemned. Papa took advantage of the dragoons' distraction and swiftly shepherded his family down the hall to their room.

Once he had closed the door on the excited buzz from the dragoons mobilizing to hunt down Huguenots, questions poured forth.

"Papa? What now?"

Papa didn't answer immediately. His head turned up as he stared into the distance, listening to his heavenly Father. It was worth waiting to hear what he received. But Jeanne had to move. She had to do something.

"Papa, Maman, I'll go downstairs and help Marion finish the midday meal. The return of a few day workers has relieved some of the pressure on her, but she's still quite overwhelmed with the demand."

Maman started to object, but Papa agreed. He nodded in her direction. Jeanne read trust in his eyes and possibly even a new level of respect.

Jeanne hurried out of the room and down the hall to the servant's stairway. She drew a deep breath, grateful to escape the confines of the bedroom and to head towards the relative warmth and comfort of the kitchen. Thankfully, the soldiers still seemed to have no interest in that particular room as long as meals were forthcoming.

One layer of Marion's stress lifted when Jeanne entered the kitchen. She was glad to help, and once again, practical work provided an outlet for pent-up anxiety. It also gave her the space to process the terrible new developments.

The "lesser consequences" were appalling. Pastors condemned to death! Would that be the next step for them all if they did not conform to the King's demands? Jeanne racked her brain for a new plan on how to live through this unprecedented season.

A gust of wind scratched branches across the window. Startled, Jeanne peered outside to where the barren ginkgo tree stood tall, surrounded by its carpet of golden leaves. One scene after another passed through Jeanne's mind: Massador and Soulier beneath the tree, waiting for their deaths, surrounded by dragoons and the King's officers. Pierre and André, also there, hands bound. Massador's fear-driven denial of his faith and Pierre's firm exhortation to not give up. Then Massador's choice to hold on to his beliefs, even unto death. And above all, the *glory* of the presence of God that descended on him. She'd never forget the radiance of his face.

In each of those moments, life and death were on display. Jeanne had seen and believed for the first time that God was indeed present, even in the midst of suffering. Maybe especially in the midst of suffering. She'd always thought God's protection meant nothing bad would happen. What she had witnessed was hard to understand, but she couldn't go back to unbelief. *Father, you know all things. What do we do now?*

Another blast of wind detached the heavy *volet* outside the window from the small wood clip meant to keep it in place. Jeanne wiped floury hands on her apron and reached up to stop it from rattling back and forth. More than one window had broken when the violent Çevenol wind kicked up and the shutters banged shut. She opened the window and pushed the shutter hard against the current. Immediately a man climbed through and jumped into the kitchen. He crouched down low. Jeanne gasped and took a step back. Pastor La Roquette!

Marion gaped while Jeanne wrestled the window shut against the forceful wind. Jeanne motioned for La Roquette to follow her into the relative safety of the pantry.

Once they ducked behind the flour sacks she asked, "Pastor! What on earth are you doing here? Have you not heard? There's a warrant out for your arrest and execution!"

"Jeanne! So, you've received the King's decree?"

La Roquette shut his eyes and shook his head slightly. Finally, he drew a deep breath and opened his eyes. "The messenger who brought the news to the château knew the contents of the declaration he carried. Along the way, he stopped and bragged about it, sharing the information with some fellow dragoons. By God's grace, a loyal friend of mine overheard. He'd heard I was here in St. Hippolyte to help and bring comfort. He found me and brought me the news."

Jeanne met his eyes, trying to imagine what he must be feeling.

"You know, then, that I am a condemned man."

Her throat constricted and she looked away. She had no words. Having La Roquette right in front of her made the reality of his death sentence unbearably real.

La Roquette placed his hands on her arms. "Jeanne, look at me. Don't despair. I'm fleeing to Switzerland, to Geneva."

"Switzerland?"

"Yes. Brousson and I discussed this possibility when we started the passive resistance project, in the eventuality that it failed."

Jeanne's brow wrinkled. "But how will you get there? What will you do? And what about Elisabeth and the children?" Her questions tumbled out one after another; if the situation wasn't so dire, it might have been funny, especially as they crouched amongst flour sacks like unwanted rodents.

"Brousson has relatives there who said they'll receive Huguenots if needed. Switzerland doesn't persecute Protestants. It's a safe haven." La Roquette stopped to gather his thoughts before going on. "Jeanne, my biggest concern is for my family. Once the governor is alerted that the dragoons were unable to find me, they'll go after my wife and children." Emotion choked his voice, and he was unable to continue.

Jeanne waited a moment. "Do you have dragoons living with you already?

"No. So far, St. Hippolyte has the only *dragonnades* in the region."

"Then we must get Elisabeth and the children away from your home—immediately."

La Roquette leaned closer, his voice an almost imperceptible whisper. "I've sent word with the same loyal friend for them to come down to St. Hippolyte. I cannot leave them behind, in our home, waiting for the dragoons to come for me. I'd take them with me, but travel is slow with children, and they'd possibly be in even more danger." His voice strangled around the last few words and his palpable anguish filled the pantry.

Jeanne prompted him to go on. "And then what?"

"I've instructed my friend to escort them to the abandoned barn on the road from Monoblet to St. Hippolyte, not far from the route d'Alès."

Jeanne thought about it. "I walk over that way some days, or at least I used to. I think I know which barn you mean. It's not far from the château if you walk through the Faubourg de Planque, right? Then, it's on the left as you leave St. Hippolyte?"

The pastor nodded, misery radiating from every fiber of his being.

"Of course, they can't stay there indefinitely. It's already unusually cold for October," Jeanne stated.

La Roquette searched her face.

She lifted her chin. "I'll make sure they have food, blankets, and anything else they need until we can figure out a better place for them."

"How...?"

"It doesn't matter. I'll figure it out." She paused. "God will show me the way."

A tiny ray of hope flitted through La Roquette's eyes.

Jeanne continued, "The important thing right now is for you to get out of town safely. Before the dragoons find you here—or anywhere."

"I regret putting you in danger, Jeanne."

"Pastor, this is our new reality. I'm truly glad to be of service. We can trust our heavenly Father that we *will* find a way to keep your family safe."

Gratitude and grief emanated from La Roquette as they stood and embraced.

"*Adieu*, Pastor! Go with God!"

Jeanne led the way out of the pantry and opened the window for his exit. With one last glance, La Roquette bounded through it and disappeared across the road towards the hills beyond. Tears fell freely down Jeanne's cheeks as she offered up a silent prayer for his safety. Would she ever see him again?

Back to kneading her bread dough, she found her earlier frustration had dissolved. To her surprise, the daunting task before her filled her with something that had been missing. As she divided and shaped the dough into loaves, then set them in cloth-covered bowls near the fire to rise, it came to Jeanne what that was exactly. She now had a purpose, a goal. Also, that this was an answer to her earlier prayer. Every last trace of lethargy and frustration fled as her thoughts sparked and fired to life. She began to lay plans for taking blankets and food to Elisabeth and the children in the barn.

A small smile crossed Jeanne's face. The skills she'd recently acquired in her secret trips through town and countryside would now be put to good use. She just needed to work out how to provide for the La Roquette family. For the first time in days, she felt fully alive.

CHAPTER 41
FLIGHT NOT FIGHT

Day Nine
Thursday, 14 October 1683
Chez Lacombe
St. Hippolyte de la Planquette

Pierre slowly slid one of the oak barrels containing his experimental vintages across the floor of the wine *cave* as the mantel clock on the floor above chimed twice. He'd waited a full two hours past midnight to be sure that the dragoons living with them had completely passed out before slipping down to the *cave*. So far, they had not discovered his workshop and wines, and now he intended to do everything possible to hide their existence.

Pierre never disrupted his wine by moving it at this point in the process, but he had to do something before the unquenchable dragoons discovered his creations. The thought of the indifferent soldiers guzzling them down grated his very soul.

He appreciated having this workshop nearby, enabling him to watch over the new blends he nurtured along like so many children. While his main job was to oversee the men who worked vineyards for the Château de Planque and the production of the wine they sold regionally, Pierre's passion was right here, developing these new vintages. Right now, it was imperative to hide them well out of the sight and reach of the ill-mannered dragoons living in his home.

Pierre sighed and rubbed the back of his neck. He'd planned to hide the barrels in the narrow storage room at the *cave's* far end, then conceal the door. The unpolished chestnut *armoire* used to store their tools would do the job, but it was much too heavy for him to move alone. His father and he could do it together easily. But both Lacombe men couldn't be in the *cave* at the same time, leaving the women in their family vulnerable to the dragoons. Leering looks, inappropriate touches, and suggestive comments increased as the restless soldiers grew bolder with each passing day. The soldiers applied constant verbal harassment to convert them to the King's faith. And, as the food ran out, the dragoons demolished furniture, burning it as firewood and continually threatening worse. Another layer of tension descended on Pierre's shoulders. He needed to quickly stash the wine and get back upstairs to help his father protect his mother and sisters. But, first, he had to figure out another solution to camouflage the door to the hiding place.

Pierre gently shoved the cask along, pondering for the hundredth time how to get Gabriel out of his cave and moved to a safe place. For the past four days and as many sleepless nights, he'd thought through every possibility and still hadn't been able to come up with a strategy. Thankfully, Isabeau managed to get food and water to Gabriel and dress his wound daily, under the pretense of visiting pregnant women. She reported that he was healing fairly well and gaining strength. But that didn't solve the problem of getting him off the mountain or where he could go. There were dragoons in every home. Showing up with a young man healing from a gunshot wound would not go unnoticed.

Pierre whispered a prayer, a cry for help. *Heavenly Father, you have protected us this far. We need your wisdom, an idea and a way to get Gabriel to safety. Thank-you.*

His thoughts then wandered, across the street, to Jeanne. Not for the first time. Despite the intensity of Massador's courageous death, he'd sensed a profound spiritual shift in her as she watched from the château's second floor. It seemed impossible to know such a thing, especially from where he stood outside. Yet, somehow, he'd been aware of her doubts, layered with shock and grief. He'd observed her move towards trusting God, like the first rays of sunlight through dissipating dark clouds. Their eyes had met and his soul leapt at the light of faith breaking through her unbelief.

Pierre wedged the first barrel into the storage space. It was a tight fit, but finally, he managed to shove it into place. Only three more to go. Time was ticking away, and he needed to get back upstairs before they noticed his absence. He slid the next cask across the floor, taking care not to move too fast, conscious that disturbing the tannins upset the balance. Still, it was better than losing all his stock to the boorish soldiers.

He was aware that Jeanne, too, was in a growth process and should not be rushed. Shame colored her face every time he had seen her since her detours and deceptions to be with Etienne. If only they could have a real conversation, free and open. At the very least, they could restore their friendship.

A loud scraping sound broke through the silence. Pierre stopped, listening hard. It came from the stairs leading down to the *cave*. Which only meant one thing: someone was up there, pushing open the door. Was it a dragoon looking for him or randomly exploring their home? The hair on the back of Pierre's neck stood on end as he waited, hands frozen on the oaken cask.

A minute of silence passed. Pierre grabbed a moth-eaten wool blanket and tossed it over the barrel, determined to distract any dragoons headed down into his *cave*. No one entered. Certain the door had opened and then been shut, he crossed the room, and peered up the stairs. The shape of a man was evident, pressed against the wall on the top landing.

"Who's there?" Pierre rasped.

No answer. That seemed strange. Dragoons never held back, nor would they be timid about barging into the *cave*.

"Who's there?" he repeated.

"Pierre? Is that you?"

His entire body tensed. The dragoons had not bothered to learn his name. Was it a trick? There was only one way to find out.

"Yes, it is. Who are *you*?"

A man stepped out of the shadow and practically flew down the stairs. Josué Noguier! The two men stared at each other, then heartily shook hands. Relief and questions filled their faces.

"You're safe! We haven't had any news of you since you left my brother and mother in the cave four days ago," Pierre said.

"I'll explain; first, how is Gabriel faring?"

Pierre filled him in on his brother's progress and their lack of a long-term solution. "So, where have you been Noguier? You promised to return with help."

"I'm truly sorry I didn't make it back as promised. My every movement has been under scrutiny because I mobilized men to fight. I've been under house arrest with thirty dragoons as my guards." Distress filled his eyes. "I could only hope and pray your mother was able to tend to him."

Pierre nodded, observing the bruises on Noguier's face and his swollen left eye.

Noguier continued. "It's a miracle I managed to get away tonight. I can't explain it. I hid ten of my men in the secret room behind our *cave*. I've kept it stocked with provisions for just such an emergency. Every night, once the dragoons drink themselves to sleep, a few of the men have managed to escape. The last ones made it out tonight, leaving me free to go." Glancing around the Lacombe *cave,* he added, "I see you're in the process of concealing important items from the soldiers yourself."

Pierre patted the hastily covered barrel next to him. "Yes, and just now, I thought you were a dragoon, and my mission had failed. Why are you here?"

Noguier further lowered his voice as if the walls might remember and reveal what he said next. "I assume you heard Governor Noailles' decree today, condemning me to death for leading men to fight the dragoons."

Pierre searched Noguier's face. "So, you're fleeing."

"Yes, but there's more. When I leave here, I'll go first to Gabriel's cave."

Pierre leaned forward.

Noguier continued. "As I said, the dragoons drink themselves into a stupor each night and are usually passed out sometime after midnight. Judging from the empty streets on my way here just now, I imagine it's much the same in most houses around town."

Pierre waited while Noguier gathered up his words.

"So, with your family's permission, I plan to take Gabriel with me, to the Vivarais, north of here. My mother's family is in that region and will welcome us."

Pierre stared at Noguier and then off into the distance as he considered the proposal. *Is this your answer to our predicament, Father? Is there any other solution?*

After a moment, Pierre spoke. "You're adding considerable risk by taking him with you. Our mother says he's mending but not yet fully healed, of course."

"I figured that would be the case. But I can't just leave Gabriel behind. And you can't bring him home."

205

Both men glanced up at the ceiling, conscious of the soldiers sleeping above.

Noguier continued. "We'll take it slow, traveling as far as possible by night and resting in some hidden corner of the Cévennes forests during the day. I came to let you know my plan and to seek your permission. Are you in agreement?"

Pierre nodded slowly, his face taut. "There is no other good option. I have been seeking one for days."

"You'll tell your parents? I'll find a way to send word once we're with my relatives in the village of Mialet. It's usually a little more than a half-day journey on foot. I expect us to make it in two, maybe three nights, depending on Gabriel's strength and any random encounters with patrolling dragoons. I don't know what is going on beyond our town."

Pierre paused, searching for words. "Thank you, Josué, and please extend thanks to your family on behalf of ours. Would you tell my brother that we–that *I*–love him. We will pray daily for you both."

Swallowing hard, Pierre dropped his head for a second. Then he straightened and reached for a wine cork laying on the worktable, rolling it between his fingers, before handing it to Noguier. "Please give this to Gabriel." Emotion wavered through his voice, but the message was straight from his heart. "Tell him never to forget who he is or where he's from."

Noguier tucked the cork into his pocket. "Let me give you a hand with the barrels before I go."

Together the men fit the remaining casks into place and slid the *armoire* across the niche. Then Pierre spread dirt around the floor with his foot, filling in the empty spaces where the barrels had been.

Turning to Noguier, he clasped his hand tightly. "Now go! Quickly before our unwelcome 'guests' discover you. God be with you."

The men locked eyes. It was unlikely they would meet again in this life. *And, my brother, will I ever see him again?*

Pierre pointed to the above-ground window, nestled under the ceiling of the *cave*. "Climb on the workbench, and if the garden's clear, you can depart through there. I know it appears too small, but you'll fit." He paused, a hint of a smile tugging at the corners of his mouth. "My brother and I went through it many times, playing our games. And later, Gabriel used it to go out without our parents' knowledge." Pierre's heart constricted as the memories flashed through his mind.

"*Adieu*, Pierre."

"*Adieu*, Josué."

Noguier climbed onto the bench, and with one last look, he was gone.

CHAPTER 42

VIOLATION

(Caution: This chapter contains sexual assault.)

Day Nine
Thursday, 14 October 1683
Château de Planque
St. Hippolyte de la Planquette

Louise set her sewing down on the kitchen table and gently pressed her temples. Try as she might, it was impossible to concentrate on her needlework. She needed a change of scenery.

Yesterday, the King had published his decree; her father and Etienne talked of nothing else. Apparently, the whole of the Languedoc region was in an uproar at the condemnation of the thirteen pastors. Louise needed to process all this with her best friend. Anyway, four days had passed since she promised Jeanne to visit.

Louise grabbed her cloak, wrapped it around tight, and stepped out the door. Her heart fluttered as she remembered her father's warning and her promise not to leave the house. But like a caged animal with the prospect of freedom, she couldn't help herself and hurried on without looking back.

The icy wind stung her face, causing her eyes to water. Louise welcomed the crisp air, breathing it in like a person starved for oxygen. Her head cleared, her senses awakened. She'd make it a short visit with Jeanne and be back before Papa or Etienne noticed her absence. She didn't want to cause them additional anxiety, but already her soul sang with the fresh air and freedom.

As Jeanne suggested, she cut through back gardens, using all the secret paths and hiding places to avoid detection from random dragoons on the roads or any who might be gazing out a window. Within minutes, Louise arrived at the river and hurried down under the bridge. No recent rains meant exposed rocks, and for that, she was thankful as she hopped across the river to the edge of the château's vineyards. Winding her way through the vines, Louise headed towards the small stone storage cabin. There she'd catch her breath and scout the road in front of the château for dragoons before continuing.

At the hut, Louise opened the door and stepped inside, not seeing or hearing anything until too late. Almost immediately, rough hands grabbed her by the arms and shoved her against the wall. Dragoons! Two of them!

Before she managed to cry out, one of the men clamped his hand hard over her mouth. His face inches away, she reeled at his stink and the leer in his one good eye.

"You go first, Rossel!" his buddy laughed.

"No argument from me, Pouget!"

Rossel threw her onto the dirt floor, and she let out a strangled scream as he struggled to pull up her skirts. His horrible stench enveloped her as he lowered himself. She fought for breath, for life, trying to wrench herself out of his grasp, to keep him from entering her. Finally, a piercing pain sliced through her body, and darkness enveloped her.

When it was over, Louise blinked several times. For a minute, she forgot where she was before her ravaged body jolted her into full consciousness. Rossel sniggered as he heaved himself off the ground.

"Your turn, Pouget!" he announced with glee as he pulled his pants back up.

As Pouget leaned over, she flailed and fought, anything to stop him. Finally, her right knee made sharp contact between his legs. Howling and doubled over, rage now added to lust. He slapped her hard across the face. Louise continued to scrabble and swing whatever she could: arms, legs, feet. Rossel stepped forward and punched her on the side of her head. Wild with fear, she scraped and clawed. Rossel yelped in surprise as her nails made contact and scratched deep across his face.

"Help me hold her down, Rossel! She's mine now!"

"I'm *trying* to Pouget. She's hard to hang on to." He grabbed her hair and yanked her head back.

"*Attend!* Wait! I hear something."

Both soldiers stopped all movement. Rossel pressed his hand tight over Louise's mouth, attempting to stifle the groans rising from deep within her.

The sound of a creaking work cart bumping rapidly across the fields grew louder. Louise sunk her teeth into Rossel's hand and he pulled away with a yowl. Pouget peered out the small window.

"Someone's coming! We should go, Rossel, you know what the colonel said."

"Oh, he didn't mean it. You know how he is."

One of the wooden doors flew open, and a Huguenot man holding a shovel filled the frame. Without a word, the two dragoons let go of Louise and stared. One took a step towards the man; the other pulled him back by the sleeve. The soldiers exchanged a glance, then fled out the opening on the opposite side.

CHAPTER 43
AFTER

Day Nine
Thursday, 14 October 1683
Château de Planque
St. Hippolyte de la Planquette

Pierre stepped inside the stone hut, started to go after the men, then froze.

"Louise! Are you…" His voice caught in his throat. "Did they…?" He crossed the small structure, leaned out the door, and caught a glimpse of two dragoons retreating across the fields. Everything in him fought to go after them, to make them pay. Instead, jaw clenched tight, he turned back to Louise and knelt beside her. With a shaking hand, he gently took the hem of her skirt and pulled it down over her legs.

Louise rolled on her side and curled into herself. Blood covered the back of her skirt. Unsure of what to do next, Pierre waited. Anger surged hot through his veins. He desperately wanted to go after the men who did this to her but that was unwise. Plus he couldn't leave her alone.

Heavenly Father. I don't have words. I don't even know how to pray about this. Please show me what to do, how to help her.

After a moment, Louise turned her head and stared at him without really seeing, her face a mask of agony. Pierre gently took her hand.

"Louise, I'm here. Pierre."

She blinked but said nothing.

"The men. The dragoons who…they're gone." Pierre stumbled about for what to say, what to do. "When you're ready, I'll check if it's safe to go and get you somewhere more comfortable."

211

Panic seized Louise's entire body. She curled in tighter, looking as if she wished to disappear.

Pierre reached for her, then stopped himself. Grief and fury beyond anything he had ever experienced riveted through his body. He placed his hands on his knees, gripping them hard, and forced himself to take a deep breath. Then, praying for wisdom and guidance, he tried again.

"Louise," he spoke gently but with his characteristic calm assurance. We aren't far from the Château de Planque. I can help you get there, get you to Jeanne."

At the mention of her friend's name, Louise's eyes opened slightly. After a few seconds, she gave a brief nod.

Pierre carefully helped her to a sitting position, then to stand.

She flinched, a mangled cry like a wounded animal escaping her lips when he tried to reach around her waist for support. Pierre stopped and waited before trying again.

"Louise, I'm going to take you to Jeanne. May I put my arm around you to help you walk?"

Louise moaned and started to crumple back to the ground. Instinctively, he held her up. When she didn't pull away, he kept his arm around her shoulders.

"Now, if it's alright with you, Louise, I'm going to pick you up."

She gave a slight nod. Pierre gently lifted her and carried her out of the hut. She rested her head on his shoulder, her eyes shut tight.

Pierre prayed they'd be invisible and that no dragoons milled about the vineyards—for their safety and to ensure he didn't act on his raging desire for revenge.

Progress was slow, but they made it into the Château de Planque undetected. Pierre brought her in through the servants' entrance and helped her into a chair by the warm kitchen fire. Her hands were unusually chilled, and her body seemed to be shutting down as it blocked out everything and everyone.

Marion emerged from the pantry and came to a complete stop. Waving a long wooden spoon, she took in Louise's disheveled state. "What's this...what happened?"

Pierre raised a finger to his lips, shaking his head. Then, with a glance at Louise, he asked, "Marion, do you know where Jeanne is? Louise needs to see her."

The housekeeper stared at him. He held her gaze until she seemed to understand that, at the very least, something was drastically amiss. "Jeanne. Oh. Um, she's usually down here helping or up reading in the family's room."

Pierre stepped a bit closer to the housekeeper and spoke in a low voice. "Please go get her, and don't tell her why just yet. Just say that you need her help."

Marion ducked her head and scurried away. Pierre found a cup, filled it with water from the pitcher, and offered it to Louise. No response.

Within minutes, Marion returned to the kitchen. Jeanne followed her into the room, chatting away. She reached for her apron, then noticed her friends.

"Pierre! Louise! What are you doing here? This is a surprise!" She started to cross the room, then stopped. She clearly sensed that something was wrong. Extremely wrong.

Jeanne glanced from Louise to Pierre and back again. "What happened?" Her voice caught in her throat.

Pierre stepped towards her, keeping his eyes on her alone. "Marion, please stay with Louise. I need to talk with Jeanne privately."

The housekeeper agreed, pulled her chair up to the fire, and sat next to the shocked young woman. She picked up her knitting and began chattering away in a one-sided conversation. Jeanne followed Pierre into the pantry.

"Pierre! What's going on? What's wrong with Louise? Why are you both here?" Jeanne's brow furrowed deep as the questions flew out one after another.

Pierre's lips compressed as he gathered up the right words to explain. Then, with a big breath, he gently but clearly relayed what had happened.

Jeanne shook her head in denial. "No! It can't be! No! Not Louise," she exclaimed, holding her stomach tight and doubling over like she might lose her midday meal. She straightened and searched Pierre's face. Hot tears welled and burst, and she buried her face in her hands.

Pierre waited silently. He longed to pull her into his arms, to offer comfort, but he didn't dare. There was much to resolve between them and now was not the time. Finally, when her tears abated, he spoke in a low voice. "Jeanne, she needs to be in a warm, secure place to rest. I carried her here from the hut. I don't think it will be best or even possible for her to return home tonight."

Jeanne tilted her head; her hazel eyes fully focused on his face.

Pierre's heart skipped a beat, and he reminded himself to concentrate only on the daunting task at hand.

"Can she stay here with you? Is there somewhere safe for her, out of sight of the dragoons?" he asked.

Jeanne wiped her face with the back of her hands. "Yes." She gulped in some air. "Yes, of course. Marion has been sleeping right here, in the pantry. Louise can stay here. The dragoons avoid the kitchen."

Pierre checked out the small room. "This will work. Uh, I think she needs clean clothes as well." Color rose in his cheeks, and he flicked his eyes away.

Jeanne stared at him for a moment. "Oh, yes, all right." Tears welled again, but she stood a bit straighter. "Well, let's see. Oh, I know. Marion's ironing pile is down here. I should be able to find Louise something of mine in it and get her cleaned up."

"I should go then and leave you to it."

"Here, first help me with these." Jeanne pointed at Marion's stored bedding.

Together they reached for the blankets and, with great care, arranged the bedding into as soft a nest as possible. Doing something practical gave a tiny bit of relief.

They finished and stood in silence. Finally, Pierre spoke softly. "We need to get word to Guillaume and Etienne that she'll spend the night here." He rubbed the back of his neck. "I think it's best they don't discover the real reason why until tomorrow. She can't easily be moved before then anyway. Also, once they know the truth, they'll be agitated, shattered in fact. With nightfall coming, with both of the Gamond men's strong personalities, it might cause more problems with the dragoons."

Jeanne thought it over. "I agree. Let's send Martin with a message that she came to visit, and as it's nearing the end of the day, we thought it best to keep her here overnight, for safety." Jeanne choked on the final word, and once again, angry tears spilled over. "I don't understand! Why did this happen?" She stared at Pierre, in confusion.

He put his hand on her shoulder. "Good idea to send Martin. Why don't I stay here tonight also, to sit with you and Louise?" He hesitated, then carried on. "We could talk things over."

Jeanne nodded slowly. "Yes. That would be...." She took in a gulp of air. "That would be helpful. Thank you. I'll have Martin go by your

214

house as well, with some excuse why you're here overnight and why he's out and about. So far, the dragoons have left him alone. I guess they don't find him threatening."

"All right, you stay with Louise while I go find Martin and send him out with the messages. I'll tell him to have Etienne come early in the morning to escort Louise home safely."

Despite her deep well of grief, a spark of gratitude rose in her eyes. His throat tightened and he turned to set everything in motion.

CHAPTER 44
DISCOVERY

Day Ten
Friday, 15 October, 1683
Château de Planque
St. Hippolyte de la Planquette

Neuf, dix, onze, douze. Jeanne counted as the grandfather clock on the floor above pealed out the midnight hour. Bright, clear chimes resonated through the house and to the floor below, reaching the confines of the kitchen pantry. All else was quiet. The dragoons had finally finished their nightly drunken dinner and had passed out on their beds. Jeanne's eyes narrowed. On *our* beds. She'd never get used to the soldiers' presence, invading their space, living in her home as if it were their own.

Earlier in the evening, she'd joined her family upstairs for dinner while Marion sat with Louise. Once they finished eating and her siblings had withdrawn to their usual corners, Jeanne filled her parents in on Louise's attack.

"Non!" cried Maman, then dropped her head between her arms on their trunk-table. Suppressed rage and sorrow etched deep lines across Papa's face. He rose abruptly and began to pace. From across the room, Catherine demanded to know what was going on. Anne and Paul took it all in with wide eyes, afraid to ask questions.

Jeanne had shared her plan to stay in the pantry through the night with Louise. Papa agreed and said he'd come down in the morning to help prepare for Etienne's arrival. Papa would be the one to tell him the terrible news.

216

Jeanne now shivered in the midnight chill and pulled the woolen blanket tighter up around her shoulders. Cold seeped into her back where she sat leaning against the limestone pantry wall and seemed to reach all the way to her heart. She imagined Etienne's reaction, his rage when he found out dragoons had raped his sister. Jeanne reached down and stroked Louise's hair as she slept. It was impossible to understand the horror of what her friend had experienced. Jeanne sighed heavily and fidgeted around trying to find a more comfortable position. Her inner turmoil matched her body's discomfort in the icy, cramped pantry. She shifted so her shoulder could take a turn leaning on the cold wall, and found Pierre observing her.

"I thought you were asleep!" she said, lifting her candlestick to see him more clearly. They sat on either side of Louise, keeping watch.

"Me? No, just resting my eyes."

A trace of a smile tugged at the corners of her mouth. His light snoring for the past half-hour indicated otherwise. "Well, I'm glad Louise has slept all this time. Should we try again to get her to eat something?"

"It's God's mercy that she sleeps soundly. When she's ready for food, she'll wake."

"You're probably right." Jeanne squirmed about again, still trying to settle into a better position on the cold stone floor. Even with woolen blankets beneath and around her body, the radiating chill crept into her bones. For the hundredth time, she touched Louise's cheek, relieved to find it warm.

"But, that's just it," she said.

Pierre inclined his head.

Jeanne let out a ragged breath. "*WHERE* is God in this? Why did he let this happen to her?" The words struggled and jabbed their way out of her throat like shards of glass. Tears spilled freely down her cheeks.

"I, well, at Massador's death, something happened to me." She paused to gather her thoughts. "Even before that, when the dragoons came and moved in. They had prisoners. And then they took your father—and you." She inhaled deeply. "Well, I prayed for the first time in many years. I asked for protection for us all. But…." Each word spoken out loud further opened the dam of pent-up emotion. Shuddering, Jeanne clutched her knees to her chest and bent over them.

217

When the storm subsided a bit, she lifted her head and stared at the opposite pantry wall. "Then, they condemned Massador and Soulier *and* forced us to watch their executions."

Jeanne blinked hard and glanced at Pierre. The patience and compassion on his face gave her the courage to continue. "When Massador recanted, and then you encouraged him to stay faithful, well, I didn't know what to think. I'd thought maybe we all should just recant––become Catholic and save our lives." She brushed a strand of hair off her face and leaned a little towards him, looking him straight in the eyes. "But then, hearing your words to Massador, and seeing him die so bravely...and then the way he changed, just before," Jeanne stopped. How could she put it into words? "Courage and peace radiated from him, despite everything."

Pierre shut his eyes and nodded slowly. "Yes. The very presence of God covered and filled him." Emotion layered through his voice, a mixture rich with grief and awe.

"Yes! It was stunning, brilliant, shining, and beyond this world. *Better* than this world actually, and, well, I can barely find the right words to describe it." Fresh, clean tears flowed from Jeanne, like a crystal-clear river, unobstructed after the rains. "And I knew, in a way I've never known in my life, that God is real and that he was there with Massador, with us all."

They sat in silence for several minutes until the grandfather clock chimed the half-hour. Louise stirred, moaning in her sleep.

Jeanne smoothed and tucked the blanket around her friend, then gently stroked her back until she settled again into sleep. She whispered, sharp and low, "But now, ...this! *Why did this happen?* Louise did not deserve this—no one does. *Why* did God not protect her?"

Pierre stayed silent for so long Jeanne lifted her candle to make sure he hadn't fallen asleep. Finally, he spoke, each word weighted and tinged with pain. "I don't know why this happened. But I don't think searching for an answer to that question will ever satisfy. We tend to think that if we have understanding, we'll have peace. But there's no good reason for something as despicable as rape to occur, to anyone, ever. *No one* deserves it or somehow brings it on themselves. It's the complete and total violation of a person's body, mind, soul, and spirit." Pierre paused, shut his eyes, and sat back against the rocky wall.

218

Jeanne waited. She understood Pierre needed to process internally before speaking, just as it was with her father. And, just as it was with her father, it would be worth the wait.

When he was ready, Pierre turned in his seat to face her. "Rape is *never* part of God's plan or will. It is the exact opposite of who he is and how he is in a relationship with us. But, evil exists in the world, and men have free choice as to their actions. Without denying the terrible reality of what happened, I think it helps to focus on the bigger picture, the eternal perspective."

She thought about it for a moment. "Like what we experienced at Massador's death?"

"Yes, exactly! We saw a glimpse of eternity as Massador chose to hold onto his faith in God, even though it meant death."

Jeanne understood what Pierre was saying. What she'd seen on Massador made death shrink in comparison. He had died, of course, but her perspective on what it *meant* had changed at that moment as heaven touched the earth. She discovered a profound strength amidst the shock and anguish, along with peace and even hope. It all flowed from the presence of God with them.

"So, with Louise…" Jeanne searched for the right words to put to her thoughts. "Even without understanding *why* it happened, we can keep an eternal perspective. One that anchors us, giving us the strength to go on."

Pierre locked eyes with her. "Yes. Which includes trusting God is always with us, even now, *especially* now, as we live in extremely challenging circumstances. Our suffering doesn't define who he is. *He* never changes."

"Yes, I'm beginning to believe that's true. And even here, through all this pain, I sense his presence, bringing peace and strength," Jeanne said slowly. She lifted her candle and smiled at Pierre, grateful for this conversation, for this opportunity to process what she was thinking and feeling.

But there was more. She dropped her chin. "Pierre, I need to apologize. I've been difficult and not very kind to you recently."

Louise's steady breathing was the only sound in the room.

"Jeanne, look at me. Please."

Her heart hammered, her cheeks flushed. She raised her head.

"I forgive you."

Relief washed through her like a cleansing shower, and she sat in wonder. "Thank you, Pierre. For everything."

He held her gaze, and she was sure he saw to the depths of her soul. Jeanne sensed an essential missing piece fit into place. Contentment and something more flowed through her entire being. She wasn't sure exactly what it was; she'd have to think about that later. Profound security covered and filled her, despite all that still lay ahead.

For now, there wasn't anything more to say, and they sat in comfortable silence. Then, as the grandfather clock chimed the hour above them, Pierre reached around their sleeping friend and extended his hand to her. She received it, reveling in its warmth, which spread through her entire being as she drifted into sleep.

CHAPTER 45
NOT ACCEPTABLE

Day Eleven
Saturday, 16 October, 1683
Château de Planque
St. Hippolyte de la Planquette

Louise stirred and groaned a little as she moved. "Where am I?" She blinked slowly, trying to take in her surroundings. Then, stiffly, she sat up, brushing matted golden-brown curls off her face.

Jeanne woke at the sound of her friend's voice and rolled up onto her knees, waiting to see what Louise remembered on her own. It was early morning, judging by the light coming into the pantry from the kitchen. Pierre's spot on the other side of Louise was empty. She hadn't heard him get up. When did he leave? Where had he gone?

She turned her attention back to Louise. "Would you like some water?" Jeanne held the cup up to her mouth.

Louise's face remained blank, but she managed a few sips. Several moments passed in silence.

"Jeanne, why am I in your kitchen pantry?" She glanced down. "And wearing one of your shifts? What's going on?"

Jeanne considered her answer, breathing a silent prayer for wisdom. How could she tell her friend what happened? Wasn't it better forgotten?

Out in the kitchen, a door scraped open and shut, followed by familiar footsteps. Marion poked her head around the corner. She addressed Jeanne, careful to avoid eye contact with Louise. "Good, you're awake. Your father wants you upstairs now."

"Why? He was supposed to come down here and see us in the morning. We're just waking, and Louise is not...that is, *I'm* not ready."

"Monsieur Pierre is up there with him. Good thing too, as Monsieur Etienne arrived earlier and...." Marion stopped, flustered.

"Etienne's here? Already?" Jeanne sat up straight. "And they've been talking?"

Marion nodded. "All I know is when I took breakfast in, they stopped their discussion and asked for you. So go on. I'll stay down here with Mademoiselle Louise. I'll be right out in the kitchen preparing the midday meal."

Louise clutched at Jeanne with both hands, her eyes wild. "Don't *leave!*" Her vise-like grip dug into Jeanne's arm.

"*D'accord,* all right. Don't worry Louise, I won't leave you. Let's both go upstairs and see Papa, and Etienne. He's here to take you home."

Louise held on tight as Jeanne helped her to stand, then had her step into a spare skirt and vest found in Marion's washing pile. Jeanne attempted to arrange both of their *coiffures* without much luck. At least their bonnets would cover most of their untidy hair. Alarmed at the passive, distant look on Louise's face, Jeanne kept up a steady stream of casual chatter. At least it helped release some of her own nerves.

Jeanne reached one arm around Louise's waist and led her gently up the service staircase, then through the servants' passageway. Shouts emanated from the family's bedroom as they drew close. Suddenly, Rossel and Pouget burst into the hallway from the *grand salon* at the other end, heading towards the noise. Towards them. The dragoons and the young women all stopped in their tracks, face-to-face, outside the bedroom door.

Louise cried out and jerked back against the wall, crossing her arms tight across her body. An anguished scream rose from her depths, piercing the air like the swath of a sword. Instinctively, Jeanne stepped in to shield her, her arms spread wide. Papa charged from the bedroom, followed by Pierre and Etienne.

Louise stared only at Rossel, her face a mask of dread. "Him! It was him! He..." Despite her terror, Louise appeared lucid for the first time since her ordeal. The dragoon sniggered and elbowed his buddy.

Etienne flew at Rossel with a roar, knocking him off his feet, swinging and punching. Pierre stepped in and tried to pull Etienne off the dragoon. Jeanne gasped as Papa blocked Pouget with his body, then

222

pinned him to the wall with his shoulder. He grabbed and held the dragoon's hands before he could reach for his gun.

Louise swayed and crumpled towards the floor. Maman stepped out of the bedroom doorway, just in time to reach her arm around Louise and break her fall.

Jeanne quickly weighed the options. It was just a matter of time before more dragoons showed up. They'd be outnumbered and overpowered.

Maman hustled Louise into the bedroom and firmly shut the door. Papa somehow managed to hold Pouget off while Pierre finally wrestled Etienne off Rossel, who remained on the ground, temporarily disoriented. Jeanne caught Pierre's eye for a split second. Then, with a tilt of her head, and a pointed look at Etienne, he understood. There was a small window of opportunity to get him out of there, and she was the one to do it.

Jeanne grabbed Etienne by the arm, pulled him back down the hall, through the servants' stairway to the kitchen. She quietly shut the door and led him into the pantry, then swung around to face him. "Etienne, you need to go *now*. Go out through the servants' door, across the Route de Lasalle and to the mountains. Keep going as far as possible. Find somewhere to hide until this blows over. Maybe in the hills, the caves?"

Etienne paced two steps, then stopped.

Jeanne whispered with force, "Go! Now! They'll come after you soon."

He looked her in the eye while a myriad of emotions flashed across his face: anguish, rage, and a glimmer of something else. "I'll go. But first...." His words caught in his throat. He took a step towards her. "Please. Louise, usually, she's the one caring for others, but with–" He dropped his head, unable to finish the sentence.

Jeanne raised her chin, her jaw set. "Yes, of course, I'll always be there for her. She's strong, and she *will* recover. But, you'll support her too, once it's safe for you to return." Her voice trailed off as she understood what he was asking her.

Etienne placed his hands gently on her shoulders, his eyes intense. "After this, I cannot stay in town. The dragoons won't let my actions go unpunished."

Her stomach twisted. He was right. "But, where will you go?"

"I'd already been contemplating leaving for Geneva. Brousson told us that if things ever became untenable here, we would find refuge there. I simply can't abide living with dragoons in my home any longer. And now, well, now I *must* go."

Jeanne took a small step back, startled but not entirely surprised. Beyond conscious understanding, she'd sensed that Etienne couldn't stay in St. Hippolyte during a dragoon occupation. Despite the danger ahead, deep down, she understood this was his path.

"Go then, quickly! You'll lose your chance if the soldiers find you here. I promise you that I'll be there for Louise. Always."

Grateful for the spark of relief in his eyes, she added, "Send us word when you arrive in Geneva."

He nodded, and the two friends embraced.

"*Adieu,* Jeanne."

"*Adieu,* Etienne."

Three *bisous* of farewell, and he was gone.

CHAPTER 46
A MEASURE OF JUSTICE

Day Eleven
Saturday, 16 October, 1683
Château de Planque
St. Hippolyte de la Planquette

Jeanne closed the door behind Etienne, leaned against it briefly, praying for his protection, then ran back upstairs. The hallway outside her bedroom was empty. She hurried towards the *grand salon* and pushed through the door. For the first time since the dragoons moved in, she crossed the threshold without fear.

What had happened to Louise was unacceptable. It could never be undone, but she wouldn't stand by passively. She *had* to do something. Jeanne understood why Etienne attacked his sister's rapist, he needed to take some form of action. She also needed to respond. Exactly how, or what, wasn't yet clear.

Jeanne stood just inside the *grand salon* and took in the scene in front of her: Colonel Arnault at the side of the room, questioning Papa and Pierre. In the opposite corner, several dragoons, including Lefèvre and Duboise, surrounded Rossel and Pouget. Her blood boiled at their easy banter. How dare they act as if nothing was wrong. She bit her lip and prayed. *Heavenly Father, I need your wisdom. Please show me what I can do.*

She shut the hallway door, and every man in the room stopped and stared at her. Only Pierre didn't register surprise. Their eyes met, and her own determination mirrored his. With a slight nod she communicated Etienne's successful escape. Pierre blinked briefly in return.

Papa started towards her. "Jeanne, please, go back to the room. I'll deal with this."

225

"Papa, I *must* stay." She planted her feet, unwavering. He studied her for a moment, then acquiesced. Together, they crossed the room.

Colonel Arnault turned back to Pierre. "You claim to have found Mademoiselle Gamond yesterday inside the stone hut in the vineyard?"

"Yes, sir."

"She appeared to have been attacked? And, you say that you observed two men fleeing the scene?"

"Sir, there's no question she was attacked. Raped. Yes, two men ran away when I arrived. The same two dragoons who fought just now in the hallway."

The colonel followed Pierre's gesture to where Rossel and Pouget sat. Arnault's face darkened, and his lips compressed into a thin line.

Pierre continued. "Louise Gamond identified at least one of them as her rapist."

A heavy silence descended upon the room, layered with different forms of anger radiating from each one of them.

"How can you be sure?" asked Colonel Arnault.

Jeanne could hold back no longer. "Anyone who witnessed Louise's reaction when she saw the men, especially that one," she pointed at Rossel, "would have any doubt he attacked her. And, her face bears bruises from the struggle. Also, are there not scratches across his cheek?"

"That is circumstantial evidence at best, not proof," Arnault replied.

Jeanne's eyes flashed. "What more, sir, do you need in the way of proof? Dragoons raped my friend; of that, there is no question. Pierre found her immediately after, in a state that left no doubt about what she had endured. He witnessed these men fleeing the scene but chose to stay with her. When she was able to move, he brought her here. Now Louise has identified at least one of them as the man who attacked her."

Jeanne was aware she was pushing all the boundaries speaking to the colonel this way. She was also equally aware that every other male in the room was listening. It didn't matter, though; nothing did, except exposing the truth and finding a measure of justice for Louise. Suddenly, she understood this was an answer to her prayer earlier. God led her to fight by speaking up. She folded her shaking hands on her skirt and squared her shoulders.

Colonel Arnault stared at her and rubbed his chin. "We'll wait for General De Tessé, who will arrive shortly. As it happens, he's in town today, and as cases of this nature are his domain, I've sent a messenger to request his presence here."

Without a word, Jeanne pulled out one of the dining room chairs and sat down to wait, arms crossed. Papa's left eyebrow raised as he joined her at the table, a glimmer of pride on his face. Colonel Arnault paced the room's length, frequently glancing out the front windows for De Tesse's arrival.

Pierre remained standing and observed the whole of the room. Jeanne imagined he was processing it all, assessing the next step. She managed to catch his attention and motioned for him to join them at the table. He sat next to her, and she leaned in close. "Did the colonel ask where Etienne went?"

"No, he and even more dragoons arrived in the hallway, but not until after you and Etienne left. So the only ones who know Etienne was here are those two." Pierre tipped his head in the direction of Rossel and Pouget. "And the colonel has not allowed them to talk, at least not yet."

"That one has always been trouble," Papa added, looking towards Rossel. "The other one follows him like a pet dog." The crease between his brows deepened. "Etienne's gone?"

"Yes, Papa. But not home. If the dragoons talk, he'll be in great danger. He was already considering fleeing to Switzerland, as Claude Brousson suggested. You know there's no future for him here."

Papa sat back in his chair. "So it's happening. I hoped this day would never come." He let out a ragged sigh. "However, it's a relief that he got away and has a place to go."

He reached for her hand and gave it a slight squeeze. Jeanne relished his warm strength as a welcome reprieve from all the chaos and pain, only to be interrupted by Rossel passing gas loudly. Lefèvre and Duboise swallowed their guffaws after a fierce glare from their colonel.

Jeanne scowled at Rossel, then turned away, revolted at the sight of him. He appeared to feel no remorse and acted as if he expected this to all blow over. Anger raced through her veins, and the desire for justice increased to the point where she almost couldn't stand it. They would not let themselves be victims.

She glanced at Papa and sensed the frustration and rage just beneath the surface. And despite Pierre's rock-like exterior, his face carried a sharpness she'd never seen before as he studied the dragoons, collecting information.

227

Colonel Arnault announced the arrival of General De Tessé. Jeanne's head tightened. She had not forgotten his callous indifference during the trial and deaths of Massador and Soulier. It was unlikely that he'd bring charges against the King's dragoons. Wasn't rape considered a by-product of war? And that was exactly what this was: a war of religions.

Within minutes, De Tessé appeared through the double doors and entered the *grand salon,* followed by several aides. Everyone rose as the colonel and dragoons saluted their general. Slowly, Jeanne, Papa, and Pierre stood also. De Tessé scowled at them, then turned his attention to Colonel Arnault.

The two officers conversed quietly at the far end of the room. From time to time, they glanced at Rossel, then at the Huguenots.

When they finished, Colonel Arnault approached Papa. "Where is the young woman in question?"

"In our family's room with my wife."

"General De Tessé orders her to appear. She must testify as to what happened to her."

Jeanne stepped towards the men, her fists clenched. She opened her mouth to protest, to tell him the ordeal was too much for Louise. Instead, a quiet inner nudge cautioned her. In that exact second, she understood the necessity of Louise's testimony to achieve some form of justice. Swallowing hard, she said, "I'll go and prepare her, sir."

"Do not delay. One must not keep the general waiting."

Jeanne wanted to retort that she'd give Louise all the time she needed to collect herself. Biting her lip, she left the room.

Sometime later, she returned to the *grand salon* with a pale but calmly determined Louise. Heads held high, the women crossed the room and stood beside Papa and Pierre.

General De Tessé's eyes bored into the women. Jeanne didn't flinch but stood her ground, her spine straight. He demanded that Louise step forward. Jeanne glanced at her friend, surprised at the glint of anger in her eye. She linked her arm through Louise's, and both women stepped forward. Papa and Pierre moved behind them and stood firm.

De Tessé paused a second as if to protest but then carried on. "You are Mademoiselle Louise Gamond?"

"I am," Louise replied, her voice quiet and clear, her gaze fixed on an unseen object in the distance.

The general stepped closer, his impressive presence bearing down on Louise. "It's been reported that you were attacked by dragoons last night. Is that true?"

Louise dropped her head. "Yes, it's true," she whispered.

"*Louder!* Repeat your response!"

Jeanne interrupted, "Sir, she said it's true!"

"Hold your tongue, Mademoiselle Tessier, or I'll remove you from the room."

Louise lifted her chin and looked the general full in the face. "Last night, I was attacked by dragoons. One of them raped me."

De Tessé pursed his lips and leaned in closer. "Can you identify your alleged attackers?"

Jeanne felt Louise's body tense beside her. After a moment, Louise cleared her throat. "Yes, I can. Those two men in the corner assaulted me." Then, pointing at Rossel, she continued, "That man raped me, while the other one held me down." With each word, Louise's voice became more powerful.

General De Tessé regarded Rossel, whose one good eye focused on him, a grotesque leer lurking behind his confident demeanor. A barely suppressed guffaw escaped Pouget. De Tessé scowled at them both, then turned and peered at Louise. Jeanne was proud of her friend's courage as she met the general's intense scrutiny with great dignity, without the slightest hint of retreat. Her heart rattled against her ribs as they all waited for his next move.

General De Tessé swiveled abruptly and crossed the room to the pair of dragoons. He motioned for them to stand.

The general started with Rossel. "What do you say to this accusation?"

"I did not rape this woman, sir," stated Rossel, a tiny grin tugging at the corners of his mouth.

Fury rose in Jeanne as the hint of a wink crossed his good eye.

De Tessé stepped closer and asked again. "Did you rape this woman?"

Rossel did not answer at first. Colonel Arnault stepped towards his man, "Answer the general's question, now!"

Rossel glanced from the colonel to the general. "Well, sirs, I did what we always do. We're to suppress the heretic Huguenots, aren't we?"

Jeanne desperately wished to slap the smirk off his face. She clasped her hands together so tight her knuckles shone white.

General De Tessé raised his eyebrows, then turned to Pouget and posed the same question.

"I didn't get my turn, sir. Ran out of time." He all but cackled like a buddy sharing a joke with a peer. Pierre inhaled sharply, and Papa stirred, his fists opening and shutting at his sides.

De Tessé's fiery glare from one dragoon to the other dried up every last bit of their swagger. The general ordered them to sit and then motioned for Arnault to follow him to the far side of the room. Jeanne dared to inch a bit closer to hear their discussion. Despite their low voices, she caught certain words, enough to understand that De Tessé was ready to release Rossel and his buddy with a light reprimand, while Arnault argued for some form of punishment. He reminded his superior of their orders to not repeat the severe violence of the Dauphiné and later in the Vivarais. But, from the look on De Tesse's face, he did not appear convinced.

Jeanne's pounding heart sent blood roaring through her head. It was now or never. Evading her father's attempt to hold her back, she approached the officers. De Tessé and Arnault instantly stopped their conference, incredulous at her audacity.

She stood straight, determined to appear confident and meet the eyes of the two men towering over her. "Excuse me, sirs, but I *must* speak on behalf of Mademoiselle Gamond." Before they could interrupt, she tumbled out the words. "I ask you to do what is just and, at very least, punish the dragoon who raped my friend. We are all French, and all subjects of the King, are we not? Surely, justice must be served when one violates another." With a glance at the general, she honed in on Arnault. "Would the King approve of this man's actions? Is this what the King intended when he sent you here?" From past conversations between the colonel and Papa, Jeanne understood that he saw himself as a man of honor, carrying out the will of his sovereign and his God. She'd also sensed he found Rossel and his behavior repugnant.

Colonel Arnault stared at her, his face like flint. She met his eyes and refused to look away. The ticking of the grandfather clock echoed in the silent room.

Finally, Arnault turned to the general. "Sir, I believe the King wishes us to convert the Huguenots, bringing them back to the one true church.

230

What happened in the north..." The colonel paused and appeared to search for the right words. When he continued, his voice carried calm conviction. "Sir, I believe we should *not* allow our men to rape the women of St. Hippolyte. I do not see that it serves our cause. It is not how men who represent the King and his faith should comport themselves."

General De Tessé eyed Arnault, then began to pace the length of the room, hands clasped behind his back. The general's demeanor was unreadable as he walked the floor. Jeanne pressed her fingers onto her temples as her headache pounded out the minutes. Earlier, De Tessé had seemed ready to make a quick decision and get back to his other business. Now, he was lost in thought, taking his time to arrive at a verdict. She moved back to Louise's side and again linked arms with her friend.

Finally, the general banged his fist on the dining room table as if calling an unruly crowd to order, despite the complete silence of everyone else in the room.

"Everyone! Attention!" He pointed at Rossel and Pouget. "Bring those two men forward."

Without their guards, the accused dragoons strode forward, stood with feet apart, their thumbs hooked in their belts.

General De Tessé continued. "By the authority bestowed upon me by King Louis XIV, in whose honor, and by whose will we serve, I have come to a decision. One that will please our King." He nodded as if reassuring himself as he strode back and forth. Then, abruptly, he stopped in front of Rossel. "I sentence you to the most severe punishment for the violation of the Huguenot woman."

Rossel's habitual scorn dissolved, and disbelief etched across his face. Bewildered, he looked to Colonel Arnault, whose stony visage gave away nothing.

General De Tessé continued. "As officers of the King, we wish you to become an example, a deterrent to others. We do not need to violate the Huguenot women to obtain conversions to the one true faith. Therefore, you will be executed, beaten, and broken, upon the Wheel. Within the hour."

CHAPTER 47
AFTERMATH: COLONEL ARNAULT

Day Eleven
Saturday, 16 October, 1683
Château de Planque
St. Hippolyte de la Planquette

Colonel Arnault stared hard at the general, willing his face to remain neutral. Yes, he had advocated for severe consequences for Rossel. But this! Execution on the Wheel! Profound surprise rendered him motionless. Indeed, the whole room stood deadly silent, as if all the air had been sucked away.

Then, General De Tessé began barking out orders, breaking the spell. He pointed at Pouget and spared him from the death penalty but declared him a prisoner for his involvement in the rape. Both dragoons' sentences would serve as a warning for any others who considered going too far.

General De Tessé then turned to Arnault. "Colonel, have some of your men take the prisoners up to the servants' quarters and guard them there until further instructions. Then choose others to come with me to prepare the execution."

Arnault snapped to attention. "Lieutenant Lefèvre, you and Duboise go with the general." The men rose immediately and followed De Tessé. Colonel Arnault then pointed to four soldiers. "You will guard both prisoners upstairs. Take them away, now!"

The room erupted into chaos. Rossel's disbelief evaporated, and he howled like a madman as two of his fellow dragoons bound and dragged him away. Pouget's face registered dazed confusion as guards tied his hands and led him out of the room.

Soon, Arnault stood alone in the *grand salon*. His dragoons were all deployed elsewhere, and the Tessier family had retreated to their room, except for the father.

From opposite sides of the *grand salon*, the two men eyed the other in silence. Finally, the colonel turned away and stared out one of the tall front windows, his hands clasped behind his back. Isaac Tessier walked at a measured pace across the room and stood next to Arnault. Shoulder to shoulder, they both gazed out the window, taking in the bigger picture.

"Colonel Arnault, sir, I don't know how to say this exactly, but thank you for speaking up for justice."

"It was the right thing to do," the colonel responded.

"Yes. I believe it will have the effect of holding back ungodly violence, especially towards our women."

Arnault gave a curt nod. Isaac Tessier paused, as if he had more to say, but then turned and crossed the room. When the door shut behind him, Arnault's shoulders sagged. These people! He couldn't explain how or why they got to him on some deep interior level. It had been so much easier to condemn the Huguenots before actually meeting any of them.

There was a striking similarity between the Huguenot woman rising from the forest floor in the north after Rossel had finished with her and his latest victim, Louise Gamond. The same intangible but genuine strength shown from their eyes, despite their pain. And the audacity of that little Jeanne Tessier! He had to admire her boldness in advocating for her friend with General De Tessé and himself. Confident courage emanated from each of them, and the power of their convictions stunned him.

His eyes landed on a bare ginkgo tree down below. Its golden-yellow leaves spread across the ground, creating a brilliant carpet at the very site of the hangings. Now, under General De Tessé's watchful eye, Lieutenant Lefèvre and Duboise hustled about staging it for Rossel's execution.

The memory of Massador's brave death rose in his mind, yet another example of the Huguenot spirit. Truly, these people possessed something he did not. He knew himself to be highly loyal to the King's faith. Yet these Huguenots carried an experience of God, a relationship with him that he didn't comprehend. They talked to him like he was right there with them, like he actually listened.

Arnault turned away from the window and the scene below. He smoothed his emerald jacket and stood straight. No more time to lose in internal reveries. Earlier, the general had issued his new orders. Tomorrow morning, he'd lead his men in a sweep through the surrounding villages and towns. Montpezat's regiment of 700 foot soldiers had orders to stay in St. Hippolyte and continue to exert pressure on the Huguenot community. Arnault's lips pressed into a line. Montpezat and his men were exceptionally vulgar. But now there were limits on the atrocities they would inflict. At least, he hoped that to be true. And before God, his conscience eased a tiny bit.

CHAPTER 48
AFTERMATH: JEANNE

Day Eleven
Saturday, 16 October, 1683
Château de Planque
St. Hippolyte de la Planquette

Jeanne's hand flew to her mouth, and she stumbled back several steps, right into Pierre. General De Tessé decreed that Rossel was to die! She wasn't sure what she expected justice to look like but she had not expected execution, and in one of the worst ways possible. Rossel was to die on the Wheel, a slow and torturous death usually reserved for enemies of the King. Waves of shock coursed through her body. She swayed slightly, trembling from head to toe. Pierre steadied her, reaching his arm around her waist. They turned to Louise, who stared out the window, her body also shaking violently. Jeanne took her hand and squeezed it lightly.

Yet, Jeanne didn't regret speaking up. Indeed, she could *not* have remained silent and let Rossel get away with rape. She'd wanted him severely punished for what he'd done but had never imagined it would go this far. He'd be beaten to death while tethered to a terrifying instrument called the Wheel. The fact that General De Tessé passed this sentence on one of his own men shook her to the core.

Once the guards exited the room with the prisoners and General De Tessé with Lefèvre and Duboise left to prepare the execution, Jeanne reached out to Louise and pulled her close. Flanked by Pierre and her best friend, with her papa just behind, Jeanne breathed deep. General De Tesse's verdict was vindication for Louise. Her face showed a hint of relief, overshadowed by enormous fatigue. Jeanne glanced at Pierre, and together they led Louise out of the room, down the hall, and into the relative calm of the family's room.

Jeanne seated Louise by the fire, grabbed a woolen blanket, and gently wrapped it around her shoulders. Maman began preparing a soothing *tisane* from the *tilleul* leaves they had picked together last spring. The memory of that bright spring day caused Jeanne to blink. She could barely imagine a time when her biggest problem was avoiding the bees who competed for the linden tree's fragrant offerings. That all seemed like another lifetime, which indeed it was.

While she settled Louise, Papa returned from the *grand salon*. Jeanne crossed the room to the far corner where Papa and Pierre stood close together, locked in a whispered discussion. Then, finally, she couldn't hold back her questions one minute longer and barged right in, not caring if she interrupted. "Why? Why did General De Tessé give Rossel such a harsh sentence? I wanted him punished for what he did to Louise, but this! It never occurred to me he'd order his execution."

Pierre's deep brown eyes searched her face. "The severity of the general's decision comes as a surprise to us all. But it *is* a just response to what Rossel did."

Papa tugged on his beard. "I believe the general wants to make a point with Rossel's death. Yes, they are the King's soldiers, and their job is to force us to abandon our faith. But, it appears the King expects them to do this without 'excessive violence,' including resorting to rape."

Admiration lit up Pierre's face. "Jeanne, the fact that you stepped forward and dared to speak appears to have influenced the final decision. You mentioned the King and something activated in Colonel Arnault. I believe his subsequent exhortation then caused a shift in De Tessé's opinion. Before that, the general seemed to be leaning towards a more lenient response."

"I know!" Jeanne shook her head, still trying to understand all that had happened. "I don't regret what I did, and I'd do it again without hesitation. But, it's just that...." She paused to find the right words. "It's awful that the result is a man's death."

"The decision and the responsibility lie with General De Tessé and Colonel Arnault. All you did was speak the truth." Pierre's firm voice brought clarity and steadied her—once again.

Jeanne met his eyes, lingering there a bit. She then turned to her father. "Papa, I believe it's time for Louise to go home, if she feels ready.

I want to walk with her and have Pierre come as well. Together, we can explain everything to Guillaume. He needs to hear what happened to Louise plus Etienne's response and escape to Switzerland. Also, of course, he needs to know about Rossel's sentence."

Papa started to object but stopped. His internal struggle played out across his face. Finally, he shut both eyes. After a moment, he opened them and nodded. "Yes, that's a good plan. I'll go inform Colonel Arnault."

Louise agreed it was time for her to return home, assuring Jeanne and Pierre that she was strong enough to walk across town. She finished her *tisane,* handed the porcelain cup to Maman, and thanked her for kindness and care. She rose a bit stiffly and wrapped the shawl Jeanne offered her around her shoulders. The three friends headed out.

Once outside the château, they all stopped and breathed deep. It was already colder than usual for October; Jeanne and Louise pulled their linen caps down a bit farther to cover their ears. Without speaking, they relished the frosty air. For a brief moment, it tasted like freedom.

In silence, the trio crossed town towards the Gamond home, Jeanne and Louise arm-in-arm, with Pierre close beside. This time, they didn't sneak through the gardens and hidden passages but stayed on the main streets. It was most likely they'd soon have to return to surreptitious movements. But today, they sensed there was a reprieve due to the severity of Rossel's sentence. At least for now, no dragoon risked stepping out of line. A ghost of a smile crossed Jeanne's lips. Here was another form of God's protection, even in the midst of ongoing danger.

Jeanne imagined the dragoons would continue to be their awful selves, and it was still unclear how far they'd go to force the Huguenots to convert. However, there was a limit, a boundary drawn which the soldiers couldn't cross without the most severe consequences. In that, there was some comfort.

The three friends rounded the corner onto Louise's street, then stopped abruptly. A group of dragoons stood just past the Gamond front door, their loud, angry voices filling the air.

"Colonel Arnault warned us not to go that far!"

"But Rossel's one of ours. I don't care what he's done!"

"Rossel was always looking for trouble."

"But this sentence is more than he deserves! We're supposed to subdue these heretics, aren't we?"

"Yes, so why is the general being so tough on us?"

"It's not fair!"

One of the dragoons turned and tipped his head toward Louise, Jeanne, and Pierre standing at the head of the street. All discussion ceased immediately, and the tallest soldier strode forward, nostrils flared, hand on his saber.

"Leave them for now. They're not worth the trouble," said another, as he grabbed his friend's arm. "Wait till the execution is over, when things have settled. Then we'll get 'em."

Both sides, dragoons and Huguenots, stared at the other in silence.

Finally, the tall one spoke. "You're right! Not worth it right now. There'll be plenty of time later to make them pay."

With a fierce glare, patting his saber as a promise, he turned and strode down the street. The remaining dragoons lobbied a few more verbal threats at the Huguenots, then followed their comrade.

Jeanne, Pierre, and Louise collectively let out a breath once the soldiers disappeared around the corner at the end of the road.

"Apparently, General De Tessé's sentence is as much of a shock to them as it is to us. I don't think any of them expected serious repercussions, even for...." She trailed off, reluctant to say the word out loud in front of Louise.

"Jeanne, I know what happened to me, and I know what it's called," Louise stated, her voice calm. "I don't want you tiptoeing around me, avoiding saying certain words in my hearing."

"Oh! All right! I didn't know that's what you'd want," Jeanne stammered. This was new territory for them all.

"What I want is for you all to treat me the same as always, please," Louise said, gentle yet firm. "Not like fragile china that will shatter if not handled correctly."

"Yes, of course!" Jeanne and Pierre answered simultaneously and with such sincerity that all three chuckled a little. They met each others' eyes. A deep bond had been forged between them, born out of Louise's excruciating ordeal. Here was yet another form of God's presence, *in* suffering and pain. He knit their hearts together, with one another and with his own. They were not alone. Together, they'd walk through all that was to come, with God and with each other.

A swirl of brilliant autumn leaves blew through the street in front of the Gamond home. Louise opened the front door and stepped inside while Jeanne stopped to view the scarlet and gold leaves dance and whirl in a shaft of light, another reminder of the goodness of God. Gratitude filled her soul, and she glanced up at Pierre, who was also drinking in the beauty. He met her gaze, filling Jeanne with warmth and a surrounding sense of security.

Everything in their lives had changed irrevocably in the last eleven days, herself included. God cared! He loved her, personally, intimately, and that made all the difference. Knowing God could never fail or abandon her anchored Jeanne with enormous peace and strength. His presence with them was as tangible as the fresh air swirling around her now. She inhaled deeply. The terror of dragoons living among them was their new reality, but their heavenly Father would always remain close. His loving, powerful protection plus his guidance and wisdom provided everything they needed to face the challenges ahead. She relished the thought.

Jeanne reached for Pierre's hand, and they crossed the threshold together.

EPILOGUE

Five years later
6 October 1688
Chez Lacombe
St. Hippolyte de la Planquette

Jeanne curled up next to one of the windows in the *salon*, reading the latest letter from Switzerland. Passed from one trusted hand to another, it had arrived in St. Hippolyte earlier that day. Once the Gamonds read and absorbed its contents, Louise brought it to Jeanne.

Jeanne perused the letter, then stood and stretched, glancing out the window at the rows of recently harvested vineyards. She smiled and waved at Paul, out adding chicken manure to the earth around the vines. Not for the first time, she marveled at how tall he'd grown, how soon he'd be an adult. Yet, he still chafed for adventure. Where would that lead him?

Across the room, Louise sat by the fire, deep in conversation with Catherine. Warmth filled Jeanne as she watched Louise connect with her sister and encourage her relationship with God. Jeanne appreciated the time Louise made for others, especially as she had her own family now. Thankfully her husband loved staying at home with their toddler when he wasn't at work. Louise often brought the little one along, but today he was recovering from a cold. She'd left the two of them cozy in the Gamond family home where they lived.

Louise's process of healing had included moments of doubt of God's goodness. Hadn't he promised to protect them, as in the psalm? Had she done something wrong? Or worse, was God not trustworthy after all?

Jeanne remembered the many discussions they'd had, often with Pierre, seeking understanding. Suffering and persecution had become

240

part of their daily lives and they'd done nothing wrong, nothing to deserve any of it.

They always came back to the truth of God's real and tangible presence in the midst of the darkness. As in Psalm 91, his promised protection was there through the troubles. They'd seen it countless times already, starting with the execution of Rossel and the restraint on further rape being allowed.

But above all, it was God's unchanging goodness and love they counted on. No matter the circumstances, he was with them—strengthening, healing, transforming. Jeanne had seen this first hand, in Louise, who now passed on all she'd gained to others.

Nearby, Anne sat curled up in a corner, absorbed in her book. She raised her head from time to time to listen and then went right back to her story. Gratitude filled Jeanne for all the ways she counted on Anne's help and strength of character. She couldn't imagine managing their lives without her support.

They all still missed Maman terribly, even though four years had passed since the fever took her from them. And Papa's absence left an enormous, gaping hole they all felt daily. Right before Maman died, he'd been sentenced to row in the galley boats in Marseille harbor for refusing to convert. Although they hadn't received official word, most chained men perished within the first two years.

Jeanne's heart squeezed as the memories rose unbidden. At least the remainder of her family now lived together with Isabeau and André in the Lacombe home. After the first months of the occupation, the dragoons had finally moved into lodgings of their own, bringing some relief to the Huguenots of St. Hippolyte. Except for the Château de Planque—still inhabited by dragoons officers and used as their headquarters. Jeanne missed her former home terribly. Living next door, in the shadow of the château, reminded her constantly of all they had lost.

King Louis XIV's dragoons continued their constant harassment. They called themselves "booted missionaries" and never seemed to run out of ideas of how to torment the Huguenots. The brutal execution of Rossel had conveyed the message that the officers did not tolerate rape, yet the dragoons found many other forms of abuse. As hard as Jeanne tried to avoid the soldiers, they still lurked in corners and alleys around town, ready to grab at her clothing, to throw out their lewd profanities.

Jeanne shuddered at the memory of a dragoon spitting in Maman's face when she happened to walk in front of him at the open market. She'd never forget Maman's dignified response, pulling a handkerchief from her pocket and wiping away the spittle as if it were nothing more than a splash of rain. Jeanne's throat had filled with bile until she was on the verge of spitting out her own spray of words. Maintaining her composure, Maman had linked her arm through Jeanne's and moved them on their way.

That wasn't even the worst of it. Suspicious at the midwife's frequent comings and goings, Isabeau Lacombe had been whipped by dragoons while the men in her family were held back, detained from interrupting. André had never fully recovered from the ordeal of watching his beloved wife beaten while he was unable to protect her. On top of that, the soldiers in the Marolle's home had crushed Emmanuel's fingers with pliers and slashed Françoise's face, leaving permanent scars. Yet, for the first two years, none of them had given in and converted to the King's faith.

A spark appeared in Jeanne's eyes. Despite the soldiers' vile behavior, she was incredibly proud that only a little over one hundred of the four thousand Huguenots of St. Hippolyte had renounced their faith during that first year of the dragoon occupation. Cévenol people were often called stubborn with good reason.

But then the oppression worsened. Finally, with a stroke of a pen, the King attempted to erase their existence. He revoked the Edict of Nantes and outlawed Protestantism. The Huguenots of St. Hippolyte and all the surrounding towns finally capitulated and turned to Catholicism. At least outwardly. Jeanne filled with tension remembering that tumultuous time.

Many had fled from France seeking refuge in other countries. From the last reports, the *réfugiés* numbered in the hundreds of thousands. Jeanne still could barely believe it. Most likely, they'd never again see the condemned pastors and other Huguenot friends forced to flee.

The trace of a smile crossed her face. At least within the week of La Roquette's flight, she had been able to secure passage for his family, hidden in one of Papa's vendors' wagons. The La Roquette family were now united and well in Geneva.

242

Jeanne got up, crossed the room, and settled into a chair next to the fire. "Did you find anything I missed?" Louise asked. "Any clues he might return someday?"

"As usual, I'm not sure, which is the point, of course. Etienne does an excellent job of being cryptic in case these letters fall into the wrong hands."

"I'm amazed they get to us at all. The three days' journey from Etienne's seminary in Lausanne to us affords many possibilities for their interception."

"I am eternally grateful for the messengers. But, unfortunately, once they cross the border into France, these missives put them in great danger."

Louise took the letter from Jeanne. "Look here at this bit," she said, pointing to a paragraph near the end. "It says something about diplomas and caves and our ultimate home not being here in this world."

Jeanne leaned forward. "Yes, I noticed that too. He seems to have understood from our letters, and possibly from the messengers themselves, that we meet secretly in caves and deserted places, for our worship services. His reference to diplomas makes me think he may soon finish his studies. Do you think he plans to return to France as a pastor?"

"It's hard to say for sure. Knowing my brother, I'd say that's exactly his plan."

"Then that explains him mentioning that our final home is not here on earth. As a Protestant pastor, he'd automatically be a wanted man if he comes back to France now. His diploma would be a death sentence."

"I don't wish for him to be in danger, but I'd be incredibly proud of him if he chose to return and serve the clandestine church."

Jeanne loved the strength that emanated from Louise. She'd emerged from her ordeal with a new depth to her relationship with her heavenly Father and even more compassion for others. Of course, what had happened to her would always be part of her story, but Louise had allowed the healing balm of faith in God's ultimate goodness and love to transform her pain into a fount of empathy. Many were instinctively drawn to Louise and benefitted immensely from her care. Especially young women like Catherine.

"My brother is following his call, Jeanne. You know he always wanted to be a pastor. Now, *because* he fled to Switzerland, he's received seminary training! That would've never happened here."

"I've thought about that many times since he fled. How God turned a dreadful situation into the fulfillment of Etienne's deepest desire."

They paused, savoring the mystery of God's ways. Despite the terrible persecution they lived with, His unchanging goodness was as living water to their souls.

Louise continued. "If he does return to minister, well, that seems to be what he was born to do. Wherever it leads him."

"It'd be great to have his help with our clandestine meetings. I don't know how much longer I can travel at night, guiding visiting pastors to the caves." Jeanne patted her swelling stomach and burst out laughing when the baby kicked hard. "I think someone wants me to keep going on adventures!"

The door to the *salon* opened. Pierre entered and scooped up three-year-old Suzanne from where she played with some wooden blocks on the floor. "What's so funny?" he asked as he kissed his daughter's chubby cheeks.

"Baby Lacombe doesn't want me to stop my nocturnal adventures with the underground church."

Pierre pressed his hand on Jeanne's belly and was rewarded with a hard thump. "Yes, he's making his point! Just as well, you're far better at sneaking around at night than I am!"

Their eyes met, alive with shared memories and the significance of their current mission.

"Wait, *he*? So you're sure this one's a boy?"

"Yes, I think so." Pierre smiled. "I'd like to name him Gabriel Isaac."

Emotion welled in Jeanne. "That's perfect."

Louise asked, "Have you had any word from your brother?"

Catherine looked up, all her attention on Pierre. Paul, just returned from the vineyards, stepped closer to listen.

"Not for quite a while. I heard from Gabriel years ago when he safely arrived in the eastern Cévennes with Noguier. And then a second time after the King revoked the Edict of Nantes." Pierre sighed. "He lives in a tiny hamlet called Mialet. There are rumors that a movement is growing there among the Huguenots. They call themselves *Camisards* for their white shirts, and they train to fight the dragoons. All of which sounds perfect for my brother. I trust him to God."

Catherine sat back and stared at the fire. Louise waited a moment, then reached for her hand. She whispered a few words to Catherine, who nodded, then lay her head on Louise's shoulder.

Paul stood motionless, digesting Pierre's information. Then he glanced down at his white shirt, and Jeanne imagined him picturing himself as a *Camisard* fighter. A cold finger of fear trickled through her core, but she quickly turned to the source of all comfort, wisdom, and strength. She prayed for Paul's protection and for him to walk in the destiny for which his Father created him.

Jeanne stood and smiled at her daughter, busy tugging away on her papa's beard. Pierre reached for Jeanne's hand with his free one, and she read in his eyes that he'd followed her train of thought. His ability to read and understand her was still one of the things she treasured most.

Pierre tickled Suzanne's neck with his beard, and she giggled in delight. "Anyway, for now, Jeanne, you should continue to be the night guide. I enjoy staying with this one. Of course, I'll carry on spreading the word about meeting locations and times while I deliver wine."

"We each have our role to play. While we help the underground church exist, Gabriel plans to fight those who'd stop us. It's always been in him to do just that."

Pierre gazed out the window as if his brother would materialize under the ginkgo tree. "True, and now more necessary than ever." He turned back to Jeanne. "You know that the new governor, Bâville, is far more vicious than his predecessor. Plus, they've now finished the fort here and most of the rampart walls encircling the town." He paused, rubbing the back of his neck. "The dragoons plan to *increase* their control: who goes in and out of the city gates, keeping lists, enforcing curfews. We'll effectively be prisoners in our own town. They're already growing bolder. It reminds me of the early days of their occupation."

Jeanne's eyes darkened, sparks flew out with her words. "Of course, we'll continue to resist! We've come this far, and we'll *never* give up!"

The fire hissed and popped on cue. Pierre and Jeanne laughed a little, then leaned in closer to one another, basking in the warmth and light.

"You are made for such a time as this," Pierre said. "We all are," he added as he looked over the family gathered in front of the fire.

Suzanne reached for her maman. Jeanne smiled, sat down and pulled her onto what was left of her lap. Suzanne snuggled in and started playing with Jeanne's gold necklace. A recent gift from Pierre after a trip to

Nîmes, it carried a newly designed symbol for the Huguenots to wear and identify one another. Fashioned with the royal cross in the center, it was full of biblical symbolism, and despite everything, expressed their ongoing loyalty to the King.

Jeanne gently removed the pendant from her daughter's grasp and fingered the shape of the Huguenot cross and the dove, representing the Holy Spirit, which flew beneath. God's strengthening presence and peace were always near. No matter what lay ahead, they were never alone.

ACKNOWLEDGMENTS

I'm one of those people who read the entire acknowledgment page at the end of a book, partly out of curiosity and partly to know the author better through her connections. I'm always impressed at how many people are involved in creating a single book. Now, I understand more than ever that writing a book is not accomplished alone. My deepest gratitude goes to my French friends, who answered historical questions and loaned me countless books. Special thanks to Michel Caby, former director of the Musée du Desert, for long, informative discussions. Also to Roland Castanet, local historian and author, as well as Pascal Coulorou, Huguenot descendant and former owner of our little town's wonderful bookstore ("the center of everything"!)

Dear friends, France Huckendubler and Danièle Bastide, also Huguenot descendants, listened, prayed, and gave invaluable insight— and books. I'm also privileged to know Madame Quintin, great-niece of former owners of my home, the Château de Planque. Besides loaning me rare books, she filled me in on many pieces of the past. I am grateful for these dear sisters in Christ.

Enormous thanks go to my early readers, who gave excellent input and correction: Donough O'Brien, Liz Cowley, Timothy Hamilton, Cindy Godwin, and Kelsea Tripod.

Kimberly Schulz, editor extraordinaire, deserves a special mention. She selflessly gave her time and expertise, going over the manuscript more than once with a fine-tooth comb. The story is much better as a result.

I am indebted to graphic designer Katie Fisher, who created the wonderful cover and remained patient and helpful through my every request.

Much needed technical help came from Mickala Seabrook, who created my beautiful website. Thank you for "getting me." Also, to Michael Wallerius for bailing me out of technical complications.

The incredible experience of the "Good Lit Writers Retreat" marked me deeply. Thank you is not a large enough word or concept to cover it. Bret Lott, I continue to feed off of your perspective and insights. Thank you for your humility, honesty, and encouragement.

Bodie Thoene, your books are the gold standard. They've inspired me for decades.

The Lady Lits! Best online writers/support/mastermind group ever! Thanks to each one of you for your generosity and friendship. I'm grateful to share the journey with you.

Joe Portale, you have encouraged me regarding writing for years. Your interest and belief in me have meant so much.

Brooke and Lane Webster, words are inadequate to convey how much I treasure you. Our rich friendship is sterling proof of God's goodness to me. Thank you for the invaluable coaching, listening, questioning, encouragement and prayers. The generous use of your home in the early stages of writing was a dream come true.

I must also thank my artist parents, Phil and Michelle Joanou. They pursued their dreams fearlessly and gave me the courage to do the same.

Thank you to my beautiful children, Joshua, Jessica, Hannah, and Sarah, who cheered me on.

And to my wonderful husband, Dudley, who lived through this with me, understanding my need to process verbally. Thank you for all the listening at lunch, the helpful input and support, I love you.

Finally, to God the Father, Jesus the Son, and the Holy Spirit, who flowed, inspired, and sustained me to the end.

J anet Joanou Weiner grew up in southern California and studied French against her 6th-grade teacher's advice that she'd never use it.

Very glad she stuck with her preference, Janet has lived in France for almost twenty years. First in the Alps, followed by several years in the center of Paris.

Currently, Janet and her husband reside in southern France, in St. Hippolyte du Fort, where they've established a Christian training center, YWAM Bridges of Life.

Janet has also lived in Amsterdam, the San Francisco Bay Area, and Kona, Hawaii. In addition, she's traveled for her work in Christian ministry to over forty countries.

Despite missing her four children and four grandchildren, who all live in the US, Janet loves her life! She delights in the endless opportunities to discover past stories of depth and inspiration while soaking up the beauty, culture, and history all around her. And, of course, there's the incredible food and wine.

Janet has dabbled in writing over the years, but never found the time needed to pen a novel. After a significant birthday a few years ago, she decided it was now or never.

Based on actual events, Janet's first historical novel takes place in her village and home, the over 500-year-old Château de Planque.

janetjoanouweiner.com
blog: Fig & Vine

GLOSSARY

Adieu- good-bye; literally "Go with God"

à table- come to the dining table or at the table

aides-de-camp- assistants

armoire- wooden cupboard

arrête- stop

attend- wait

bergerie- sheep fold

bien sûr- of course

bienvenue- welcome

bisous- traditional cheek kisses used in greetings

bon appétit- literally "good appetite;" meaning, eat well!

bonjour- hello, good-day

bonsoir- good evening

cache-cache- "Hide 'n Seek"

Camisards- white-shirted Huguenots who organized and fought the dragoons

Capitaine- Captain

cave à vin- wine cellar

centre ville- town center

chataigner- chestnut tree

château- castle

chez- at the home of

coiffures- hairstyle

d'accord- in agreement, ok

désolé- sorry

dragonnade- dragoon soldiers living in Protestant homes to force conversions

enfin- finally

façade- face of the mountain
garrigue- scrubland, hinterland
grand-père- grandfather
grand-mère- grandmother
grand salon- large living room
lavoir- outdoor stone laundry basin
ma chère- my dear
maman poule- mother hen
mas- large southern France farmhouse; in original regional language, Occitan
moulin à huile- mill with olive press
oui- yes
neuf, dix, onze, douze- nine, ten, eleven, twelve
non- no
pas possible- not possible
petit déjeuner- breakfast
pont- bridge
potager- kitchen garden
quartier- neighborhood
refugiés- refugees
saucisson- dried sausage
temple- Huguenot/Protestant church building
terroir - soil, land
tilleul- linden tree leaves
tisane- herb tea

s'il vous plaît- please
sortie- outing
vas-y- go ahead!
vendanges- grape harvest
verveine- lemon verbena leaves
volets- large wooden window shutters

Made in the USA
Las Vegas, NV
04 June 2022

49781046R00144